Secret Gift of Lucia Lemon

Celia Anderson is now living the dream as a full-time writer. She was a teacher and assistant head in her previous life, but other jobs have included barmaid, library assistant and cycling proficiency tutor. Pulling pints and sorting books are two of the most useful life skills she's acquired over the years. Cycling . . . just isn't.

An enthusiastic member of the Romantic Novelists' Association, Celia spends far too much time on Facebook and posts increasingly random photographs on Instagram. Her interests include cooking, eating, walking, reading and drinking wine, usually with her husband, except for the cooking bit and not necessarily in that order. Celia feels very lucky to have two daughters who have not only presented her with two equally lovely sons-in-law and grandchildren, but are also very keen on putting apostrophes in the right places. Such a relief.

 @CeliaAnderson1
 CeliaJAndersonAuthor
 @cejanderson

Also by Celia Anderson
59 Memory Lane
The Cottage of Curiosities

The Secret Gift of Lucia Lemon

CELIA ANDERSON

HarperCollins*Publishers*

HarperCollins*Publishers*
The News Building,
1 London Bridge Street,
London SE1 9GF

www.harpercollins.co.uk

HarperCollins*Publishers*
1st Floor, Watermarque Building, Ringsend Road
Dublin 4, Ireland

First published by HarperCollins*Publishers* 2021
1

Copyright © Celia Anderson 2021

Celia Anderson asserts the moral right to
be identified as the author of this work

A catalogue record for this book
is available from the British Library

ISBN: 978-0-00-846844-6

This novel is entirely a work of fiction.
The names, characters and incidents portrayed in it are
the work of the author's imagination. Any resemblance to
actual persons, living or dead, events or localities is
entirely coincidental.

Set in Birka by Palimpsest Book Production Limited, Falkirk, Stirlingshire

Printed and bound in the UK by CPI Group (UK) Ltd, Croydon CR0 4YY

For Ida and Levi – wonderful lockdown bonuses

None of us want to be in calm waters all our lives.

JANE AUSTEN, *PERSUASION*

The ancient device in its leather box sits deep inside the crate, waiting silently for something to happen. Years of mystery lie within the case. Centuries of explorations and of choices, of good times and goosebump moments. Sometimes, just occasionally, the choices made have been the wrong ones, but that doesn't happen often because this is an instrument that knows its own mind. If the lucky person benefiting from its special powers decides to ignore the advice it provides, that's their look out.

It's been a long time since the last change of owner. Tommy Lemon is a maverick and never short of ideas, but just lately he's been a bit of a let-down. Hopefully, the next one will inject a whole new lease of life into the tired mechanism. Who knows where they'll go together? It's time to fly again. The open road, the unknown . . . freedom. Marvellous adventures are about to begin.

Chapter One

'It's the endless flabby sandwiches and anaemic quiches that are going to be the death of me. Well, those and the grey potted meat. And the hideous trifle. That's the worst of all.'

'What's wrong with the trifle?'

Tommy Lemon shudders. At 70 years old, he's still as fit as he was when he was 40, as he tells himself regularly, but pink custard with hundreds and thousands upsets even his iron constitution.

'The only good thing about trifle is a hefty slug of sherry and nobody seems to have told the cook that. Maybe they think the excitement would be too much for us. Feels like going to a really bad wedding or a wake every single day of the week.'

'Have you quite finished grumbling?' The woman with the tea tray frowns down at him. She looks as if she'd like to fold her arms and huff but her hands are full.

Tommy pulls a face. 'Sorry, Chrissie. I know it's not your fault. You just work for them. Anyway, nobody forced me to come here. I've only got myself to blame.'

He leans back in his lounger and surveys the view spread out in front of him. It's a cool spring morning,

3

but it's better to be out here well wrapped up than in the overcrowded lounge trying to avoid the morning armchair Pilates session. The gardens of the retirement complex are extensive and well-manicured, with very tidy flower beds dotted here and there. The lawns go all the way down to a stream which is carefully fenced off, presumably in case any other residents feel as depressed as Tommy.

'You're still regretting burning your boats then?' Chrissie stoops to present Tommy with a plate of assorted biscuits. There are three. Somehow the kitchen staff have managed to choose exactly the kinds he hates most.

'Tell me something, Chrissie,' Tommy says. 'Does anyone over five actually like Jammy Dodgers?'

She shrugs. 'Dunno. It was just that we got them free. Job lot from a grateful relative.'

'Ah. That explains it,' he said darkly. 'I'm not sure if I'm regretting coming here. I was so sure it was time for a change . . . but maybe this move was a mistake. It certainly feels like one, and I'm no stranger to cock-ups.'

Chrissie brushes a piece of invisible fluff off her apron and sniffs. 'Some people like it here.'

'Oh, I know they do, and the staff are sweethearts, except for our leader. She could turn milk sour with one look. But, for pity's sake, talk about God's waiting room? I thought having a café on site for us residents would be heaven but once you've chosen what sort of sandwiches you want for your tea and queued up to order them, the

4

day's excitement is over. I remember the day pitta bread was suggested. Everybody hyperventilated.'

'Hey now, that's enough moaning. Most of the residents love being looked after properly!'

Tommy relents and pats Chrissie's hand. 'You're right, of course you are. I'm being grumpy. Ignore me. And they do make great chocolate cake.'

She laughs. 'I can't understand why you *ever* thought moving in here would be a good idea. You're much too young. You don't strike me as the sort of man to spend the rest of your days playing dominoes every morning, with only bingo to look forward to.'

'No, but the heart attack knocked me for six. I thought I was just biding my time before the next one hit me. I felt crushed.'

'I know, you told me. But as it happens, you're not. It was only a minor one and you're back on track now, aren't you?'

Tommy reaches for his mug of tea and takes a tentative sip. He screws his face up again.

'*Now* what's wrong?' Chrissie is about to set off back to the kitchen and Tommy is mortified at the hurt look on her face. She's one of the best here, and she always tries to make everyone feel at home.

He grimaces apologetically. 'I'm sorry. It's just that this isn't the life I imagined for myself when I checked in here. Even my old mate Pete said I was mad giving up my own place, and he never gives advice as a rule. I told him I was more than happy for someone else to do the cooking and cleaning but he just laughed and said there was more to life than housework.'

'True enough.'

Tommy's eyes are on the horizon now and he's silent for so long that Chrissie starts to fidget and look at her watch. He rallies.

'Anyway, as you so rightly say, I've burned my boats now. They'll get used to the idea, just like I'll have to. Especially when they find out what I've got lined up for them. They all need a good shake up. Chandlebury is hardly the hub of the universe.'

'What are you talking about, Tommy? Who is it that needs a shake up?'

Tommy looks at the floor for a long time before answering. Chrissie reaches a foot out as if she's about to prod him with her toe, so he starts to speak again, fishing out a rather battered photograph from his pocket.

'Des, his wife Lucia and their introvert of a son Isaac. They're all stuck in a giant rut. It's even worse than mine.'

'Oh, I get it now. Didn't you say Des was your nephew?'

'No, we're second cousins, Des and me – there are a whole lot of us Lemons but we're spread out all around the globe these days. My dad was his godfather and I kind of took on the role unofficially when Pa died. Des's lad Isaac actually *is* my godson. He's a good boy but he needs a rocket under him. My new scheme might just do the trick and tip him out of the nest.'

'You make him sound like a cuckoo.'

'Ha! That's not a bad description of Isaac. And Lucia's

a lovely, clever woman but our Des doesn't go in for much deep thinking.'

Chrissie takes the photograph that Tommy's holding out and looks down at it as Tommy leans to peer over her shoulder. A tall, rangy man is standing in a garden with his hand on the shoulder of a serious youth with exactly the same build. The woman by their side is laughing, looking at something to the right of the photographer. Lucia's skin is lightly tanned and her body is voluptuous, with luscious curves and just a hint of cleavage beneath the neckline of the rather austere navy sundress. She's much shorter than the other two, barely reaching her husband's shoulders but she's not wearing heels. Her shoes are the sort of sensible sandals that Chrissie wouldn't be seen dead in unless she was at work. Large, glamorous sunglasses create an image of intense privacy.

'What a weird mixture that woman is,' she remarks, peering more closely at the photograph.

'How do you mean?'

'Well . . . on the one hand so . . . kind of . . . sexy and yet . . . not.'

Tommy pulls a face. 'Under-appreciated, that's our Lu. I think she's missed out, somewhere along the line.'

'Missed out on what?'

'Oh, I don't know. Would you think I was a soppy old fool if I said . . . adventure?'

Chrissie seems to be about to say more but then goes back to her perusal of the photograph. 'So what's the

7

problem with Des? He's a good-looking man, I'll say that for him, and so is his son. A right lot of Lemons. You can tell you're all related.'

'Is that a compliment?'

'Hey, stop fishing. You know half the old ladies in here have got a crush on you, with your all-year-round tan and your dimples. Mind you, the competition isn't great, to be fair. You're the only man without a cardigan and zip-up slippers. Anyway, you haven't answered my question. What's wrong with this guy?'

'Des? Oh, there's nothing *wrong* with him. It just bothers me that neither of them has ever got to follow their dreams.'

They sit in silence for a while, lost in their own thoughts. Chrissie glances at her watch and Tommy sits up straighter.

'Anyway, back to the present,' he says quickly.

'I thought we were already in the present?' Chrissie wrinkles her nose. She's had words with Tommy before about talking in riddles. He grins.

'No, the *present* as in the gift. The money. My legacy. I've finally sold my house in Chandlebury. It was my parents' place and it needs a family to live in it to bring it to life. I don't need much cash for the future. Let's see what happens when Des, Lucia and Isaac suddenly realise they've got options.'

'You've given them some money to spend? Wow.'

'Wow indeed. And more importantly, there's something else even more useful. I'm passing on . . . the extra thing.'

'It sounds as if you've been more than generous, Tommy. Who wouldn't be happy with an unexpected dollop of cash? But what do you mean by the *extra thing*? I'm intrigued.'

Tommy doesn't answer for a moment. Then he smiles, one of the mysterious ones he keeps in reserve. It's good to keep people guessing sometimes. Chrissie is still waiting, tapping her fingers on the table between them. Eventually he cracks.

'It's not just the money that'll give them their freedom. The decider will be what I'm sending with it. Something very precious to me. I haven't found it easy to let it go, but the time's right. Nobody keeps it forever. A great upheaval is on the way for the Lemon family. Life in a sleepy English village is about to get a whole lot more interesting. You mark my words, the poor buggers won't know what's hit them.'

Chapter Two

Lucia Lemon sits at her desk, wrapped in a thick sweater over her oldest jeans. The Easter holidays ended three weeks ago and the month of May is here already, but the sun is refusing to come out this morning. The overcast sky matches Lucia's mood perfectly. She looks down at the little dog at her feet, and sighs.

'I'm so bored. There's nothing new to do any more apart from my reading group on a Wednesday morning. And the bloody summer fair. Oh, Nigel, I'm absolutely furious with myself about that. Why didn't I say no to organising the school fair? I don't even work there now. I'm just a mug. I must be going around with a sign on my head saying *sucker*.'

Nigel seems as unimpressed as Lucia with this character assassination. He rolls onto his back and waits for her to tickle his tummy, then drifts off to sleep again with his paws still in the air.

'I know how you feel. It's a dull old life, this early-retirement lark, isn't it?' Lucia says. 'Although I guess you can't really call it retiring when you're given the push.'

Outside the living room window, the garden stretches away, rambling and untidy. Lucia and Des don't do much in the way of weeding and planting these days so nature has run riot in places, although their dutiful son Isaac makes a point of mowing the lawn once a week and keeping the patio clear of leaves and twigs so that his bird table and all the dangling containers for fat balls can be a neat focal point from his bedroom.

This is great in its way, but Isaac is only twenty one and he seems to have slipped into the role of a much older son looking after his ageing parents. Having their only child later rather than sooner in their marriage was a delight and a blessing after years and years of trying but surely by now he should be ready to branch out on his own more? That abortive university course has knocked his already fragile confidence completely for six. Lu wishes she could find out the real reason why he dropped out. She has a feeling a girl was involved but Isaac clams up if she ever tries to get to the bottom of why he came home so suddenly.

Lucia leans her chin on one hand and watches a blackbird helping himself to the mealworms Isaac put out before he cycled off to work early this morning. He never forgets. If he put as much effort into making friends as he does with feeding the birds, he might not spend so much time alone in his room, she reflects sadly, but friendships have always been hard for Isaac. Has she been wrong not to battle with her feelings about leaving her comfort zone for all these years? If she and Des had made more of an effort to get out there in the world, Isaac might not be so isolated now.

Hearing the throaty chug of the Skoda as it pulls onto the drive, Lucia gets up rather stiffly and makes her way into the hall. Des must be back from his trip to the supermarket. It's his one concession to helping with the running of the house.

The front door crashes open and Des manages five steps along the hall before he drops a large crate at Lucia's feet.

'What on earth have you got there?' Lucia asks, moving closer.

He straightens up and rubs his back. 'I bumped into the delivery man as I got out of the car. There's something else too.'

Lucia bends down to peer at the crate more closely. It's made of light, unvarnished wood and is padlocked shut.

'Is there a key?'

'How do I know? I'm hoping it's in the parcel that came with it. Here you go.' Des kicks the front door closed behind him at last, shutting out the chilly blast, and hands over a bulky padded envelope. He shrugs off his waterproof, revealing a well-worn sweater that has somehow grown in the wash.

Lucia turns the package over, peering at the sender's address on the back.

'It's from the people at Tommy's old house. How weird. Bring it through to the kitchen, would you? It's freezing out here.'

Giving the box one last look, Lu heads for the kitchen to put the kettle on. It'll be her third cup of tea of the morning, but who cares? There's not much else to do. If she was at work now, it'd be break time. They'd all be in the warm staffroom finishing up the Easter chocolate supplies and talking about going on diets next week. Being made redundant is taking some getting used to. She knows Des feels the same. At 63, he's five years older than Lu. Des's career was meant to take him right up to retirement. They're just not ready for this.

'It must be from Tommy. I wonder why he didn't tell us to expect a delivery? Well, aren't you going to open the parcel?' her husband says, pulling up a chair at the kitchen table and shivering slightly.

Lucia puts the envelope on the table while she makes the tea, suddenly apprehensive. Why would Tommy go to all this trouble to send them something so substantial when he made such a big deal about dispatching everything unnecessary to the charity shop before he left his old home?

'Can we have the heating on?' she prevaricates.

'You are joking, aren't you? We said if we were both going to be at home permanently, we'd have to economize.'

Lucia sighs. 'It's just that I hadn't realised how warm it was in school. You must feel the same, you just don't want to admit it. If anything, your office was always too hot, you used to say.'

They grimace at each other over their steaming mugs of tea. The cat flap creaks open and a large fluffy creature eases its way in, placing each paw down very carefully as if the floor were made of ice.

'Hello Petula,' says Lucia, sighing as she sees the strange angle the cat's paws seem to land at as she skids across the laminate floor.

'The old girl's made it home then,' observes Des, leaning down to stroke the cat, who purrs and then nips him before going over the basket in the corner and flopping into it with a wheeze. 'Every time she goes walkabout I half expect her not to come back,' he says, rubbing his damaged hand. 'This place is turning into a rest home for sad old pets and tatty furniture. Everything here's seen better days. We need to declutter and decorate. We should smarten everywhere up now there's more time.'

'Well, we've got plenty of that now, haven't we?'

'Too right. Well, what are you waiting for? Go on, open Tommy's parcel.'

Lucia decides to ignore the sharpness in Des's voice and reaches for the package. It's sealed with three layers of sticky tape but eventually she gets through the barrier and draws out an oblong parcel encased in bubble wrap. Underneath is a smaller envelope, this time white, and with the words *A message from Tommy* in purple letters across the front.

Wordlessly, Lucia slits open the flap and slides out a small key, her fingers closing around it as Des reaches for the package and rips off the bubble wrap, revealing a tiny black tape recorder. 'I haven't seen one of these since the eighties,' he says, turning it over in his hands. 'I used one for dictation in the days when I had a secretary. Before we were restructured and I had to type my own letters.'

'Well, come on then, press play.' Lucia has never had much patience, and watching her husband turn the machine over and over in his hands is making her want to scream very loudly. A lot of things are making her feel like that at the moment, now she thinks about it.

Des gives up on his examination of the Dictaphone and presses a button, adjusting the volume as the voice of his uncle booms out.

'*Well, hello, you unfortunate folks up there in the draughty Midlands. I'll cut to the chase. You both think I've gone mad, don't you? Shutting myself away in the depths of the countryside, with just a bunch of octogenarians for company, and selling Coronation Villa? I know you both loved the old family home.*'

Lu hears the chink of crockery in the background and someone shouting about it being tea time. She hopes they're making Tommy's tea how he likes it. Imagine the luxury of having all your meals and drinks made for you while you relax in a sunlit conservatory. The brochure Tommy sent them when he moved in made the place look more like a five-star hotel than a retirement complex. She thinks about the tinned soup in the kitchen waiting to be opened. Vegetable. Des doesn't like anything too fancy.

'*Right then, if you're reading this, the new folk in Coronation Villa must have done their bit to spring my surprise. I asked them specifically to wait until I gave them the okay, to give me time to settle in here. Just to prove the point that I haven't lost my marbles and I can still make decisions, I've decided to dish out some of your inheritance*' *now, while you're still young enough to enjoy it, because although I plan on living a good long time, there's nothing much to spend all that lovely cash on here. So, my beloved relations, to that end, I'm giving twenty grand to Isaac. He still might not make it out of the nest, but at least he'll have a bit of scope to get a decent car. And as for you two old stick-in-the-muds . . .'*

Lucia opens her mouth to speak, eyes flashing but Des shushes her.

'Exactly how long are you planning to moulder in that backwater? Oh, don't get me wrong, as villages go, Chandlebury's fine and dandy. Much too far from the sea, of course, but you can't have everything. Anyway, it's high time you branched out. Take Lucia somewhere exciting, Des. You don't appreciate that gorgeous wife of yours enough, I've always said so.'

Des laughs. 'Yeah, right.'

He sees Lu's face flinch at the sarcasm-loaded words and backtracks hastily. 'Only joking, love.'

Lucia blinks away sudden tears. She's always laughed off Des's digs about her appearance but since she lost her job, they're not even mildly funny somehow. Des shrugs and rewinds the tape to catch the bit they've just missed. Tommy's voice booms out again.

'So in my humble opinion, you're both way overdue a few adventures. For that reason, I'm giving you some of my spare dosh now, instead of after I've popped my clogs. Fifteen thousand quid between you. If you check your bank account and tell the lad to do the same, you'll find it's

already safely in there. Now DO SOMETHING! You've worked hard all your lives. Get out there in the world and shake your tail feathers.

'*In the box, you'll find my collection of photo albums. You'll see that over the years, I've seen a heck of a lot of places and had shedloads of japes. Take a flip through and see if they inspire you. I really hope they will. Have some fun of your own, for pity's sake, and then come down here to see me. I'll get the bubbly in, plenty of it.*'

There's a crash in the background and a loud shriek.

'*Oh dear, the new girl in the kitchen's not doing too well. I hope that wasn't my second-best mug. There are two more things to mention. Des, I'd really appreciate it if you could check on my old mate Pete to see if he's okay. He seemed a bit down when I last spoke to him. To be frank with you, in my mind that's part of the deal. In return for this dollop of cash that I hope's going to put a spring in your step, you have to go and see Pete. It's only fair, right? Pay it forward?*

'*Finally, there's the other gift. Des will recognise it and he'll explain why it's important, Lu. I haven't found it easy to give it to you both, but it's the right time, I'm sure. And chaps, don't over-think all this, like you usually do. Just go with the flow for once, okay? I'm presenting you with the gift of freedom.*

'*Give the lovely Lu a kiss for me, Des. Bye for now, both.*'

Chapter Three

Lucia is speechless, staring at the recorder as Des clicks it off. He holds his hand out for the key and deals with the padlock.

'I hope this isn't one of Tommy's weird jokes,' he says. 'I'm half expecting a jack-in- the-box to hit me in the face.'

They both lean forward. When Des makes no further move, Lucia tentatively lifts the lid. The box opens with a creak. They wait. Nothing untoward happens, so Des reaches into the pile of albums, lifting them out two or three at a time. Silently, he spreads them on the table, as if he's performing a card trick. He studies them for a moment, picks one at random and opens it at the first page.

A middle-aged man with a long, tangled mass of fair hair and a wide smile has an arm around a woman in a bikini. They're both deeply tanned and the man is a head taller than his companion, with a lean, well-muscled body. There's a beach in the background and the tide's out a very long way. Des frowns.

'Those are donkeys and you can hardly see the sea. My mum and dad used to take me there when I was a kid. It's Skegness, Lu. Why would he want us to go to sodding Skeggy, of all places?'

'I've got no idea, but there are plenty more pictures here. Look, the books are all labelled.'

She begins to pick up the albums, one by one. They're all different colours. Some are leather bound and classy, others plastic-covered and more garish. Each book has a sticker on the front. She recognises Tommy's messy handwriting and trademark purple pen.

'What a great life he's had. Look, this one's full of Spanish pictures. And here's one that covers the Lake District and the Scottish borders. Wow.' The envy in Lucia's voice surprises her, and she can see that Des is startled too.

'I didn't know you felt like that. Do you think we should've travelled? Done more . . . stuff?'

'Like what?' They're straying into territory Lucia doesn't want to explore too closely. Being so busy at work and only having school holidays at their disposal have always been the excuses they have used to anyone who's asked why they don't go on trips away from home. 'Way too expensive and a complete rip off,' Des has often said, of airline prices and suchlike at peak times.

'Well, where is it, then?' she prevaricates.

'Where's what?'

'My kiss? Tommy said you were to give me a kiss for him.'

Des stares at Lu in obvious bewilderment. Then he shrugs, gets up and walks round the table, planting a quick peck on her cheek. 'There you go. Now can we get on with the job in hand?'

Lucia stands up and grabs her husband's arm before he has the chance to get to his chair again. 'Hey, come on. That was pathetic,' she says, trying to make her voice light and flirty. 'When was the last time you kissed me properly, Des?'

He freezes to the spot and looks down at Lu. She stands her ground and waits. After a moment he puts his hands on her shoulders and bends to touch his lips to hers. Lucia tries hard to feel something . . . anything . . . but she can tell by the fact that Des's eyes are wide open and he's making sure the rest of his body doesn't touch hers that it's the same for him. He lets go and sits down again. Lu does the same. The silence seems to drag on. Des puts his head in his hands.

'Des? What's going on? I know we've both been a bit fed up lately, but . . .'

'A bit fed up? Is that what you think this is?'

'Well, what *is* it then? Tell me? I'm not a bloody mind-reader.' Lu's breath is coming in gasps now. She follows all her usual panic attack strategies but her head's spinning. She's been avoiding this conversation for months. The ostrich technique hasn't let her down before.

'Are you happy with me, Lu?'

The words shock her, spoken in a voice so unlike Des's usual matter-of-fact bluster. 'Of course I am,' she answers automatically. What else is there to say?

'Then why do you look so sad all the time?'

'Sad?' Lu repeats the word as if she's never heard it before. 'I wouldn't say that . . . exactly.'

20

'How would you describe it then?'

'Well . . . it takes everyone a while to get used to big life changes, doesn't it? We're not unusual.'

'Aren't we?' He looks up, and Lu can see the pain in his eyes. She flinches.

'No, I don't think so. You've worked all your adult life and I loved my job at the school. I felt useful. Now, we're just . . . us.'

'And that's the problem, isn't it? What actually is "us"?'

Lucia's breathing is under control now. This is silly. Des must be having a delayed mid-life crisis, or something. But as hard as she tries, she can't think of an answer to his question. The clock on the wall carries on its loud, slow beat, as if emphasising their life ticking away, second by second.

Eventually, Lucia clears her throat. 'So, where were we?' she says, pulling another album towards her.

Des rubs his eyes and blinks. He sits up straighter. 'I think we were talking at cross purposes. You sounded as if you're wishing you'd been to all these places. Have I got it wrong all these years? I thought you liked our *staycations*.'

Lucia takes a deep breath. She loathes that word. 'I did . . . I do. It's just . . . oh, I don't know. Maybe we've been missing out. Isaac's never had a proper holiday because of the way we feel about being away from home, has he?'

'But Isaac's never liked being far from his own bedroom either, you know that. It's just how he is. He used to throw a tantrum if we so much as suggested he went to

21

someone else's house to play. Days out have always been quite enough for all of us. Travelling's over-rated.'

'Is it though? Maybe we should have tried not to be so boring. My mum and dad were the same, especially after . . . after what happened . . . with Eddie . . .'

They stare at each other. It's been years since Lucia has referred to that time.

'Don't upset yourself, Lu. It's in the past. There's no point in digging it all up again.'

'You *would* say that. You're just happy to brush everything under the carpet and pretend it's all okay. And because of Eddie I've cramped our style haven't I? Yours, mine, Isaac's?'

Des sighs.

'What's got into you today?'

'Me? What about you with your stupid questions?'

'Leave me out of it for now. You've been going on about kissing, and now all this comes pouring out. There's no point in thinking like that just because Tommy's suddenly decided to interfere.'

There's another uncomfortable silence during which Lu has time to reflect that there have been quite a lot of these lately. She tries to think of a way to divert the conversation into safer waters but Des beats her to it.

'Talking of Tommy, I had no idea he had so much money going spare, did you?' he says. 'And why would he spend it on us anyway?'

Lu shakes her head and Des continues. 'I knew Tommy wasn't hard up even before he sold Coronation Villa, but this is seriously weird. Money for Isaac and us too, but the catch is, he wants to say what we should do with it. That's outrageous, isn't it? Why should we want to have a holiday when there's so much to do in the house? Dumping his friend Pete's problems on us too? And what if I don't want my tail feathers shaking?'

Ignoring the last question, Lucia thinks back to the many riotous parties she's attended at Tommy's house. 'That's a point, tell me more about Pete. Why is he so important? I'm sure I've never come across anyone of that name in Tommy's gang, have you?'

Des scratches his head. 'I've only spoken to the guy a couple of times, and it was a good while ago. Sir Peter Cavendish is his full title. He's a baronet. Tommy met him when he used to volunteer at Meadowthorpe Manor, before he started teaching. You must have heard of it? I think the old house has been going downhill for a long time, but there's a huge estate, and Tommy always liked getting his hands dirty.'

'What's he like? Is he Tommy's age?'

'No, he's older. He seemed like a good bloke, but no idea why Tommy's so concerned about him. The man lives in a stately home, what problems would he have, apart from bats in the belfry?'

Des gets up and starts to prowl around the kitchen. Lucia grits her teeth. Looking for biscuits again. He'll probably hunt down the chocolate digestives she was saving for the weekend, eat four and then say he doesn't want lunch. Des surprises her by giving up the search quite quickly and sitting down again.

Lucia rubs her hands up and down her arms to warm herself. The tip of her nose feels chilly and she's cold right to her bones. She and Des gaze at each other for a moment, and then he shrugs his shoulders and stands up to switch the boiler on. It hums into life, the ancient pipes clanking as water begins to flow through them.

'Shall we see what else is in the box now?' he says.

Shaking off the thought of Tommy's baronet with some difficulty, Lucia reaches both hands into the crate and begins pulling out the rest of the contents. 'It's just a heap of old maps under these albums,' she says, puzzled. 'Why would Tommy think we need these?'

'Haven't got a clue. He says he wants us to have an adventure, doesn't he? But we've got a perfectly good Sat Nav, even if it is worth more than the car. Anyway, like I said, we haven't got time for dashing around the country.'

'N . . . no, I guess we haven't.'

'Lu, you're not thinking of going along with this, are you? We definitely agreed we were going to get this place straight before we went on any holidays. Everywhere's dingy and Isaac's room hasn't been touched for twenty years. Since he was born, in in fact.'

'That's because he hardly ever comes out for long enough for us to decorate it.'

Des smiles rather sadly. 'Yes, he does love his own space, doesn't he?'

'At least he's showing more interest in food these days. He's actually started baking now and again, thanks to

Polly. He used to love experimenting in the kitchen before he went away. I thought we were right to persuade him to go to Uni but he's never been the same since, has he?'

'No. There was something weird about that. And ever since he came home, he's spent even more time on his own than he did before.'

'He's always on his laptop. If I hadn't pushed him into applying for that job in the lab he'd never leave home at all. We could always ask him to change rooms while we give his a coat of emulsion, I guess. But now Polly and the baby are in the other big bedroom, there's only the box room spare and it's full of junk.'

They exchange glances again. Long years into this marriage, they can say a lot without words.

'Perhaps Polly likes painting and stuff,' Lucia says hopefully. 'We don't really know much about her, do we? Only that she's got Reggie to look after and she loves cooking. She's started to teach Isaac how to make a few of her favourite veggie dishes. Anything that gets him downstairs is a good thing, I reckon.'

Des lowers his voice as he answers. You can never be sure when their lodger will appear. She's usually barefoot and she makes no noise approaching, unless Reggie's in one of his bellowing moods.

'I can't believe we ended up with another twenty-something kid under our roof. And not only that, a baby thrown in. It was Rowan's fault. I know she's your friend but she can be bloody interfering sometimes.'

Lucia smiles. Rowan runs the village post office with

25

great efficiency but she also likes to take a hand in people's lives if she thinks they need what she calls 'a leg up'.

'If she hadn't seen Polly putting up the card on their shop notice board to find somewhere to live we wouldn't be short of a spare room now,' says Des. 'Goodness only knows why she thought we needed to rent it out at this point in our lives. We've got enough going on.'

Lucia is painfully aware this is another subject to avoid. She reaches into the bottom of the crate and lifts out the only thing left in there. It's a square object swathed in red tissue-paper, about the same size as a Terry's Chocolate Orange. Tommy knows they're Lu's favourite indulgence and always makes sure she gets one at Christmas. Her stomach gives a hopeful rumble but Des seems to read her thoughts and shakes his head. His eyes are fixed on the parcel as she tears off the paper and reveals a battered leather case.

'So *that's* what Tommy meant,' he says slowly. 'I was afraid it might be.'

Chapter Four

Lu hesitates. This must be a gift for both of them. 'Shall I open it or will you?' she asks. 'What can it be?'

Des doesn't reply, and when Lu looks up, she's shocked to see how pale he is. 'Go on, you do it,' he says huskily.

Mystified, Lucia reaches out and lifts the lid of the leather case. The hinge creaks slightly as she reveals a lining of faded blue silk. Resting in the centre of the box is something so unusual that Lu can hardly speak.

She reaches out and takes the object from its nest. It's perfectly circular and smooth, with the pleasing heaviness of the sort of large stone you might select to bring back from the beach, made of something that looks and feels like cool, rippled marble. She gazes down at the sea green curves. At first glance an inset right in the centre looks a bit like a clock face, although when she looks more closely, Lu can see that it must have more than one use.

Cradling the beautiful thing in the palm of her hand, Lucia takes it over to the window. A sudden shaft of sunlight catches the colours in the enamels of the dial. She sees azure and emerald green joined by a pattern of feathery gold filigree. The brass edging is well-polished, and gleams as brightly as the fragile hands and needles

27

that are now spinning around madly as if unsure what to do next.

Lucia can't help smiling in delight.

'It's got two purposes,' she says slowly. 'I can see now that the ring round the outside is an old fashioned barometer like the one my gran had to predict the weather. The middle part is a compass. I think the stone in the centre is a sapphire and there are tiny diamonds on each compass point. Des, this must be worth a fortune. Why has Tommy given it to us?'

'I haven't a clue. It's been his most precious possession for years but he hardly ever shows it to anyone. He . . . well, he actually tried to give it to me once when I was visiting not so long ago and I was really down in the dumps.'

'So why didn't you take it? Hang on a minute, why were you so fed up? Did I know about this?'

Des frowns at his wife who's come to sit opposite him again, placing the object halfway between them.

'Oh, it was about the time the rumour of redundancies was going around at work. I guess he could tell I was coming up to a bit of a crossroads. But I suppose I didn't want to deprive Tommy of one of his favourite treasures.'

Lucia waits. There's got to be more to it than this because her husband has got his shifty look on, the one he gets when he's forgotten their wedding anniversary or when he's had a silly row with Isaac, but Des has clammed up.

'Hmm. Anyway, it's ours now. It's so pretty, isn't it? I can't stop looking at it. Those colours . . .'

Lucia leans closer, admiring the way the jewels glitter and the brass gleams even in the weak sunshine. 'So it can tell us the weather and it knows the direction we're going, but what are we meant to do with it?'

'Oh, *we* don't do anything with the compass, my love. It's what it does with us that you need to worry about.'

Lucia swallows hard. Des's words seem to hang in the air between them. The only sounds in the kitchen are the whimpering of the little dog as he chases squirrels in his dreams, and the mesmeric hum of the fridge. 'Tell me more,' she says.

There's a pause in which Des reaches out to touch the compass but pulls his hand back. Finally he grasps it and holds it in the palm of his left hand. With the fingers of the other hand he makes circles in the glass over the dials, lightly at first and then more forcefully.

'It's no good,' he says. 'I didn't think it would be really, it didn't like me last time either. This is Tommy's treasure. It probably only works for him.'

Lucia leans forward and takes the compass from her husband. 'I don't know what you mean. What were you expecting it to do?'

He looks at her for a long moment as if assessing something, then sighs. 'I bet you'll think I'm mad, but it . . . kind of . . .gives you guidance. So, if Tommy was unsure of what to do about something, he would hold it, like I just did, and wait for its reaction.'

He scowls a little as he sees her expression. 'You see, I knew you wouldn't get it. You're smirking.'

Lucia tries to look serious but this whole thing is getting more and more farcical. 'Go on then, show me.'

Wordlessly, Des pushes Tommy's gift towards Lucia and she cradles it in her palm for a moment, the smoothness and the weight somehow calming her jumbled thoughts.

Automatically, as if following an age-old pattern, she forces her mind to focus on the two golden needles which immediately begin to quiver and then spin slowly around their respective dials. The barometer readings are similar to those on the one Lucia's grandfather kept in their hallway and tapped every day as a matter of course. At the bottom of the dial is the word stormy. Going clockwise, the next is *cloudy*, followed by *variable*. The topmost word is *change*, then still moving clockwise the last two are *steady* and *fair*.

'It's moving,' she breathes. 'What does it mean?'

There's still no reply from Des so Lucia waits for the delicate mechanism to settle and looks more closely. The barometer needle is pointing towards the 12 o'clock position on the dial and the word *change*. The compass is pointing to south west.

'Des, I think it's broken. The house faces north and anyone can see it's about to rain.'

'I don't understand either. Maybe it doesn't work without Tommy.'

Des doesn't meet his wife's puzzled gaze. Lost in thought, Lucia considers the conundrum, something else occurring to her as she ponders. 'Why does Tommy think he has to give us the gift of freedom, Des? It's not like we're in prison. What's he getting at?'

Des shrugs and stares at the floor. Lucia waits, the word *prison* seeming to echo around her head. After an uncomfortable minute or two he looks up.

'It's a dig at me, if you must know. Tommy's referring to something he said to me about you just before we got married. On my stag night, as it happens. Totally out of order, and I told him so.'

'Go on. I'm listening.' Lucia is intrigued. This is the first she's heard of any stag night argument but thinking back, she recalls a distinct frostiness between Tommy and Des around that time. She'd assumed it was because Tommy resented Des settling down and getting on the property ladder when he was frittering his money away on fancy holidays.

'Oh, come on, you know he's always had a soft spot for you. He was spouting some rubbish about me clipping your wings, because you were so young, as if I'd captured you against your will. You were just as keen to settle down if I remember rightly, love. I had the house, there was no point in waiting, was there?'

Lucia is trying to think of an honest answer to this when Polly appears silently, padding into the kitchen with a bundle of washing. Their lodger bends to load the washing machine, then straightens up and turns, eyes widening at the sight of the maps and the photographs, but it's the glowing colours of the compass that really catch her attention. She comes closer to take a better look.

'Wow, that's cool. What is it?'

Lucia glances up at Polly and is struck afresh by how attractive she is. Not traditionally pretty, but with long dark hair flowing down her back in rippling waves, and clear green eyes that seem to miss nothing. A light dusting of freckles over the bridge of her nose only enhance her pixie-like air. She's delicately built with narrow shoulders and a tiny waist but there's an unmistakeable strength about her, especially in the capable hands that seem to be able to do any household task much more quickly and efficiently than any of them.

'Its . . . well it's . . .' Lucia sees Des frowning at her and continues anyway. 'Isaac's godfather has given it to us, along with some money and maps and photo albums. He wants us to plan an adventure.'

'Cool! What an amazing present. Where will you go?'

Des stands up. His body language is so frosty that Lucia flinches but Polly is undaunted. 'What's up, Des?' she asks.

'Nothing's up. I just don't see the problem with wanting an easy life after all those years paper-pushing and jumping when the boss says jump. Why would we want to go away all the time, racketing around the country in an ancient car that might conk out at any moment, following a stupid scheme that Tommy's cooked up for some crazy reason of his own?'

The kitchen door slams shut behind Des as he leaves the room. It's not often closed, and it rocks slightly on its hinges, as if shocked to be in use. Polly pulls a face at Lucia.

'Sorry, Lu. I think I touched a nerve there. You know me, I always say too much.'

'I like it. My gran used to be the same, calling a spade a spade is how she described it. We know where we are with you, Poll.'

She grimaces. 'Yes, but some people take offence. I reckon Isaac thinks I'm . . . a bit too much.'

'Isaac's always found everybody too much, pet. You carry on being yourself. We'd be lost without you and Reggie now.'

'*You* might, but I think Des would be quite glad to see the back of us. I didn't mean to upset him though. It just sounded such a great idea, to go travelling. You've surely both earned it?'

'Well, I . . .'

'And it's none of my business but you're always at the school doing something or other. I'm guessing they don't pay you for any of it now you've officially left the place?'

Lucia feels the band of tension that's never far away tightening around her temples.

She places the compass carefully on the table before speaking. She picks her words carefully, not wanting to sound defensive.

'Polly, I know you and Des and Isaac think I'm silly doing all these random jobs for other people. I just can't seem to say no somehow,' Lucia says, feeling exhaustion wash over her when she remembers last year's bitter fight over who was going to run the cake stall. The repercussions lasted until at least Christmas.

'I don't know. It depends how much you enjoy it, I guess.' Polly goes over to the door to listen for Reggie. 'Sorry, Lu, I just want to make sure he isn't awake. He was up three times in the night with his poor sore gums so he's having a lie in. That's why I've got these bags under my eyes.'

'You look lovely. You always do. About the jobs though. I'm not sure if I do enjoy them all that much, definitely not the summer fair anyway.'

'And why would you? I reckon it's time for a complete break from all of it. The whole lot. This present from Isaac's godfather has come just at the right time. Go for it!'

'Really?

Polly comes and sits at the table and takes Lucia's hands, holding them tightly in her warm grip. 'Look, Lu – you saved me and Reggie from having to take some crumby place with damp and cabbage smells and . . . and probably cockroaches. You're a helpful, kind person and you deserve good things to happen to you.'

Does she? Lucia looks again at the beautiful gift, lying between a map of the western isles of Scotland and one of the coast of Normandy. Freedom. There's a buzz in the air that she can't explain and so many emotions are fighting for prime position in her head. There's no way of knowing which one will win, but Lucia has an unexpected, overwhelming desire to see the sea.

Chapter Five

Three days later Lucia and Polly are on the train into town, giddy with excitement at what they are about to do. Polly has asked Lucia's good friend Rowan to look after Reggie for a couple of hours. Rowan runs the village post office with effortless efficiency, adores babies and always makes a big fuss of Reggie. Polly is somewhat edgy about leaving him to begin with but once she's had a message with a picture of the little boy playing happily, she relaxes and throws herself into the escapade.

'But what's Des going to say when he finds out you've blown nearly all Tommy's present on an old camper van?' Polly says, not for the first time. 'He's going to go mad, Lu. He really is.'

Lucia shrugs. She's not ready to admit that Polly could be right. It's her turn to make a decision, for once. 'He'll get used to the idea,' she says, straightening her shoulders and ignoring the little worm of doubt creeping into her mind. 'He'll be happy about it once I've filled him in on all the places we can go. Isaac must come too.'

'Right.' Polly looks out of the window. 'And I suppose if he doesn't come round, you can always sell it again.'

'Why are you being so defeatist, Poll?' Lu says, turning

to face the younger woman. 'I thought you'd be all for the idea. You're always saying we should have more fun. Well, this is the start of it. A whole new chapter.'

'I'm not trying to slap you down. I just don't want you to be disappointed when . . . I mean if Des doesn't jump for joy at the thought of a long holiday with you.'

'And Isaac. Don't forget him.'

Polly is silent for a few moments. Then she says quietly 'I haven't known you all very long, I guess, but Isaac doesn't strike me as one of life's great adventurers, Lu. I've never actually seen him go anywhere except to work.'

'Exactly. That's why we need to do this, before it's too late. Isaac's world is his room and his flipping computer. I don't know what he finds to do on it all those hours, do you? I've thought this through, Poll. I hardly slept last night. It's the right thing to do, I know it is.' Lucia reaches into her bag, fingers automatically searching for the cool comforting feel of the compass. Polly stares at her.

'You've been acting very suspiciously ever since you got that gift from Tommy, touching it it all the time when you think nobody's watching. You're doing it now, aren't you? Come on, Lu, what's all this about?'

Lucia feels her cheeks burning. She's checked the barometer several times today already and she still thinks it might be broken. The needle is stuck on *change* and the compass is firmly set to south west.

'Look, we're nearly in Stowhampton,' she says with relief. Explanations can wait.

Lucia and Polly hurriedly follow the directions on Polly's phone and reach their destination with five minutes to spare. Lu's out of breath and her hands are shaking. She clutches Polly's arm as they approach the house where the vehicle in question is parked in the driveway.

'Oh . . .' Polly gasps.

Lucia blinks. 'He didn't say it was decorated,' is all she can think to say.

As they stand gazing at the amazing spectacle of a converted transit van with a giant rainbow painted all down one side, the front door of the house opens and a willowy man comes towards them holding out both hands. His grey hair flows down his back and his feet are bare apart from several jewelled toe rings.

'He's going to get gravel rash in his feet if he doesn't watch out. That or frostbite,' murmurs Polly.

Lu snorts, but quickly pulls herself together. 'Erm . . . Donovan Partridge?' she says. 'We spoke on the phone yesterday. I'm Lucia Lemon.'

'Of course you are. What a wonderful name. How did you choose it?'

'I . . . well . . . my mother picked it for me, I suppose, and then I married a Lemon.'

Lucia can hear Polly's strangled giggles now and she coughs loudly. 'Yours too, your name I mean. It's . . . unusual.'

'Donovan after the greatest folk singer this county has ever known. You know 'Catch The Wind'? No? 'Universal

37

Soldier'? 'Mellow Yellow'?' he adds rather desperately. Polly's face says she thinks he's speaking in tongues but Lucia nods.

'Absolutely,' she says firmly, nudging Polly hard with her elbow. 'And Partridge?'

'In a pear tree?' Polly says, and then has to cover her mouth.

Donovan fixes her with a glare. 'The Partridge Family. Home of David Cassidy and the marvellous Shirley Jones. Anyway, enough about me. Here . . .' he gives an expansive flourish, 'Here she is.'

'She?'

'Flora the Explorer. It breaks my heart to let her go but we're emigrating to Thailand next month and I can't take her with me.' He sighs, and ushers Polly and Lucia around to the other side of the van.

Lucia opens her eyes wide and Polly lets out a squeak of pure admiration. The rainbow on the driver's side is beautifully executed with all the colours clear and bright but the passenger side is completely covered with flowers of every kind. Polly sees lilies, tulips, roses, daisies and a whole host other kinds that are like nothing she's ever seen blooming.

'Wow. Just wow,' Polly breathes.

It takes all Lucia's well-learned powers of calming excited children to get her friend back on track, but soon Polly has her head under the bonnet, moving speedily on to taking them for a test drive on the bypass and casting stern looks at Lucia as they negotiate a fair price.

While Polly's busy doing a final check and Donovan has nipped inside to the loo, Lucia slides the compass's case from her bag and flips open the lid.

The feel of her new treasure in her hand is reassuring. Her fingers slide over the smooth surface and almost immediately the needles react. A shiver of excitement runs right through Lucia's body. The compass is still pointing to south-west but the word on the barometer dial where the other needle rests is *fair*. Of course it is.

Donovan turns out to be deceptively shrewd when it comes to his finances but Polly and Lucia together are more than a match for him. In next to no time Lucia has done a direct transfer of cash and having checked it's gone through he waves them off, albeit with tears in his eyes.

'Goodbye darling Flora,' they hear him cry as they chug away down the road. 'Happy exploring! I know you're going to . . .'

His voice fades away as they turn the corner and Polly giggles. 'I hope he wasn't going to say, "I know you're going to break down as soon as you get on the motorway" because my impressive knowledge of engines doesn't include being able to replace one,' she says.

Lucia is too busy getting used to this cumbersome new vehicle and way too full of joy in her ownership to pay any attention. It's not until she pulls up beside the Skoda at home and the van splutters to a standstill that the enormity of what she's done hits her. She and Des have never had that amount of money in the bank just sitting there for no reason, and now most of it has gone. As she climbs down from the drivers' seat, she sees her husband's astonished face at the window.

'Now we're for it,' Polly mutters.

The row that follows is one that Lucia will never forget. Des is incandescent with rage when he realises what his wife has done 'without a by-your-leave'. He stomps around the living room bellowing about ridiculous women who have no common sense and zero consideration for others and it isn't until Reggie is delivered home by Rowan that he stops shouting.

The house is very quiet when Des has slammed out of the door to go for a pint at the pub, but Lucia and Polly are soon distracted by showing the new purchase to Rowan and then again to Isaac when he arrives home on his bike. Rowan is full of admiration and is easily persuaded to stay for dinner with them all. Isaac says very little.

Rowan goes upstairs with Polly to help bathe the baby and Lucia finds herself alone with her son in the kitchen. Before he can escape up to his room, she hands him a knife. They sit down at the table and begin to peel potatoes, a companionable silence falling between them until Isaac clears his throat and says, 'So I'm getting the hint that Dad wasn't impressed with your masterplan?'

Lucia rolls her eyes. 'You could say that. It's best to give him time to calm down. A pint or two and a game of darts should do the trick.'

Isaac doesn't reply, and Lucia glances across at him with a ripple of motherly pride. She knows she's not the only one who thinks her son is an extremely good-looking young man. At almost twenty-one, Isaac is even taller than his father, with a slimmer build but strong muscles from all the cycling he does. His fair hair is cropped very short so there is no sign of Des's greying curls or Tommy's wild mop of white locks. The Lemon males are a handsome bunch, Lucia thinks, with their brilliant blue eyes and their tendency to tan easily. The memory of month after month of disappointments and then the gruelling round of fertility treatments were worth every painful step along the way to her dream of being a mum.

'So what about you, Isaac?' she asks after a few moments, swallowing a wave of emotion. 'I'm guessing you'll have heard from Uncle Tommy by now? About the cash?'

'I have. I wanted to talk to you about that. It's a hell of a lot of money, Mum. Why would he do that? Should I refuse it, do you think?'

'Refuse it? Not on your life. He just wants to help us all out. It's Tommy's choice what he does with his savings surely? Did you get an email telling you about it?'

'Yes.' Isaac rubs a hand over his face, reminding Lucia of the little boy who had always been deeply troubled by surprises. 'He seems to think I should make a splash. Buy a car, put a deposit on a flat, that kind of thing.'

'Is that what you want?'

Isaac busies himself cutting potatoes into chunks before answering and Lucia holds her breath. Bringing up Isaac has never been easy, not helped by her feelings of guilt at holding him back. 'I'm sorry I haven't been a better mum to you,' she blurts out eventually.

'What are you talking about?'

Isaac looks genuinely confused by the sudden apology, so Lucia ploughs on. 'I mean, I should have encouraged you to be more outgoing when you were small. I gave in too easily when you didn't want to go places, because well, I was always happier staying put too, if I'm honest, love.'

'What's brought all this on? I'm not complaining.' He grins at her and Lucia tries to smile back but there's a lump in her throat. That smile. It's always melted her heart. 'Anyway, what about Dad?' Isaac continues. 'He's not exactly led the way, has he? When did he last suggest going out?'

'True enough. Anyway, I've been doing a lot of thinking,' Lu says. 'I want us to have some fun in the future, like a proper family. Outings, holidays . . . it's not too late. Are you up for that?'

Isaac shrugs. 'What does Polly think about all this?'

He's avoiding her eyes now and there's a faint flush on his cheeks. Lucia smiles to herself. Aha. So Isaac isn't impervious to Polly's charms. She suspected as much.

'Polly's all for it. Maybe we could persuade her to come with us.'

Lucia flinches at the thought of not only getting Des onside but persuading him that any road trips should include their lodger, not to mention her small child, with the additional challenge of talking Isaac round, but she swallows her doubts and gets on with the dinner preparations. Shortly afterwards, when she receives a text to say Des will be eating at the pub tonight, she heaves a sigh of relief. There will be plenty of time to make plans when the dust of the fierce row has settled. However Des doesn't return home until much later, when his exhausted but exhilarated wife is already in bed and fast asleep.

Chapter Six

Weak sunshine is already creeping through a crack in the curtains when Lucia wakes the next morning. She rubs her eyes and sits up. The place next to her is empty, with only the faint dent in the pillow suggesting that someone else has slept there. The alarm clock on the bedside table tells her it's half past six but Lu's been out cold for hours so she doesn't mind waking early. She hasn't slept this well since the day she lost her job.

'Des?' she calls. No answer. He can't be in the shower – the pipes are so noisy in this old house that you can't even clean your teeth without waking up the world.

Lucia slips out of bed, pushes her arms into the sleeves of her old towelling bathrobe and heads for the stairs. She hears a plaintive cry from Polly's room. Reggie's stirring now, and shouting for attention. Polly's voice answers sleepily and he subsides into a contented crooning. Isaac's door is firmly closed.

Where on earth is Des? Maybe he's planning to surprise her with breakfast in bed. Lu snorts. That'd be a first. She potters downstairs, automatically glancing out of the hall window. Their car isn't in its usual place under the oak tree. Strange. She leans to look round the back of the house where she eventually parked her new pride and joy. Flora the Explorer is a substantial affair, not terribly attractive apart from her decorations but solid and roadworthy, with only a few dents and scrapes.

The previous owner has customised Flora in various ways. Inside, everything you could possibly need for a camping holiday is stowed away in neat little cupboards. Lucia clasps her hands together and takes a deep breath to calm the fizz of joy that sweeps over her. It's the first vehicle she's ever chosen by herself, and already she loves it. Tommy's money has made this possible, she thinks, smiling as she goes to hunt for Des. It's going to be the start of a whole new chapter. Des just needs a helping hand to start to live again. Perhaps they both do.

Downstairs, only their elderly dog is waiting in the kitchen. 'Where is he, then, Nige?' Lucia asks. Unsurprisingly, Nigel doesn't answer but goes over to his bowl and looks up hopefully. It's only then that Lu sees the letter on the table. It has her name written in Des's trademark capitals across the front.

She reaches for it, pulling out a chair, ripping it open with mounting unease. Like Tommy, Des never writes letters if he can help it. Inside the envelope are more capitals, closely written on two sheets of blue Basildon Bond paper. There's a sinking feeling in Lucia's stomach as she begins to read.

Dear Lu,

There's no easy way of saying this. I'm leaving you. Well, not just you, I'm leaving everything in this godforsaken house. Our reclusive son who seems to dislike me more every day, which tears me apart, it really does. I love Isaac so much and I've tried so hard with him, but it's no use. We're like strangers these days. Then there's the lodger. Lovely though she is, I'll never understand why you had to bring Polly and her noisy baby in just when we were heading for some time of our own. And the geriatric pets, who break my heart every time I think about losing them, but, let's face it, smell a bit. Everything is just too much, Lu, don't you think so too?

Right on cue, Petula staggers through the cat flap, meowing pitifully, but Lucia ignores her. She reads on, one hand over her heart like a Victorian heroine in a melodrama.

You must have got the message by now. I don't want to live like this. Surely Isaac shouldn't be so antisocial? They said at school he had comparatively mild Autism but his behaviour doesn't seem very mild to me these days. Mild compared to what? Why can't he talk to us instead of playing those computer games day and night? And he ought to be planning for his future by now. I had my life all mapped out by the time I was his age. You know that.

All I wanted was for us to have some time for ourselves. To enjoy the house for a change, and spend some time doing it up, but once you'd heard Tommy's message and seen the maps and everything, that went out of the window, didn't it, Lu? I've got a feeling you're ready to break out, and maybe I am too, but not in the same way. We should have talked more over the years about why neither of us have felt able to travel, I realise that now, but taking off completely into the unknown isn't the answer for me.

I don't want to go trundling around to places I've not got the slightest desire to visit and I don't know why you would want to do that either. I love you but we've been drifting around aimlessly for ages, haven't we? I need peace and quiet for a while so I'm going to stay with Bob to think things through. He'll understand. He always did.

I'll be in touch. You can keep the motorhome. I never wanted it anyway.

Des.

Lucia takes a deep, shaky breath. 'He's left us,' she tells the cat and dog. 'But . . . but Des never goes anywhere. And why go and visit Bob anyway? As far as I know they haven't seen each other for years. Surely he could have found someone who lives nearer?' The pets stare at her, unblinking. Upstairs, Reggie starts to cry. Putting her hands over her eyes, Lucia joins him.

After a while, hearing Isaac moving around upstairs, she gets up from the table and tears off a wad of kitchen roll, mopping her face quickly. Tears alarm her son, always have done. She busies herself at the sink, washing the few dirty pots as Isaac enters the kitchen, returning his mumbled 'Morning' but keeping her back to him. She hears him begin his breakfast preparations and then, unusually, he stops clattering and comes to stand beside her.

'What's up, Mum?'

Lucia is so surprised she drops a mug, but Isaac catches it deftly in one hand and places it on the draining board before taking her gently by the shoulders and turning her around to face him. She stares up at him, reminded sharply of Des as the faintly worried blue eyes gaze down at her. She longs to reach up and smooth the short fair hair, but she resists. He doesn't appreciate that sort of contact.

'Come on, tell me what's happened. I heard you crying from upstairs,' he says. 'Is it Dad? He went out really early. What's he done to upset you this time?'

There are so many surprising things to take in here that Lu can't think of anything to say. Firstly, Isaac hardly ever notices other people's worries, but *this time* suggests he's aware of the tension in the house since Lu and Des finished work. Also, this is the longest speech he's made for ages, and he's still holding her shoulders, which in itself is odd.

'Mum?'

Lucia takes a couple of deep breaths. 'It looks as if your dad's walked out on us . . . well, on me . . .' she says. 'You'd better read his letter.'

Too late, she remembers the words that Des has written about his son, but Isaac's already let go of her and is skimming the two pages. His face gives nothing away as he reads. A loud shriek announces Reggie and Polly's arrival in the kitchen and Lu's heart sinks. Now she's going have to go through all this again and she's not even taken it in herself properly.

Des leaving? They've been together for years, ever since they bumped into each other, quite literally, at Stowhampton ice rink when Lu was almost seventeen. Des was twenty-one at the time and already well on his way to a steady well-paid career as an accountant. With a hefty dollop of cash donated by his parents, he'd even got himself a mortgage on a tiny cottage on the edge of the village.

This all seemed impossibly grown up to Lucia, and she was impressed. For a long time she'd gone along with his strongly-held opinion that they were better off as a couple and children were an unnecessary complication. By the time she'd persuaded him otherwise, her body didn't seem to want to cooperate. The joy of finally having Isaac overshadowed Lu's frustration at not being able to get through to her husband how desperately she wanted a baby and she has never seriously looked at another man since she fell for Des in such a big way. Life without him is unimaginable.

'Hiya guys,' says Polly, handing the baby to Lu as she goes over to warm some milk for his cereal. He gurgles happily in her arms, one arm clutching a battered wooden bird and the other reaching for the gold locket she always wears. Lucia hugs Reggie's warm, cuddly body and removes his sticky fingers from her necklace with some difficulty, kissing the top of his head and inhaling the delicious scent of baby shampoo and sleep as Polly busies herself mixing up his porridge.

'I didn't know you'd given Reggie your precious bluebird, Isaac,' she says, momentarily distracted from the turbulent thoughts of Des.

'It's only on loan. Isaac said Reg could borrow it because he saw it on its perch outside his bedroom door the other day and made a grab for it. Morning, Isaac,' Polly says, belatedly. 'What're you reading?'

Isaac looks up with a start. He's hardly registered Polly's appearance in the kitchen. He drops the letter on the table and rubs a hand over his face. 'It's from Dad,' he says. 'He's gone.'

'Gone where?'

'Just gone. Left. He never goes anywhere,' says Isaac, echoing Lu's first thoughts.

'Oh. Right. That's . . . a bit of a shocker, isn't it? Well, I just need to get Reggie's bib from upstairs if you don't mind holding him a bit longer, Lu. Back in a minute.'

Polly leaves the room rather hurriedly and Lucia is grateful that she's given Isaac a moment to deal with what he's just read.

'What's all this about, Mum?' Isaac says, as soon as Polly's out of earshot. 'What he says about me isn't true. I'm not reclusive or antisocial, I just like staying in, that's all. And I'm not *playing* computer games, I'm . . .'

'You're what?' Lu says, when Isaac doesn't continue.

'Oh, nothing. And also, why does he have to bring in the other word? I hate it when he describes me like that, as if that's all I am.'

Lucia sighs. 'I know, love. And I've told him countless times not to phrase it in that way. He should say "Isaac is Autistic", not refer to *having Autism*, as if it's like measles or something. He doesn't mean to upset you though.'

'He shouldn't need to say anything. It's up to me if I want to explain about myself.'

Lucia sighs, still feeling the faint hiccoughing after-shocks of her sobbing bout. 'Look, Isaac, it's not just about you. He's basically left *me*. I'm his wife, remember?'

'Yes, and he says he loves you. He's got a funny way of showing it.'

Tears threaten again. Lucia's stomach is churning now and her whole body aches with the effort of holding herself together and keeping a fresh storm of anguish at bay. The reality of the letter is sinking in. He's really left her. Des, who was meant to walk arm in arm with her into old age as they cared for each other and made light of grey hair and wrinkles.

Reggie beats his one free fist against Lu's chest and then nuzzles into the crook of her arm just as Nigel heaves himself out of his basket and comes over to lay his head on her bare feet. Polly bustles back in and puts Reggie's bowl of porridge down on the table in front of Lu. She stands behind her chair, putting her arms around Lucia's neck, while Isaac, shaken out of his reverie, heads for the kettle to make tea. Suddenly surrounded by all this warm love, she's overwhelmed. The hard edge of the wooden bluebird digs into her ribs but she hardly notices.

'Right Lu, you feed Reggie, and I'll make us a proper cooked breakfast,' says Polly, 'You can help me, Isaac. It's about time you tackled scrambled eggs. I'm very particular about not over-cooking them. We all need something to get us going today. I've got veggie sausages, there are loads of mushrooms and we'll have baked beans and grilled tomatoes. No arguments.'

Isaac nods, and unexpectedly beams at Polly. 'Sounds good. I'll ring in and say I'm taking some flexi-hours, I'm owed plenty. You okay, Mum? Sorry I was a bit of a git just then. It's just that I never imagined Dad felt like that about me.'

'I'm sure he doesn't really, it's his whole life he's disillusioned with, or so it seems.'

Polly opens her mouth to speak but then appears to think better of whatever she'd been about to say. 'Okay, but what are you going to do about it?' she asks eventually, as Lu starts to shovel porridge into Reggie's open mouth. He drums his feet against her knees and crows with delight.

'Do? Well, first I'm going to eat the most enormous

breakfast ever, and then . . .' She pauses for a moment, 'then I'm going to get out Tommy's maps.'

Lucia thinks about Flora, waiting outside on the drive, and Donovan waving goodbye, barefoot on the gravel. *Happy exploring,* he'd shouted. Fat chance of that at the moment.

Isaac clears his throat and Lucia returns to the present.

'I'm still going!' Lucia declares loudly. Isaac and Polly look at her in surprise. 'I'm still going on the adventure. Clearly Des has voted with his feet, but if no one wants to come with me, I'll go on my own. Now!'

'You absolutely won't go alone, Lu.' Polly says, sending Isaac a meaningful look. 'We'll come, Reggie and me.'

Lucia beams. 'Where shall we go first?' she asks eagerly. 'Shall we go with the compass reading and head south west? How about Cornwall? Let's go as soon we can, shall we? How long can we be away?'

'I'm a free agent,' says Polly. 'We'd need to sort a few things first though, we can't just go charging off without packing properly.'

'Isaac?' Lucia prompts, when the silence is getting uncomfortable.

'I've got quite a bit of annual leave stacked up, and they're always on at me to take it,' he says slowly. 'I think I can come. I've got a bit of a project on my laptop but I can do that anywhere.'

'For work?' Lucia is intrigued.

'No. For me.'

Lucia decides not to mull over why Isaac is being

so secretive again or to marvel at his willingness to join her on the road – she's too excited. Clapping her hands, she says, 'Let's get cracking then! What do we need to take?'

Over the next frantic hours, Lucia has cause to regret this last question on more than one occasion. Polly is fiercely practical and soon has her own and Reggie's belongings organised, but once Isaac has made the decision to come with them it's clear he would like to bring most of his possessions along too.

'Isaac, you can't take three pairs of trainers, your wellies, your walking boots *and* those bloody awful crocs,' Lucia hears Polly shout as her son makes yet another trip out to the van, heavily laden with assorted bags.

'But we don't know what the weather's going to be like. It rains a lot in Cornwall, I've heard. I haven't even started to sort my coats yet.'

Lucia finds that Polly's vocabulary is much more extensive than had previously appeared, although she notes that the younger girl is careful not to make the air blue if Reggie is around. In the end she says yes to Isaac's portable barbecue, his tent and a carefully chosen box of kitchen equipment but a firm no to thirty assorted paperbacks and his giant boom box.

'You've got your Kindle and Polly says she'll sort the music on her phone or we can play CDs in the van, love. Go on, put them back,' she says, hardening her heart as his face falls. This is huge progress for Isaac and she knows he needs to take some of home along for security but there are limits, for heaven's sake.

Taking advantage of their distraction, Lucia slips away to her bedroom for a moment and gets out the compass. Deep breaths help to calm her agitation and stave off the exhaustion she's been feeling since she got up this morning. It's been a very long day already. She settles the compass on her knee. Gradually, she empties her mind of all thoughts of Des, the remaining packing and the tasks still to come. Glancing down, she realises that the needles are moving even though she hasn't even run her fingers over the surface yet.

The compass needle is the first to stop, and this time it points towards north east.

Lucia shivers. She's already half decided to make a quick call on Tommy's friend Sir Peter before they set of on the main journey, and his home is definitely in that direction. It's uncanny.

The barometer reading wavers for a long moment, undecided. For a few seconds it veers between *change* and *variable* but then swings back to the former. 'You're not wrong,' whispers Lucia. 'Never in this family has there been so much of that commodity.'

The next morning seems to take an age to arrive but at last they're as ready as they'll ever be. Lucia has cause to feel grateful for her friend Rowan once again. Not only does she love babysitting but she turns out to be a willing house-sitter too. She arrives with her suitcase, full of promises to keep them all posted as to Nigel and Petunia's health and wellbeing.

'Stop thanking me,' Rowan says, holding up a hand to stem the tide. 'You're doing me a massive favour. I'm getting my flat decorated at the moment and I'm more than happy to be away from the stink of paint. It's brilliant. Now go before the poor old pets rumble what's going on.'

As Lu watches Isaac carefully strap Reggie into the van, the constant ache of Des's desertion is for the moment submerged in a wave of euphoria. She's done it. They're off.

Chapter Seven

Sir Peter Henry St John Cavendish, or Pete to his friends, sits in his favourite wing-back chair in front of a gas fire that's seen better days. *A bit like me*, he thinks to himself as he leans forwards to twiddle the knobs on the side of it without much hope of more heat. *We're both ready for the scrap heap and we don't function properly.*

He glances out of the long window to his left and sees one of the few remaining estate workers jogging by, on his way to see what damage limitation jobs can be achieved today. The young man is dressed in a warm fleece and thick track suit bottoms, and a bobble hat is pulled down well over his ears on this brisk May morning.

The Baronet (how he hates that ancient title) looks down at his own more formal attire and half-wishes he could let go of his standards and dress for the weather, instead of keeping up this ridiculous pretence of looking like a well-heeled landed country gentleman. His tweed jacket is threadbare in places, with leather patches carefully sewn onto the elbows by the faithful Mrs Jacques. His trousers aren't designed for snugness, more for sartorial elegance, and his socks are way too thin for today. The brown brogues are well polished, but he sometimes

57

longs for a pair of the fur-lined boots Mrs Jacques favours for work. Not attractive, it must be said, but she never seems cold.

Leaning back, lost in his memories as he gazes at the feeble flicker of the gas fire, Sir Peter reflects that one could do with someone impartial to talk to right now. There are things one can't discuss with Mrs Jacques or the other staff, and Miles, reluctant heir to Meadowthorpe Manor, is far away in California, probably basking in the warm sunshine at this very moment as he wanders around his extensive vineyard.

The grandfather clock in the corner creaks gently as if it's clearing its throat and begins to strike. On the eleventh stroke, Mrs Jacques enters the room backwards, pushing the door open with her generous bottom as she carries the morning coffee tray over to its usual table.

'It's a bit parky again, duck,' she says, 'You should get a jumper on. That jacket's not enough to keep you warm in this draughty old house. I keep telling you, but do you listen?'

As she finishes her regular diatribe the ancient doorbell clangs out a warning. They look at each other in alarm. The only visitors to the manor lately have been the ones who want an answer.

'Whoever it is, I'll tell them you're busy,' Mrs Jacques says, bustling out of the room.

Sir Peter sighs and drinks his coffee. It's strong, black and in his favourite cup because Mrs Jacques knows his tastes very well. She's brought him ginger biscuits today.

They're home-made and beautifully crumbly, reminding him of the Cornish Fairings his wife had adored when they holidayed on the Lizard Peninsula all those years ago, in that tiny rented cottage with the spiders and the damp. How happy they were.

He blinks hard to get rid of the sudden wash of tears that threatens to overwhelm him. If only Frances were still here. They could talk this thing through and he's sure his difficult decision would be easier. Or even if his son was more approachable and not so damnably far away. All Miles has said on the subject is that it's up to his father to choose what to do.

Puzzled, Sir Peter listens to the babble of voices coming closer. He frowns. Why has Mrs Jacques let them in, whoever they are? There isn't anyone he'd like to see today, except possibly Miles, and that's never going to happen. As his housekeeper opens the door he gets to his feet. The gesture is one of habit rather than politeness or welcome.

'Sir Peter,' says Mrs Jacques formally, 'there's a lady to see you. Apparently she's been sent by your old friend Tommy Lemon to see if you are well.'

She purses her lips and Sir Peter can't hide a grin. Mrs J doesn't approve of Tommy. There was an incident in the orangery with one of the maids . . . he puts that out of his mind and comes forward, holding out a hand to shake.

'Good morning,' he says. 'You say you're here because of Tommy? What's he been up to now and why on earth does he think I'm ill?'

The woman who's been standing behind Mrs Jacques steps forward to greet him and Peter is dazzled by the warmth of her smile. She's petite and curvy, with bright brown eyes and a look on her face that says she's embarrassed to intrude on his privacy.

'I'm so sorry to drop in on you like this,' she says, 'but Tommy seemed worried about you. I'm not sure why. I would have phoned first but . . . well . . . we've made a snap decision to go on an adventure and so I won't be around for a while. I'm Lucia Lemon, and I'm married to . . .' She pauses for a moment, her face awash with sadness. 'I mean, I *was* married to Des, who's one of Tommy's many relations. I don't know if I am any more. Married, that is.'

Lucia falters to a standstill and Sir Peter looks round vaguely. Did she say *we*? If so, who are the others and where are they? He was sure he'd heard more voices just before she came in. He shudders. Visitors were not in his plan for today.

Mrs Jacques clears her throat. Sir Peter had quite forgotten she was still in the room. 'I'll make some more coffee, shall I? And how about a nice scotch pancake or two? I expect the others would like a snack when they get back from their walk. That's a very bonny baby. Your grandson, is he?'

Lucia shakes her head. 'No, Isaac's my son, but Polly and Reggie are our lodgers. They insisted on coming on the trip with me. I was quite glad of the offer of company, if I'm honest. Oh yes, coffee would be lovely if it's not too much trouble. I haven't had a scotch pancake since my gran used to make them, but she called them drop scones.'

Sir Peter looks around, seeming to see the room from someone else's perspective for a change. The heat from the gas fire is being supplemented by two gently whirring fan heaters and the sense of peace in the room is palpable. It's shabby but very clean, with the elusive scent of lavender furniture polish in the air. A vase of yellow tulips stands on the sideboard, a splash of colour reflected in an enormous oil painting hanging over the fireplace featuring acres of golden corn and a sun-drenched meadow.

'Make yourself at home, my dear,' he says. 'You look as though you could do with a rest.'

'Yes, it's been a whirlwind getting ready to go away so quickly,' Lucia says, settling back into the chair. 'Isaac and Polly wanted to get organised and set off right away. He has some leave due.'

The telephone at Sir Peter's elbow shrills and he picks it up before Mrs Jacques can reach the kitchen extension, apologising to Lucia with a wry expression. She stands up and moves away a little and he is touched by her discretion, but since his hearing has been deteriorating slightly, Peter finds it hard to talk quietly on the telephone.

'Hello? Who's that? Well, of course I remember you. We only spoke last week, didn't we?'

He listens carefully, feeling chillier by the minute.

'Yes, I *did* speak to my son on the telephone, if briefly.

I have to admit I feel as if so much discussion at this point seems a little . . . precipitous?'

The voice on the other end of the line burbles away for several minutes. The Baronet opens his mouth to speak a couple of times but he can't seem to think of the right words to interrupt the flow. Finally there's a brief break in the diatribe.

'Yes, I see your point. It must look as if I've been stringing you along and I apologise for that. I know I said my decision was made all those weeks ago, but this isn't easy, you know.'

The ancient fire hisses and pops rather alarmingly, putting him off for a moment, but the next words he hears take his breath away.

'You need a final answer by this weekend? I must look for the forms in that case, and have another read through. Yes, I'm aware I said I'd already signed everything and that's quite true, but surely I'm not the only person to have had second thoughts?' A quick look around the room reveals that piles of papers lie on every available surface. He's been having a huge sort-out just in case . . . but no, mustn't think about that. He pushes the unwelcome thought away.

The Baronet listens again. 'Yes, that's as it may be,' he says eventually, passing a hand over his weary eyes. 'I do understand. But you must also take into consideration the magnitude of what you are suggesting. I need more time. Why don't you give me a call in a couple of weeks?'

The voice on the other end of the phone is a little louder now. 'Very well, let's chat again about all this later today. Yes, I know you're absolutely ready to proceed and to move your people in but I . . . very well . . . I'll await your call. Yes, I promise to have made some sort of final decision by Saturday at the very latest. I will discuss the matter with . . . with . . . well anyway, I'll think hard about it. Goodbye.'

Peter turns to Lucia who has given up the pretence of not listening to his end of the conversation and is looking deeply concerned. 'My apologies,' he says. 'That was rude of me. I don't have a mobile telephone I'm afraid, can't be doing with the things, but it means I couldn't take that annoying call elsewhere.'

'I'm sorry too,' she says, 'because I couldn't help over-hearing. It sounds as if you've got big worries. You don't have to talk about anything now if you don't want to but I'm happy to listen if you need a sounding board.' She smiles at Peter and he immediately feels less dismal. 'Any friend of Tommy's is a friend of mine,' she continues. 'Besides, I've got problems of my own. We could take turns. Like an impromptu therapy group?'

Mrs Jacques bustles in with the coffee pot on a tray loaded with assorted jams, clearly home-made, and a pretty blue and white china butter dish, plus knives, plates and spoons and Sir Peter waits until she's left the room again before speaking.

'That's a most generous suggestion, my dear,' he says, pouring coffee for them both. 'I wouldn't normally burden anyone else with my troubles but in this case I'll make an exception. Providing you agree to go first.'

Lucia helps herself to a scotch pancake and butters it. She seems to be struggling with where to begin. She clears her throat and launches into the tale of Tommy's legacy finishing with 'You see, I've been given all that money to make changes, or actually it was meant to be shared between Des and me but I blew it all. Do you think I'm awful, Sir Peter?'

'Just Peter, please Lucia. Unless of course you'd like me to call you Mrs Lemon? An interesting name, if I might say so?'

'It's not always fun being a Lemon,' she says. 'People tend to laugh when I introduce myself and ask if I ever feel like one. A lemon, I mean.'

'I can imagine it's a mixed blessing. A lemon can add so much to life though, remember that. Mrs Jacques makes a very fine lemon drizzle cake, and my evening gin would be lost without a slice or two. Anyway, I digress. Carry on, my dear. You've filled me in on Tommy's generous gift, but now I'd like to know more about Lucia Lemon.'

'Oh, I'm not very interesting. I never do anything. You'd be bored stiff in two minutes.'

'Go on, try me. I don't get many visitors, my dear, you're like a breath of fresh air.' Encouraged, Lucia begins to describe in brief the way her life has panned out so far. Sir Peter gets the impression it's a relief to talk about the years of staying near home and all the tasks she's taken on to fill the time. Running out of words at last, she leans back and butters the two small golden pancakes on a delicate china plate provided by Mrs Jacques while Peter sips his coffee and takes the story in.

After a few moments, he gets up and goes to stand in front of the fireplace, warming his back as generations of his ancestors must have done before him in this room full of faded velvet and chintz, although in those days the fire in the large stone grate would have been a blazing inferno of logs from the estate woodlands.

'I don't want to pry,' he says after a moment or two, 'but I can't help feeling that there's something you're not telling me.'

'How do you mean? I told you I'm not very interesting. There isn't any more.'

'Now, tell me to mind my own business if you like, Lucia, but as someone who's known great sadness in my life, as I get older I seem to be able to recognise it in others. My own crippling grief is for the dear wife I lost. What happened to you?'

Lucia takes a sip of cold coffee and pulls a face. Sir Peter waits patiently, his eyes on the far horizon that can be seen from the long windows leading to the terrace. He has the strongest feeling that this sweet woman who came into the house a stranger is going to be very important in his life in some way. Lucia takes a deep breath and begins to speak.

Chapter Eight

'When I was fifteen and my brother . . . Eddie . . . was twelve,' Lucia says, her voice not much more than a whisper, 'there was a terrible accident and he . . . he died. My parents blamed me. They didn't explicitly say so but I know they did. They're both dead now but afterwards we spent a long time edging around each other's pain and then I decided to harden my heart and just see them now and again.'

Lu wraps her arms around herself and shivers. On an impulse Sir Peter goes over to the armchair and pats her shoulder. He wonders fleetingly how long it is since he's had any sort of physical contact with another human being. He and Mrs Jacques don't go in for that sort of thing. He smiles at the image of how she would react if he admitted he sometimes yearned for even the briefest of hugs. Lucia carries on rather shakily, unaware of how much Peter is appreciating her sharing her troubles with him so confidingly.

'Now there's just me at home with Isaac, Polly and baby Reggie. My husband has left me with only a short, spiteful letter to explain why. I'm unbelievably sad, furiously angry and I feel like a complete failure as a wife and a daughter. But most of all, I failed as a big sister all those years ago. I'd do anything to have Eddie back. I just want to explain to him . . .'

She reaches into her pocket for a tissue and blows her nose. 'I really don't know why I'm telling you all this. You must think I'm insane. I don't usually pour my heart out to complete strangers, but you don't feel like that somehow.'

'I've been most honoured to listen to your story, my dear, and I agree we're not strangers anymore,' Peter says, when she's gathered herself again. He hesitates for a moment. 'I wonder if you'd still allow me to return the compliment by sharing my problem with you?'

'Of course.' Lucia beams up at him, clearly touched. 'How can I help?'

'Well, as you probably gathered from the telephone conversation, I am shortly going to have to make the biggest decision of my life.' Peter rubs his lower back as he speaks, stretching his shoulders until the bones crack. Lu flinches.

'I'm sorry, my dear. When you get to my advanced age, the old carcass gets somewhat creaky. So, my big question . . .'

He pauses. The comforting hiss of the gas fire and the sound of birdsong drifting in through a crack in the window give him confidence to continue.

'This is the crux of the matter,' he says. 'I have got to make my mind up almost immediately as to whether I hand my family home over to a privately owned trust.'

Sir Peter swallows hard. Saying the words out loud is making them all too real. He tries again.

'They're a very well thought of organisation and I'm confident they'll do a good job in restoring what needs to be preserved and getting the old place fit to be seen by the public. To be fair, I'd already told them my decision but I'm suffering from cold feet, and they're understandably getting frustrated.'

There, it's said. His big problem in a nutshell. He waits, hoping his new friend will understand the magnitude of the dilemma.

'You don't have a family to carry on the tradition then?' Lucia asks tentatively.

'I have one son and my wife is dead, as I mentioned.'

'Oh. And your son doesn't live here?'

'No, Miles owns and runs a vineyard in California and he has no children. Nor does he have any real affection for Meadowthorpe. He regards the Manor as something of a burden, and I'm very much afraid that when I'm gone, it'll be turned into one of those hideous health spas or an old people's home for geriatrics with a bit of extra cash.' He shudders.

'But what'll happen to you if you give your home away? I can see that it'd make a wonderful visitor attraction, people would flock from miles around to see it, but where will you go?'

'Now there's the rub. Where indeed? But if I stay, I'm watching the old place get more and more decrepit. I can't even afford to get that window replaced.' He nods to the cracked pane. 'And you must have noticed the awful holes in the drive. The roof is leaking in several places too, and those problems are merely the tip of the iceberg. Meadowthorpe Manor is falling apart around my ears.'

Lu is silent for a moment and Sir Peter senses that she's thinking hard.

'I wonder . . . could you offer it to them on the condition that you keep a corner to live in? Or convert a few outbuildings for a flat?' she asks. 'How would that be?'

Peter strokes his chin, hearing the faint rasp of bristles. He chides himself for not shaving this morning. He certainly would have done so if he'd known he was going to have such a charming visitor. 'I suppose it's worth asking. I hadn't thought of that. I must admit the only option seemed to be a clean break, just like our friend Tommy decided to do. As I said, I made the mistake of telling the Trust several weeks ago that I'd made my mind up to hand over the property but since then I've had many doubts. The only thing is, Lucia, I'm so very, very lonely here.'

Peter's voice cracks as he ends his explanation and he turns his back on Lu while he takes out a brilliantly white cotton handkerchief to wipe his eyes.

'So . . . do you think getting away from your old home, even if only for a while, might help you make a decision?'

The thought is enticing, but where would he go? Echoes of previous holidays and trips abroad flit through Sir

Peter's mind like an old-fashioned Cinemascope in black and white. Suddenly, a longing to escape fills his being.

'But I haven't been anywhere for so long. I . . .'

'Look, I'm sorry, I didn't mean to put you on the spot. I was out of order. Shall I clear the tea things?'

Lucia's question seems to be intended to give him time to collect himself and Peter is grateful for her tact but the floodgates have opened now and he finds himself unable to stop the tears flowing. He mops his face, mumbling an apology.

Lucia gets up and goes to stand near Peter. The grandfather clock in the corner begins to whirr, preparing to strike. It seems polite to wait for the twelve chimes to finish. As the sound dies away, she says something that shocks him profoundly.

'You should make a move,' she says, putting a hand on the rough tweed of Peter's jacket. 'It's time to let someone else have all this responsibility. And not only that, you need a break and we've got plenty of room in the van for an extra one. You should bite the bullet and come away with us, right now.'

Sir Peter feels his head begin to spin. His sharp intake of breath alerts Lucia to the fact that she's dropped these two ideas on him much too suddenly. She hurriedly guides him to a chair, apologising all the way, and pours him another cup of tea, adding two sugars. He drinks it absentmindedly, staring into the fire.

'Are you definitely telling me to leave my home? How can you know for certain that's the right thing to do?'

he asks. 'And how can you just invite me to crash your trip? The others don't know me from Adam and you and I have only just met.'

Lucia appears to struggle for words to explain how sure she is that Peter must give his home away. 'It's kind of a gut feeling,' is all she can come up with. 'But Tommy gave me something apart from the money and maps and photos. It's a kind of compass-come-barometer. I'll show it to you if you come with us. I don't know how, but holding this beautiful object in my hands gives me a powerful sense of all the other people it must have guided in the past. It's already giving me a strength to make decisions that I've never had before.'

'How very odd.' Sir Peter can feel his strength coming back now, and although the idea of not only leaving his home but setting off on a mad excursion with strangers is alarming, it's also filling him with a sudden wild excitement.

'Can you and your little party stay for lunch while I think about all this, Lucia? It's been lovely to have such a charming visitor and I do want to meet them all. They might take one look at me and be horrified at the thought of an octogenarian companion on their trip.'

Lu glances at the clock. 'I'm sure they'd love that, but we must be going immediately afterwards to get to our first port of call. We're heading for Cornwall eventually but there will be a couple of stops on the way. It's a very loose plan.'

'And that, in my opinion, is the very best kind. I'll

just go an inform Mrs Jacques that we have luncheon guests. No, don't start looking worried, my dear, she'll be delighted to have someone other than me to cater for. I expect she'll rustle up some of her marvellous omelettes and she's always got freshly baked bread on the go.'

Keen to make a good impression, Peter insists on donning his overcoat and escorting Lucia out into the grounds to round up her troops for lunch. He crams a battered old trilby onto his head and steps out smartly.

'I want to see this marvellous vehicle,' he says.

When they reach the van, he walks all around the van, whistling admiringly. 'It's stunning,' he says, patting the side of the van. 'So cheerful with the rainbow and all that marvellous foliage.'

'You like it? My husband thought Flora the Explorer was a silly name and a ridiculous vehicle.' Lucia smiles up at him. 'I'm not going to nag but I really hope you decide to come along for the ride with me and my odd little family and give the Trust the okay to take over, providing you can keep your own space? If you find you're allowed to hang on to a small apartment, you could probably get it fixed up while we're away. How does that sound?'

'I rather think I will, if the others are in agreement of course. You've given me a great deal of food for thought, and your listening ear has been much appreciated. You're a very warm and comforting person, Lucia, and I have a feeling that now's the time for you to blossom.'

'Really?'

'Yes indeed. This is probably a terribly trite thing to say but we only get one life and we both need to make the most of ours, don't we? I'm so glad you came here today.'

Peter sees the rest of the party approaching across the fields. Lucia waves to them and they wave back. A tall young man looking to be in his early twenties is pushing a buggy containing a chuckling baby with round, rosy cheeks. A girl walks beside them, her long hair flowing in the breeze. They look supremely happy to be in each other's company on this fine blowy May morning.

As they draw nearer, Peter finds himself holding his breath as questions whirl around his brain. Will they like him? Can he cope without his home? Is he crazy to be even considering his new friend's impulsive suggestion? As the girl calls a cheerful greeting and the baby flaps his arms, he straightens his shoulders and grins. The Cavendish family coat of arms bears the words *Carpe Diem*. If there's even the slightest chance of it, Sir Peter is about to seize the day.

Chapter Nine

Sir Peter's packing takes him less than half an hour after lunch and astonishes them all.

'Where's your suitcase?' Lu asks him as he comes downstairs.

'A suitcase? Why would I need one of those? You did say you'd have room for me to put in a sleeping bag and pillow, didn't you? And my old camp bed can fit under the back seat?'

The old man looks alarmed and Lu pats his arm. 'Yes, of course, but where are all your clothes?'

'Lucia, my dear, it's the glorious month of May. I got the impression we were heading south west, not to the Antarctic. The weather will become beautifully warm the further we go. In this rucksack I have a rolled-up raincoat, several changes of clothes, soap, shaving tackle, a small towel and a lightweight dressing gown, plus three books I've been meaning to read for a long time. What more would I need? When my clothes are dirty, I shall wash them in the ablutions area, as I always used to. I have my own small washing line and miniature pegs in here, and a travel size packet of washing powder.'

'Oh . . . well . . . that's fine then,' says Lu faintly,

thinking of the contrast with Isaac. Polly's eyes meet hers and they grin at each other. How comforting it is to have another woman to understand the pitfalls of being Isaac's mother. Lu hasn't felt at all disloyal sharing her exasperation at her son's mode of packing because Polly is clearly very fond of him too even if he aggravates her at times. How fond, it's too soon to tell.

It's after three o'clock by the time the somewhat overloaded van trundles through the extensive grounds of Meadowthorpe Manor and turns left onto the road that will eventually take them to the motorway. As Lucia hoped, Reggie is already fast asleep in his child seat, looking adorable in a fluffy all-in-one suit with bunny ears.

Isaac is taking the first leg of the driving and Lu's glad to see he's already looking less tense. Uprooting her son from his comfort zone hasn't been as difficult as she'd expected after the initial decision was made, considering how he's resisted travelling for so many years. He's chatting away to Peter in the front passenger seat as if he's known him all his life, which in itself in a minor miracle. Isaac's friendships are few and far between, really only including Rowan, Polly and Tommy.

The journey threatens to be tedious with the tea time traffic building up as they head down the M5, but Polly's made a good playlist and they're all in the holiday mood now, singing along quietly so as not to wake Reggie. Sir Peter appears a little bemused at some of the songs but after a few false starts, manages to sing along to the chorus of 'Dancing Queen' quite valiantly and almost in tune, beating time with Reggie's rattle.

'Have you heard from Dad to say if he got his clothes parcel?' says Isaac, after a few miles. 'He's got a nerve, taking off like that and then expecting you to send his stuff on. Did he text to say thank you?'

'What do you think?'

'That's a no then?'

Lu nods. 'I'm beginning to wish I hadn't bothered. It took me ages to get everything checked off that list and then the courier didn't turn up until the very last moment of the time slot *and* he was really rude too. I don't know why your dad needs all those things. Two of the T-shirts on the list are in Nigel's basket now anyway. He stole them while I was sorting the heaps. He can keep them.'

'Des doesn't deserve you,' says Polly shortly, closing her eyes as Isaac overtakes a very slow lorry with some difficulty and slides back into the slow lane again as fast as he can. This old van isn't built for speed, but Lu's proud of its progress. She's joined a breakdown service just in case, but although the engine chugs a bit, so far all is well.

Bang on cue, Reggie wakes with a wail as they pull into the services near Bristol. Once he's fed and cuddled and everyone else has had an impromptu picnic in the van, of strong coffee and assorted sticky pastries from the motorway café, the last short lap of their first journey passes without incident.

'It was a good idea to stop near Bristol, Lu,' says Polly as she squints at the map. 'Then we can get straight back on the motorway tomorrow and head for . . . well, wherever we decide. It's a good job we didn't make all the plans before you joined us, Sir Peter. This way you get to chip in too.'

'Please do try and call me Peter,' the older man says, for around the tenth time. 'I feel uncomfortable with you all using my antiquated title when we're going to be spending so much time together.'

'It's quite hard forgetting you're a sir,' says Isaac. 'I've never met one before. I know Uncle Tommy calls you Pete but that seems even worse, even though you're one of the gang now.'

'I don't mind either way, I'm just happy to be in your lovely gang,' he says, reaching back over his shoulder to tickle Reggie under the chin. 'I feel as if I've gained a whole new set of friends, and all in a couple of hours. It's so very good of you to include me.'

'Well you're going to have to stop being grateful soon,' say Polly, as Reggie starts to grizzle. 'A few days in the company of a teething baby and you'll probably wish you'd stayed at home.'

Peter shakes his head but says nothing. He seems to have something in his eye.

The Sat Nav is telling them that they're nearly at the first camp site now, and Lucia reaches for the notepad where Isaac has jotted down the name and phone number of the site.

'Forest View Nature Park,' she reads. 'We should be almost there by now, keep a look out, Polly.'

They carry on for another five miles with the chequered flag on the dashboard telling them they have *reached their destination,* but nowhere is there a sign to say they're in the place Isaac booked.

'Are you sure this is the right name and post code, love?' Lucia asks doubtfully. 'You did do it in an awful hurry last night.'

'I think so,' Isaac says. 'The woman on the phone asked if I'd like her to email us a brochure but I thought there wasn't much point. All the other places I tried were full so it wasn't as if we had a choice.'

After turning back and driving more slowly along the lane, Polly finally spots a sign more than half covered by overhanging trees and bushes. The beginning and the tail end of the wording is just visible and there's a small picture of a caravan so Isaac pulls into the driveway with a sigh of relief. He jumps down from the cab to stretch gratefully and heads for the reception hut, which is very small but brightly painted in blues and yellows.

When he comes back out, he's clutching a piece of paper in his hand. 'The site owner left us a note because she's busy organising a barbecue over on the far side of the site, and she says everyone else will be there already but we're welcome to join them if we're hungry.'

'That's kind,' says Peter, 'I'm not a big fan of cremated burgers, personally, but I expect you young folks would enjoy it. I've brought plenty of indigestion tablets, so no need to worry about my elderly tummy.'

Isaac follows the directions he's been given to a quiet

pitch under a giant oak tree and backs the van in expertly, to the accompaniment of everyone's admiring comments. It takes them a while to get themselves organised to set up the awning that came with the van, and Lucia finds that Peter's language isn't always what she previously might have considered suitable for an aristocrat, but eventually they have a camp that satisfies them all.

Isaac has a tent in the corner of the pitch, Peter's camp bed is at one side of the awning, and Lucia and Polly will be sleeping in the van with Reggie in a travel cot that can be slotted in when the beds are up. It all looks very cosy, Lu thinks as she stands back to view their efforts. Peter is relaxing in a camping chair now with a mug of tea, Polly's giving the baby his dinner and Isaac's just back from filling the water barrel.

'It's like a ghost town out there,' he says. 'There's nobody about. I can hear voices from behind the trees though and I smelt fried onions so the other campers must be enjoying that barbecue the site owner mentioned.'

'What a friendly idea,' says Peter. 'I think I'll take a stroll over and see how the land lies. Maybe there will be an alternative to the burnt sausage platter. Fish, perhaps?'

He finishes his tea and saunters off. Lucia sees him disappear into the trees and turns to Polly and Isaac. 'I'm so glad we asked Peter to come along. You don't mind do you? I know I sprung it on you both but it just seemed like the right thing to do. I was looking at Tommy's compass again last night, watching the needle spin as if it were alive and thinking how calming it was to hold it, and I just felt . . . I don't know . . . kind of decisive. I'm beginning to realise that change can be a very good thing.'

'I'm glad too,' says Polly. 'He's lovely company. And the compass is so beautiful. I'm surprised Des didn't take it with him.'

Lucia knows the answer to this. The compass is apparently no use to Des. There are still a few unanswered questions though. He'd definitely looked furtive when he said '*Oh, we don't do anything with it, my love. It's what it does with us that you need to worry about.*'

As she ponders, Lu sees Peter in the distance, but instead of his previous leisurely pace, he's now striding towards their pitch at a speed that looks far too fast for an elderly gentleman.

'What's up?' Isaac shouts going to meet him. 'Is something wrong?'

Peter can't speak for a few seconds. He holds on to Isaac trying hard to catch his breath, before gasping out five words.

'They're all absolutely stark naked.'

Three startled faces greet Peter's words. He's rendered the others speechless, giving him just enough time to get his breath back.

'I walked down that path and came to a clearing in the trees,' he says, gesturing to the wood on the far side of the site. 'They're all there, sitting around a camp fire. I can't help but think it's dangerous. There could be a flying spark. There are adults there, children . . . wrinkly people . . .'

His horrified expression sets Polly off giggling and in seconds Lucia has joined in. They cling together helplessly, tears pouring down their faces as Isaac hurries to fetch the leaflet with the hastily scrawled instructions on the back. He opens it out, smoothing the creases as he reads 'Forest View Naturist Site'.

Chapter Ten

When Polly and Lucia have recovered slightly, they all climb into the van and Peter closes the sliding door firmly behind them.

'What are we going to do?' Isaac hisses, shame and embarrassment making him hot and clammy. 'We can't stay here. They'll make us take our clothes off.'

This starts Polly and Lucia off sniggering again and Peter frowns at them. 'They can't do that, Isaac,' he says kindly, 'and it's an easy mistake to make.'

'Easy mistake?' gasps Lucia, wiping her eyes. 'Which part of *this is a place for people who like to run around with their kit off* didn't you understand?'

'It wasn't like that,' Isaac protests, his face getting redder by the moment. 'She just asked if I'd read the site rules and I said yes because I was in a hurry and I was just so glad to find somewhere with a vacancy.'

Lucia takes pity on her son's mortification and tries to give him a hug but he doesn't respond. This is terrible. He can't even look at Polly.

'It's fine, love,' Lucia says, controlling a new fit of giggles as they all spot a man wearing only a pair of trainers and a sunhat cycling past their pitch. 'We're leaving first thing tomorrow so if anyone asks why we've still got our clothes on, we'll say we're new to this lark and we're just getting acclimatised.'

'Oh, I don't know,' says Polly. 'I might just join in, and Reg always prefers to be naked.'

She sees Isaac's agonised expression and holds up a hand. 'Joking. I wouldn't subject anyone to the sight of this skinny body in the buff. My mum used to say I looked like a bag of chisels when I was in the bath.'

Isaac's cheeks are hotter than ever now at the thought of a naked Polly. He looks at Peter in the hope that the older man can offer reassurance, and sees such a look of kindness on his face that he almost starts to cry, which would be even more embarrassing.

'Let's all have a cold beer or a glass of wine,' Peter says. 'I'm sure we've got enough food with us to have an indoor picnic tonight, and when we need to go over to the shower block, we'll all go together. Safety in numbers, eh?'

'Great idea.' Lucia's got herself under control now. 'We'll make a buffet and sit round the table in here. It'll be a bit cosy but we can have our planning meeting at the same time. Oh!'

Isaac turns to see what's made his mum gasp and is horrified to find a large blonde lady waving to them through the window.

'Coo-eee,' she shouts, gesturing for someone to open the door. Peter obliges but keeps his gaze on the woman's face.

'Can I help you?' he asks politely.

'I'm Delia, from the site office,' she says. 'Just popped over to welcome you as you didn't make it to the barbecue. Goodness, you must be hot in there with all those clothes on.'

Lucia leans forward and delivers the prepared excuse and Delia nods, causing her generous breasts to wobble vigorously. 'Yes, it's not easy for everyone to start with, naturism, but as soon as you experience the joys of feeling the wind round your . . . well, anyway, you get the picture,' she continues hurriedly, shooting a venomous glance at Polly who has let out a strangled yelp and has her hand over her mouth. 'I'll leave you to settle in. I expect I'll see more of you tomorrow.'

'Not that much more,' mutters Peter as she vanishes, buttocks wobbling.

After this, the evening goes with a swing, helped along by a few bottles of beer and one of red wine provided by Peter from the remains of his excellent cellar stock. When they've all finished eating, a torrential rainstorm causes even the most ardent of the nudists to scuttle into their vans and tents, and Isaac begins to relax.

'This is actually quite good,' he says.

'What is?' Lucia's only half listening, in that blissful state of being warm, cosy and cradling a sleeping baby.

'I know what you mean. There's something about rain on a caravan roof that makes me feel very, very peaceful,' says Polly. 'It reminds me of . . .' she stops suddenly and busies herself putting the kettle on.

Isaac waits to see if any more information is forth-coming. He knows very little about Polly's life before she arrived in Chandlebury and she fascinates him. When it's clear Polly isn't going to reveal any intriguing caravan memories, Isaac gets out his notepad and pen.

'It's time to make a proper plan. The adventure starts here. We're heading into the unknown now. So where do we begin?' he asks.

Polly lifts Reggie from Lucia's lap and takes a moment to snuggle him down on her bed.

'We'll bring his cot inside when we turn in for the night,' she says. 'It's okay, we won't need to whisper now he's gone off, Reg'll sleep through a tornado once he's settled. Right, how shall we decide our route? This is so exciting.'

Isaac's heart seems to contract as he looks at her sparkling eyes in the glow of the fairy lights that his mother has strung backwards and forwards across the van walls. If only he could get Polly's face out of his mind and focus completely. With every day that goes by, she's taking up more of his thoughts. Leaning over to the window, he opens it a crack, just enough to let some fresh air in. The scent of wet grass and the last vestiges of barbecue smoke drift in, making this seem more like an adventure than anything has so far.

Isaac waits for the rush of panic that usually comes with new experiences. It doesn't happen. The others are still waiting for him to speak.

'I guess we should take turns in saying where we'd

like to go,' he says slowly. 'Mum and I have got absolutely no experience of planning holiday of any kind.'

'Neither have I,' says Polly. 'We didn't go in for them much when I was growing up. There were a few, but my dad left when I was small. We didn't have much money to spare for trips out and when we did, Mum did all the organising.'

'Oh, it was just you and your mum then?' Lucia is eager to follow this train of thought but Isaac can see by the tightness around her mouth that Polly is less than keen. He's not usually good at reading other people's emotions but somehow with Polly it's different.

'Let's all say a couple of places we'd like to visit, never mind how far apart they are,' he says. 'Then we can get Tommy's maps and photos out and see if we can pull them all in. How long do you think we'll be away? I know Polly's happy to make it a long break and so is Mum. What about you, Peter?'

Peter looks thoughtful. 'I can't go home until my apartment's done,' he says. 'I think the Trust people were so happy I was prepared to give them the go ahead when I telephoned them this afternoon that they'd have agreed to anything.'

'Well done,' says Polly, giving him a thumbs-up. 'No going back now.'

'Thank you.' Peter looks only slightly alarmed at her words. 'I left the forms for Mrs J to hand over, and I've suggested she has a good long holiday to go and see her sister in Scotland. She's wanted to do that for months but for some reason she refuses to leave me to fend for myself. In any case I can always go to a hotel while I wait for my rooms to be ready, so no rush for me.'

As the others start to discuss possible destinations, Isaac's mobile begins to ring and Tommy's name flashes up on the screen. That's odd. He grabs his raincoat and slides the van door open, checking all around to make sure there are no damp, naked people lurking in the bushes, and then shows the caller display to the others and mouths 'see you in a minute'. He heads for the shelter of the nearby trees. The air is fresh and cool after the fuggy inside of the van and Isaac breathes deeply as he answers the call.

'Tommy? Is something wrong?'

The older man laughs. 'What makes you think I'm not just phoning for a chat? I don't only ring you when I've got a problem do I?'

'Erm . . . yes you do, actually, and it's usually something technology-based. Is that new iPad playing up?'

'No, I've got the hang of the b . . . blooming thing now. It's just that I wondered how you were, that's all.'

'Oh. You've spoken to Mum then?'

Tommy seems surprised. 'Yes, I had a word with her a couple of days ago. Why, has something happened?'

'So you've not heard about Dad leaving?' The words burst out of Isaac almost before Tommy's finished speaking and he carries on, unable to stop the flow now he's begun. 'I still can't believe it. Why would he just take off? And to dump her like that? Not even face to face. The bastard, I just want to punch his lights out.'

'Er . . .'

'Yes, it left me speechless too. He's not been in touch since she read the letter as far as I know, apart from to demand that she send his clothes. No text, no call. Did Mum tell you what he said about me? Reclusive? Antisocial? I don't think so.'

'Oh, I . . .'

'But it's Mum I feel sorry for. She was really looking forward to them both using your maps. You know she bought the motorhome off her own bat with some of your money, don't you? Thanks again for mine, by the way, I can still hardly believe it, but Dad hated the van, for some reason.'

Tommy still hasn't said anything is response to all this. Isaac presses on. 'So, anyway, we've set off on a road trip. Polly's with us.'

'Polly?'

'Yes, you know who I mean. Our lodger? With the baby?'

'Aha, I'm with you, Polly's the girl with the wonderful green eyes and the freckles. I only met her briefly when I bumped into Lucia in Stowhampton just before I went away. She's being helpful then, this Polly?' Tommy says.

'Definitely. And we called on your friend Peter like you wanted Mum to do, and guess what? He's come along with us! He's letting some trust or other have the Manor and he's going to keep a corner for an apartment.'

'You're kidding? Pete's with you? The old bugger. I didn't expect that but it's excellent news. I'm so envious . . .I wish I was with you.'

'Yes, he's a great guy. I feel as if I've known him forever. And I really needed to get away from that job. I hate it, Tommy. I wish I could do something else.'

Isaac pauses for a moment as a wild idea begins to take shape in his mind and Tommy manages to get a question in. 'So, just remind me why Des said he was leaving?'

'Well, I think he was just fed up,' says Isaac uncertainly, 'With us all, really. He's gone to Huddersfield to stay with his mate Bob.'

'Oh, I *see*. Yes, I remember Bob. Your dad met him years ago when he was doing an accountancy course. I didn't realise they were still in touch.'

'Dad says he needs space to think.'

'Ha! That's the understatement of the year.'

There's a pause while Isaac ponders once again on how weird it is that his stay-at-home father has taken off out of the blue.

'Look, Isaac,' Tommy says, breaking into his thoughts. 'Let's forget your dad for a minute. I'm chuffed to bits that you're all taking advantage of my legacy. What about . . . the rest of the gift?'

'What do you mean? Oh, the compass thing? Mum loves it. She's brought it with us on the trip. I saw her holding it while I was driving earlier. It's a bit unsettling really. She's always looking at it, as if she's miles away.'

'Is she indeed? Good. And Isaac . . .'

'Yes?'

'Give my love to Lucia, won't you? If she wants to come and visit me any time, there's a great little pub nearby. I could maybe take her for lunch, or something. I could do with a diversion. This place is . . . anyway, I'm not going to whinge. I've made my decision and that's that. Keep me posted about your travels. I want to hear more about this lovely Polly of yours too.'

'Oh, she's not mine.'

'Not yet she isn't.'

'But . . .'

'Bye for now, lad.'

Isaac hears Tommy heave a deep sigh as he ends the call. He wonders what that's all about but his thoughts soon swing back to Polly. Nothing's ever going to happen unless he can get over this stupid shyness whenever he's alone with her. With a buzz of joy, Isaac thinks back to the breath-taking moment last week when he almost kissed Polly. She'd just given Reg his bath and he went in to say goodnight to the little boy. The scent of the bubbles she uses still hung in the air, mingling with Reggie's lovely warm clean-baby smell.

Up until his dad decided to make everything go pear-shaped, Isaac has been reading the bedtime story to give Polly a break and he loves it. Reg waves his fat little arms and gurgles as soon as he sees the pile of books. Isaac never had anything to do with children before. That particular night, after sharing five tattered board books and a song or two, when Reg was finally nodding off to sleep and Polly and Isaac were both standing out on the landing watching him through a crack in the door, he glanced down at Polly just at the second she looked up at him.

'You're so pretty, Poll,' Isaac finally says, after almost five minutes of hesitation. 'Just like an elf.'

She laughed. 'That's not very flattering. Like one of Santa's helpers, you mean? Great! Is it my pointy ears that give it away?'

Isaac thought about it hard. He knew what he meant, sort of ethereal and delicate. Why did he always get the words wrong? 'Like a nymph then,' he said. 'Is that any better?'

'Getting there. It'll do to be going on with, but you need to practise your chat up lines.'

That threw Isaac completely. He didn't realise he was trying to chat her up. He could feel himself going redder and redder. That's when he nearly just pulled her into his arms, like they do in the movies. But then Lucia shouted up to see if they wanted a drink and the moment passed. Isaac plans to go on YouTube and see how you chat girls up. Next time he'll get it right. Surely there'll be the odd chance to get Polly to himself now they're on their travels?

Daydreaming, Isaac lets himself imaging a scenario where the little boy is fast asleep, the others are busy elsewhere and he hands her a glass of wine as they sit under the stars, talking about life, the universe and everything. He'd lean towards her and brush a strand of her hair away from her face and she'd smile at him, at peace with the world. After that, it'd be the most natural thing in the world to kiss her. If only he had the nerve.

Isaac is never quite sure whether his discomfort with girls is just due to crippling shyness or if it's all tied up with what he prefers to think of as his neurodiversity. He's different, that's all. He's well aware why he's had such difficulties with fitting in at school and work, and adapting to sudden changes to schedules, but the very word Autism feels like an ill-fitting coat. Whether it's that the term itself is too big or his feelings about it too complex, he isn't yet sure.

As he walks back to join the others, Isaac puts his hand in his pocket and feels the folded letter that he's never delivered, written in purple pen. It was Tommy that gave him the idea of using a dramatic colour. Letters always seem more important somehow in purple. Last week he wrote to Polly, explaining exactly how he feels, thinking it would be better than mumbling something all in a hurry and embarrassing himself totally. The words tumbled out of the pen, one after another, burning with intensity. He doesn't need to get the letter out, he knows it off by heart.

Dear Polly

I'm putting this down on paper because I'm so useless at saying what I think. Since you came to live with us, I've been happier than I've ever been

*in my life. That doesn't mean things were bad before
. . . well, not really . . . but now, every day starts
with the thought that you and Reg will be around
the place, bringing the house to life and making
everything better.*

*Relationships have never been my thing. I can't
seem to understand what other people are thinking
most of the time, especially girls. But with you, it could
be different if I could just stop being completely
tongue-tied when we're on our own.*

*You're so beautiful, Polly. You're natural, funny,
caring and . . . I love you, that's the thing. There, I've
said it.*

Isaac.

He reaches the van and makes the decision to tear up
or burn the letter as soon as he gets a chance. It would
be awful if she found it by mistake. He's not ready to
make his feelings known. Not now. Not yet. Maybe never.

Chapter Eleven

Lucia waits for Isaac to return from taking his call and to settle back into his seat before she begins the first proper planning meeting. It's hard to know where to start. The responsibility of dragging this motley crew away from their homes is suddenly alarming. Was it the right thing to do?

The fingers of her left hand trace the shape of the compass by her side for reassurance. Its smooth surface brings the usual feeling of calm and sneaking a quick look down, she sees that the barometer is set to *fair* and the compass needle is back in its usual place, pointing south-west.

Her heart is thumping painfully and she wraps her hand right around the reassuring weight of the compass. Lu feels an unusual burst of confidence and wellbeing flood her body. She glances down again, almost expecting to see it glowing, so strong is the wave of good feeling. She's never felt so warm and confident in her life. Far from feeling anxious about their spontaneous adventure, she's now full of hope and joy at the thought of all that might lie ahead. She can try to make headway with getting to know Polly better, give Sir Peter something to

94

look forward to and best of all, help her son to come out of the shadowy world he's chosen for himself. Encouraged, Lucia reaches out with her other hand to touch Isaac's shoulder.

'Right, let's make a proper plan,' she says. 'There are four of us now, all with our own ideas. Reggie counts as part of you in this,' Lucia adds, so as not to offend Polly. 'As we said before, we can choose two areas each to begin with and then pull them all together into one big trip. There could be other stops in between if the distances are too big, just random ones whenever we see somewhere we like?'

Polly's eyes are shining. 'I love that idea,' she says. 'It's a great compromise between a totally open-ended wander about and a rigid plan. What do you think Peter?'

'What an excellent scheme. I'm all for it. I'd love to hear everyone else's favourite destinations,' says Peter. 'How about you, Isaac?'

'I'm all for sorting out a route. There's just one thing though. I'm worried about Tommy. I told him about Dad leaving, Mum. Is that okay?'

Her son looks a little shamefaced and Lu smiles. 'It's fine, I wouldn't have expected you to keep him in the dark about your dad doing a runner. I should have told him myself. Why are you worried though?'

'It was only after I came off the phone that it struck me how down he sounded. That's not like Tommy, is it? The place he's staying . . . well, it's too dull for him, I think.'

'Yes, I did wonder if that might happen,' says Peter. 'Bored silly, probably, poor chap. The Tommy Lemon we know and love wouldn't fit into to a geriatric establishment just yet.'

'So what are we going to do about it?'

Lucia looks at her son in surprise. It's unlike Isaac to sound so forceful or to be much interested in what his family are up to. He's not uncaring, just . . . distant, as a rule.

'I suppose we could call and visit him?' she says. 'Get the map out, love. The retirement complex can't be too far from here. He said Somerset, didn't he? I haven't got round to looking exactly where it is.'

After a brief search, Isaac unfolds one of Tommy's west country maps. It's adjoining the area where they're staying. 'Yes, it's here,' he says, stabbing a finger at an area surrounded by green splodges. 'It's very rural, by the look of it, but there's a village nearby.'

Lucia's heart sinks as she thinks about what Isaac and Peter have said about Tommy. He's always been a good friend to her and she's never known him even slightly gloomy. An image of that livewire of a man incarcerated in luxury but wishing desperately he was somewhere else comes into her mind and at the same time, the hand cupping the compass registers a very slight buzz. She looks down. The needle on the barometer is quivering madly, and as she watches, it swings round to point directly to the word *cloudy*. At the same time, the compass needle drifts from south west to almost due south.

'Isaac, how far are we from Tommy and . . . erm . . . what direction would we need to go in to visit him?'

Isaac looks at Lu rather oddly but checks the map. 'Around twenty-five miles I think, and it's pretty much south from here. Are we going to go? That'd be great! He's the one who's given us the chance to do all this. Flora, the exploring, everything's due to Tommy being so generous.'

'Yes, you're right,' says Lu, glancing down at the compass again. *Cloudy.* That won't do. It won't do at all.

Chapter Twelve

Tommy leaves the relative peace and quiet of a book-lined side room and makes his way across from the main building to what he now must call home. He unlocks the door of his apartment and splutters as he takes a gulp of chemical-laden air. The cleaning staff who come in twice a week are efficient but they do love bleach, and one of them has plugged in a strange hissing air-freshener that pumps synthetic flower scent into the atmosphere every few minutes.

He sighs, thinking back to his old home, fragrant with the scent of wood smoke mingled with garlic and spices from his most recent curry experiments. The bleach only came out when he was tie-dying T-shirts.

Why did you do this? He thinks to himself. *You should have talked about it more with the people whose opinions you trust instead of taking the first offer that came in for the house and signing up for this godforsaken place. Stupid, impulsive old fool. Just because Somerset's a beautiful county it doesn't mean you should end your days in it.*

There's a burst of loud music as Maisie in the neighbouring flat turns on her TV for her favourite quiz show. She bangs on the wall, which is the sign for Tommy to go round and watch with her. He's gone along with this so far, partly because he can sense her loneliness but mainly to pass the endless time until supper appears in the communal dining area. Supper is the rather lofty term they use for a milky drink and the leftover sausage rolls and pink trifle from tea time, but it's a popular time of day for most of the residents, and usually gives Tommy something to look forward to before a long night of counting sheep and chasing sleep.

Sighing, he picks up a packet of his favourite biscuits, a contribution to the viewing fun, and heads for next door. Maisie is sitting in her wing-back reclining chair pressing the remote control furiously.

'Pesky batteries have gone again. You got any?' she shouts, breaking wind noisily. 'Oops, sorry, fried onions for lunch today and they always play havoc with my internals.'

Tommy flinches. Spending so much time with people over a decade his senior is giving him an alarming glimpse of what the future might hold. He shakes his head, and takes the controls from Maisie, slotting back the batteries that have fallen on the floor.

'Genius,' she bellows. 'Well, don't just stand there, open the ginger snaps.'

Chrissie knocks in a business-like way and sticks her head round the door. 'Both okay in here? Tea?' she asks, wrinkling her nose as the unlovely fragrance hits her. She peers at Tommy suspiciously but he jerks his head in Maisie's direction and Chrissie nods, withdrawing quickly.

Tommy goes over to open a window but is harangued

before he can manage it. 'Do you want me to catch my death, young Tom? It's perishing out there.'

'It's a lovely evening now the storm's passed, Maisie. Actually, I think I'm going to give the show a miss today and go for a walk,' Tommy says, making a sharp exit before his elderly friend can complain.

He sees Chrissie approaching with yet more insipid tea and dodges out of sight down a corridor that leads to the back of the flatlets. Gaining speed, he slips out of the door and down the well-lit lane that skirts the property. When he reaches the road, Tommy pauses to look back.

The complex is as attractive as the designers could make it, built of local stone with the low-rise blocks of apartments flanking the glass and pine communal areas. It could pass for a set of holiday lets anywhere in Europe. As Tommy walks briskly down the lane, he asks himself why he's feeling so unbearably glum. The accommodation is perfectly okay. The flat is double glazed, heated and air-conditioned, so the temperature is always exactly as he likes it. The gardens are stunning, tended by a team of diligent workers who manicure the lawns to within an inch of their lives and plant swathes of glorious if rather municipal displays of flowers. There's no hint of boiled cabbage or other more distressing smells in the communal areas. Surrounded by lush woodland in the heart of the Somerset countryside, with a fishing lake nearby for those able enough to reach it, there's something for everyone. Even the weather's improving. So why, why, why can't he just stop feeling sorry for himself?

Tommy chose his new home from pictures online. There's nothing wrong with it, apart from the fact, he thinks bitterly, that it's full of old people. Why didn't he take notice of his most reliable guide? He'd been so busy with his plans for passing his precious compass on to its next owners that he'd ignored its final advice. The indicator on the barometer repeatedly swung to *stormy* when he was mulling over his future and the compass needle refused to point in the direction of the west country.

Turning his back on the place that feels more like a jail every day, Tommy heads for the village pub. With luck, he can find a secluded table in the garden if there's a sheltered seat that's missed being drenched. He badly needs a bit of time to himself. If only life had turned out differently all those years ago.

Tommy squares his shoulders and pushes the bar room door open. There's never been room for regrets in the past and he's not about to start now. It's his own fault he's bored out of his skull. At least he's given Lucia a shot in the arm and an adventure or two to liven up her world. You can't have everything, he tells himself. The landlord puts a foaming pint of bitter in front of him and he raises his glass in a private toast.

He takes his beer and a newspaper from the bar out to the garden and prepares to while away an hour or two as the dusk deepens. It's time to face up to the fact that this is his home now. He had choices and he made them quickly. He's only got himself to blame if they were the wrong ones. It's not a bad existence. It's just not the life he wants.

101

Chapter Thirteen

Lucia takes a deep breath, a powerful surge of excitement flooding her body at the thought of what's to come.

'So that's decided,' she says. 'We'll call and see Tommy and then . . .' She pauses for effect and the others lean forward, all eyes fixed on her face. 'Cornwall,' she says decisively, reaching across the table for the three maps covering that part of the country.

Both Isaac and Polly whoop with excitement and Peter smiles at them all. He's already taking on the air of a benevolent grandfather, Lucia notices happily, the sort anyone would be delighted to have as a relative.

'I hoped you'd say that,' Polly says. 'We went there for a holiday when I was growing up a few years after my dad left. We stayed in a caravan near Padstow. It was a tatty old van on a run-down site but the holiday itself was great.'

There's a wistful look on Polly's face and Lucia thinks not for the first time that she knows nothing about the girl's family background, other than the fact that she's from Yorkshire and her father isn't around.

'Was it just you, Poll?' she asks. 'Have you got brothers and sisters or were you one on your own, like Isaac?'

102

'I . . . I can't remember much about it really,' she mumbles.

'But if there were more of you maybe it was too pricey to go away. Me and my mum and dad didn't travel that much. They said it was too expensive. And afterwards . . . later on . . .' Lu stops, feeling the treacherous lump back in her throat.

Polly doesn't speak for a long, awkward minute and Lu begins to wish she hadn't brought this up, but the urge to know more about their lodger is strong. She's becoming one of the family and it's strange to be so unaware of her life before this. Eventually, Polly breaks the silence: 'I had a sister. She died.'

Isaac glares at Lu as she starts to apologise for prying. 'You see, Mum, that's why you shouldn't try and make people tell you things. If anyone should know that, you ought to. You're always doing it.'

'No, I'm not! I was just being friendly, that's all.'

Polly raises a hand to stop Isaac going any further in her defence. 'It's fine. I just don't like talking about her, that's all. It only happened towards the end of last summer. It's still way too fresh in my mind.'

'Poll, I'm so, so sorry. Isaac's right, I shouldn't have pried into your business, especially at the moment when I'm hating everyone doing it to me so much. I won't ask again.'

'I'll tell you all about it sometime. Let's talk about something cheerful now. Cornwall?' she adds brightly, scrubbing at her eyes and sitting up straighter.

Isaac takes the three maps from Lucia. 'Right, that's the first stop settled. Where in Cornwall would you like to go?'

'Does it have to be just one part? Or can I choose a couple of places if they're close together?'

The others nod enthusiastically and Lucia reaches for Tommy's photograph album labelled *Cornwall and the South West of England.*

Narrowing the choice down is easier said than done. There are countless snaps of surfing-type beaches and villages with narrow streets going down to rocky bays. All of them are places that look as if a diet of scones and clotted cream would be easy to follow.

As Lu looks at the array for what seems like the twentieth time, she spots a photograph showing a sandy beach in a deep rocky bay. In the background is some sort of building that looks like a hotel, with chalets flanking it. A steep path winds up the cliffside. Tommy, bizarrely, is wearing a tuxedo, and posing on the shore next to a smart woman in heels who looks as if she's sinking into the sand. She feels a pang of envy for the location and the relaxed, familiar-with-each-other air of the two of them.

'Hey, I think I know that cove,' Polly says. 'I reckon I was there a couple of years ago. If I'm right it's a well-known wedding venue near that big surfing place. Newquay isn't it? My friend Shelley invited me. It's the only place in Cornwall where you can get married right on the beach, or so she said.'

She tells them the name of the resort and Isaac quickly finds it on his laptop. 'Let's go down to Newquay and find the wedding place then. We could maybe book in at a pub or a small hotel. I don't mind sleeping in the van if you lot want to have proper beds and a cot for Reg. Mum?'

'That sounds good to me. Here's my second choice.'

Lucia holds up a photograph of a view of a steep, cobbled street with a sign on one of the cottages saying *Memory Lane*. At the bottom, blue as a periwinkle, glints the sea.

'But how will we find this place?' asks Polly. 'It could be anywhere.'

'Look on the back.' Lucia turns the snapshot over and sees the word *Pengelly* scrawled in Tommy's writing.

Isaac Googles the name and soon finds the village, which is not too far from Newquay. 'That's easy enough to combine with the first stop,' he says. 'What about you, Polly? Where would you like to go?'

'Oh . . .I don't know . . . do we have to decide now?' Polly's biting her lip and the frown line that sometimes appears between her eyes is deepening.

'Why don't we just play it by ear? We've got the beginnings of a plan,' says Peter, stretching stiff shoulders. 'I'm all for the idea of taking it a step at a time. What a delightful idea, Polly. One is so used to having life mapped out to the last degree. This is all very refreshing. And to share this adventure with such splendid new friends is more than I could ever have wished for.'

The others all raise their hands and cheer as quietly as possible so as not to wake Reggie. Peter wipes his eyes with one of his trademark spotless white handkerchiefs and Polly does a little dance in her seat, careful not to knock into anyone in her enthusiasm.

'There's a bottle of bubbly in the fridge that I was given when I left the school, I thought it was a shame to leave it at home. Shall we celebrate being decisive?' Lucia says.

'What a magnificent thought.' Peter seems about to say something else then changes his mind. His eyes seem to be drawn to something happening outside the caravan.

'Something the matter, Peter?' Isaac says.

He looks out of the window as he asks the question and the others follow his gaze. It's a warm evening now the rain has stopped, and it seems some campers are taking advantage of this. A very thin, elderly gentleman is just emerging from the next door van followed by a much more ample lady. Neither of them have any clothes on but they're both wearing wellington boots. They're carrying a boules set and as they begin to set up their game on the damp roadway outside, bending frequently to place the silver balls in readiness, Lucia is overcome at the sight of so much exposed and rather wrinkly flesh. Polly is giggling again and Peter covers his eyes.

'I think I'll chose the next site if you don't mind, Isaac,' says Lucia, getting up to draw the curtains. 'I didn't think I was a prude, but I think I've changed my mind today.'

It's not long before everything is cleared away, the

bunks are ready and Isaac and Peter go outside to settle into their own beds. A wave of exhaustion washes over Lucia as she wriggles into her sleeping bag, but her overwhelming emotion is hope. The future is looking a lot brighter. They've all made a new friend in Peter, Polly's a step nearer to letting them into the secrets of her past, and Isaac has taken on board their various travel plans. Even better, tomorrow they'll see Tommy again. That thought is immensely cheering.

All Lucia needs to do now is to rid herself of the nagging feeling that she and Des are still very much unfinished business. How on earth is she going to tackle that problem?

Chapter Fourteen

The following morning is breezy, which seems to put a damper on at least some of the naked frolicking. Polly has Reggie dressed and fed in record time. The others busy themselves packing the awning and tent away and having a hasty mug of tea.

'We'll stop for breakfast when we're on the way to see Tommy,' Isaac says rather breathlessly as he jumps into the back of the van as Polly starts the engine.

They cruise out of the site, trying not to look at the family of five, who it's clear are very soon to be six, playing a very energetic game of volleyball on the play area.

'Good Lord,' murmurs Peter. 'I'm glad Frances isn't here to see this. When she was expecting Miles I seem to remember her wearing a series of very pretty flowing cotton dresses.'

Lucia pats him on the arm. 'I know what you mean,' she says. 'It must be lovely to be so free of inhibitions though, don't you think?'

'No,' says Peter firmly, and closes his mouth like a trap.

After a drive through beautiful wooded countryside, they find a roadside café where the smell of bacon cooking mingles with a heady aroma of toast. Polly and Isaac order fried egg sandwiches and Lucia fetches bacon cobs for herself and Peter, while Reggie, small nostrils quivering eagerly, has a little taste of everything.

'It's only just over half an hour's run to Tommy's place from here. Shall I ring to warn him we're on the way?' Isaac asks Lu.

'Hmmm. I guess we should let him know. He might be going out somewhere. I think they have trips and so on,' she says, reaching for her phone.

Tommy answers the call on the first ring.

'Lu, darling?' he says. 'I was just thinking about you. I . . . I wish you were here.'

'Well actually, we nearly *are* there,' she says, worried at his desolate tone. 'We're on the way to Cornwall and we thought we'd stop over this way for the night. Can we pop in and see you? We'll be about ten minutes.'

'Are you joking? You're really coming to see me? In the van? What a wonderful thought! I'll meet you on the drive and we can sit outside and have a drink. Hurray! This is the best thing that's happened since I got here.'

As they cover the final few miles, Lucia relays the conversation to the others. 'I can't bear the thought of poor Tommy mouldering away at the back of beyond way before he's ready to settle down.'

'You're right, my dear,' says Peter. 'It was a huge mistake. I tried to tell him as much but I think I was too preoccupied with my own troubles to get more involved in his plans. I should have tried to stop him.'

'I feel the same. What are we going to do? We can't leave him there. He sounds so unhappy,' says Lucia. She thinks for a moment, suddenly nervous. Will the others go along with her idea? 'We could take him with us,' she finally blurts out.

'Have we got room?' wonders Polly. 'It's the sleeping problem. There's a spare seatbelt but where would he go at night?'

Isaac's looking edgy. Lucia knows he would hate to share his space, but Peter sees the problem and comes to the rescue.

'I'm sure we can find some sort of camping shop on the way to Cornwall and pick up some extra bedding and a blow-up bed. There's plenty of room in the awning.'

'But what about tonight?' Lucia has visions of Tommy squeezing into the van with her and Polly, and her heartbeat quickens. It'd be embarrassing in the extreme. He's not really her relation and he's always seemed . . . well . . . more manly than most men. She cringes at her own Victorian attitude, acting like a delicate little flower of shy womanhood, but the feeling won't go away.

'If I know Tommy Lemon, he'll be more than happy with a couple of cushions and a blanket or two just for tonight. He used to camp out on the floor of the ballroom at the Manor when he was working on the hedging project. He's a tough cookie, is Tommy,' says Peter.

Lucia isn't convinced but she supposes they could give

him the choice of whether to rough it for now. It depends how keen he is to escape. The more she thinks about the idea, the better it seems. As Isaac says, Tommy is the generous soul behind this escapade. He should at least be given the chance to come with them.

The man waiting on the driveway outside the sprawling complex looks about as desperate as they come. It's a matter of moments before he's opened the back door of the van and is ushering them all out.

'Come on, it's warm enough to sit outside in the shelter of the house. Chrissie's bringing us coffee, although a large brandy might hit the spot better.'

They troop after Tommy, gazing around at the grandeur of the sweeping grounds. Lucia has sudden qualms about suggesting he should leave such luxurious surroundings to sleep on the ground and join the washing up rota. She must be crazy. Maybe they shouldn't even mention the idea.

Tommy is, as always, an excellent host. He settles them comfortably around a picnic bench, beaming at everyone. 'It's good to meet you again, Polly. We bumped into each other briefly during your shopping trip with Lu, do you remember?' Tommy bends down to smile at Reggie. 'Is the little chap warm enough? Yes? Oh my goodness, I'm so glad to see you all. You might as well all know. I've been a fool.'

He makes sure they're all clutching steaming mugs of coffee before he carries on. 'I jumped straight into the idea of living in this place when I was still worried about having been ill. It looked like a cushy number and I've always loved Somerset. My house was too big for me and it just seemed like the right thing to do.'

'And now you think it wasn't?'

'Lu, darling, it's so boring in there, you wouldn't believe. I'm sure I'm going to fade away from lack of excitement. To cap it all, this morning I had a dreadful row with the woman in charge. She's a nightmare.'

'Good heavens. What was the row about?' Peter asks.

'She said I wasn't allowed to have a dog.'

'Oh.' Lu's lost for words. She knows that Tommy was lost after Bruce, his old German Shepherd, died a couple of years ago but he's never said he wanted another.

'And dogs are *not allowed*,' says Tommy, spitting the last two words out with venom. 'Nor are cats, guinea pigs or even tropical fish, apparently. It's *against regulations*. The old gorgon said she thought I'd have bothered to read the rules before I moved in. Lu, you should have seen the rule book. I'd still be reading now if I'd bothered with all that malarkey.'

Lu puts an arm around Tommy's waist, leaning in to kiss his weathered cheek. He smells of fresh air and his favourite aftershave, light and spicy. The familiar feel of his strength and the warmth of his skin give her a shock of something unexpected. It's just affection, she tells herself sternly. I'm worried about him, that's all.

Peter shudders. 'It sounds horrendous, my friend,' he says.

Tommy puts his head in his hands. Even his mad white curls look sad.

Lu can't remember seeing him even slightly dejected before, let alone as unhappy as this. She decides to test the water after all. 'So what are you going to do about it?'

'To be quite honest, I was just contemplating packing my bags and ordering a cab to take me to the nearest train station and then . . . well, I suppose I'd have come back to Chandlebury and you wouldn't even have been at home. I should never have sold up in the first place. Mind you, it was worth it to be able to give you two a boost. At least something good's come of me being an idiot.'

Isaac, Peter and Polly are all casting meaningful glances at Lucia now. She takes a deep breath. 'Isaac said you were feeling blue. We were just wondering, Tommy . . . how do you fancy joining us on our road trip in Flora?'

He stares at Lucia open mouthed. 'Tell me you're not kidding,' he says after a few moments. 'I can't think of anything I'd like better. Do you really mean it? All of you?'

They all nod enthusiastically and Peter leans over to slap Tommy on the back. 'It's unanimous,' he says. 'You, my old chum, are the missing piece of the jigsaw. With you on board, my happiness is complete.'

Tommy is speechless but his shining eyes say it all.

'How quickly can you be ready?' asks Lucia, looking at her watch. 'We're on the way to Cornwall and we should get going soon so we don't hit the teatime traffic at the other end.'

'Lu, darling, give me ten minutes to throw a few things into my old haversack and another five to tell the matron where she can stuff her potted meat and I'll be in that van raring to go.'

Lucia sighs with relief as they watch Tommy leap to his feet and trot into the main building. He's almost as good as his word and they are soon back in the van and heading down the lane towards the main road. Tommy leans out of the window as they pass the sign for the home.

'Hasta la vista, baby,' he yells, 'And thank the Lord for friends like these.'

They drive on until they reach the next campsite, where fortunately everyone is wearing a full set of clothes. Tommy insists on booking them in, paying for the night's accommodation and reserving a table in the onsite restaurant for an early dinner.

'This is pure bliss,' he says, as they pitch camp. 'I should have known I was doing the wrong thing throwing in the towel. At least now I'm back on track with an adventure thrown in.'

'But how could you have predicted it'd turn out badly?' asks Polly. 'Sometimes you don't know until you try.'

'Oh, I think I knew. I just didn't let myself see the signs.'

Polly, Isaac and Peter begin to set up the tent and Tommy edges closer to Lucia. 'You get what I'm saying, don't you, darling?' he says, quietly. 'I gave away my guiding light before I'd let it do that one last job properly, and ignored the warning signs it had already given me. I hope you're getting on okay with it? No problems?'

Lucia stares at his anxious face. Her eyes automatically go to her bag, where the leather case is tucked safely away. 'So far, so good,' she whispers. 'I wanted to ask you . . .'

'All in good time, darling. We'll have lots of chances to talk now you've rescued me from a life of disgusting biscuits and pink trifle. I should have paid more attention before I let my treasure go though. Don't you make the same mistake, Lu. It's yours now. In the right hands, that little compass is dynamite.'

Chapter Fifteen

Another early start sees the party on the road again and after breakfast in the nearest services, they head south west with only a couple of stops to make Reggie comfortable and to stretch their legs. They make a brief diversion to a huge camping emporium where Tommy kits himself out with a brand new roll mat, sleeping bag and pillow but scorns an air bed.

'Were you comfortable enough last night, Tommy?' Lu asks, still feeling guilty that he'd only had the ground-sheet and a few cushions to lie on.

'Those blankets you gave me were lovely and warm and I've slept on more floors than you've had hot dinners,' he says, when she tries to persuade him to have more luxurious bedding. 'I'll be happy on this mat listening to my old mate Pete snoring. It'll be just like the old days at the Manor. He always used to camp out with the team.'

'My old bones can't stand hard ground any more,' says Peter ruefully. 'It'll be good to share a billet with you again though. And I'll have you know I've never in my life snored.'

Tommy snorts but says no more. The rest of the

journey passes peacefully but by the time they reach Newquay, Lu is so tired she can hardly stay awake long enough to direct Isaac to a suitable car park near one of the glorious beaches.

They all tumble out of the van, travel worn and crumpled. 'I need hot food, and I need it now,' says Isaac, stretching and yawning. 'What are the chances of finding a café that does veggie lunches, has a table for six free, changing facilities and a highchair?'

'We don't want much, do we?' Lu looks around vaguely, breathing in the fresh sea air and hearing her stomach rumble. 'I've already had about a week's supply of coffee today but I still need more. Where's Polly?'

Polly and Peter have been on a scouting mission up the road with Reggie in his buggy by this time. 'We've found somewhere,' she shouts, beckoning them forward.

'You two don't waste time,' says Isaac admiringly, looking around at the beach-style ambience of the busy little restaurant. The walls are timbered and painted in a faded sage green and there are small arrangements of driftwood and sea glass on each table and pictures of lighthouses and boats on the walls. The wide windows take in the enormous sweep of bay, and a waitress is already bringing a sturdy wooden highchair for Reggie.

'I'll fetch you all a jug of water and some bread and olive oil while you look at the menus,' she says, dishing out small hand-written cards. 'We can warm up baby food if you like, or there are a few things that people often pick to mash up.'

'Have I died and gone to heaven?' asks Polly.

'I'm ordering the vegan paella,' says Isaac. 'It sounds like something we should try making when we get home. Or in the van, why not? The ingredients are all listed here.'

'We'll never remember them though,' Polly says.

'I'll take a picture on my phone. Anyway, I can.'

'Can what?'

'Memorise them.'

'He's always been able to do that,' says Lucia proudly.

'That's true. Exams and tests were a doddle for you, weren't they Isaac? He got great grades,' Tommy tells Polly. 'He's brilliant at memory games too.'

Isaac shrugs but Lu can tell he's pleased. It's a depressing thought that unconditional praise hasn't come his way very often in the past. She makes a mental note to highlight his talents more often, especially in company. At least she can lead the way as subtly as possible and the others will probably follow. It's a start.

'What are you having to eat, Poll?' Isaac says. 'The waitress is coming back now. Quick, before someone else catches her eye.'

'I'll have the same. Reggie loves anything with rice so he can have some of mine, and some bread to be going on with. Let's order straight away. He's getting hungry and if he starts to yell . . .'

Their order taken, Lucia leans back in her chair and flexes her tired shoulders. Time seems to slow down as she takes in the glorious smell of food cooking and the gentle babble of various conversations. Isaac and Polly are playing a game with Reggie that mainly involves him throwing his rattles off the high chair tray and Peter and Tommy are chuckling about something that happened many years ago. Sitting back, idly people-watching, Lu notices a contented-looking young mum on the next table breast-feeding her tiny baby, both discretely swathed in a soft floral shawl. The woman meets her eyes and they exchange smiles, an unspoken sisterhood joining them for a moment.

'I remember how hard it was to feed Isaac in the beginning,' Lu says to Polly, 'but I got the hang of it with the help of a patient health visitor. Did you feed Reggie yourself?'

The shutters clang down again, and Lu can see she's touched a nerve, cursing herself for being nosy again. Maybe Polly feels bad because she didn't get on with the feeding, or something? It was just an innocent question, though. Crikey, this is like walking on eggshells at times.

Polly looks over at the nursing mum and then down at the table. 'Reggie was breast fed for a little while,' she says defensively, closing her mouth with a snap. 'There was a lot of pain and soreness involved. I hate it when people make assumptions that just because someone doesn't find it easy, they're not a good enough mother, don't you?'

'Yes, I do. It's not fair at all. Well, that's great, anyway. They say the first bit is the crucial part, with the mum passing on immunities and so on,' Lu babbles. 'Oh look, here's our lunch.'

They eat watching the waves and Polly visibly relaxes again. 'The tide is definitely going out,' she says.

'And because of that, we've got two choices now,' says Isaac. 'We can either drive round to the parking area near the hotel beach or leave the van here and walk along the shore. It'll probably take an hour there and back but the sand looks firm so the buggy would be fine. If the tide was in, we wouldn't be able to reach the place that way.'

'We're not going to get cut off, are we?' Polly asks. 'I remember my sister and I once . . .' her voice tails off and she concentrates on mopping Reggie's face with a baby wipe. He protests loudly and Lu begins to collect their belongings together.

'I'm for the beach, if everyone agrees?' Lu says. 'We've been sitting still much too long today.'

Soon they're striding across the damp golden sand, all barefoot except Peter, loving the feel of the brisk sea breeze in their hair. Polly looks much more carefree now, with whatever troublesome memories that bothered her earlier firmly put to one side. She and Isaac, jeans rolled up at the ready, have a race to the sea for a paddle while Peter pushes Reggie at a statelier pace, the basket under the buggy loaded with their shoes. Lu and Tommy follow them all, searching for shells. As she wanders, Lu thinks about Polly's earlier strange mood. There's so much she doesn't know about the girl.

Tommy turns to look at her. 'You're unwinding at last,' he says. 'The worry lines are being smoothed away. These last few days have been a big strain on you, haven't they?'

'Yes they have, but the same goes for you, doesn't it? Uprooting yourself, when you thought you were there for good? It must've been difficult.'

'Leaving that benighted place was easy, but we've both had to face up to big changes. I can't help thinking though, we might come out the other side happier than ever.'

'I wasn't happy anyway.' The words are out before Lucia can stop them, and Tommy frowns.

'That bad, eh?'

Lucia bites her lip. It's so tempting to pour out all the frustrations of recent weeks and the overwhelming feeling that her life was pretty much over at 58 years old. Nothing to look forward to but decorating the house and watching Isaac become more and more reclusive. But now all that's behind her. She feasts her eyes on the glorious sweep of the bay and the sight of this new extended family all enjoying themselves.

'Come on, you guys,' shouts Polly from the shoreline, already dipping her toes in the water. 'Reggie needs to do this too.'

When she reaches them, Lu sees that Peter has already lifted the baby out of his chariot and handed him to Polly. Isaac is further up the beach now, out of earshot, but Lu hears Polly whisper, 'Your daddy loves the sea too, Reg.'

Intrigued, Lu listens to see if there will be more, but Polly's busy helping Reggie to splash his toes in the water. Who is Reggie's father and more to the point, *where* is he? Why doesn't he want to be involved in seeing this amazing little boy grow up? Lu is suddenly very angry with this mystery man. She resolves to talk to Polly properly about Reggie's father, but to pick her time carefully.

'Are you paddling, Peter?' she asks.

'Of course I am, and so is Tommy.'

He takes off his beautifully polished brogues, slips his socks inside them and rolls up the legs of his trousers. The thin, bony ankles and calves revealed look as if they haven't seen the sun for many years, but he strides into the waves manfully, hitching his trousers up further and only flinching when a particularly lively breaker threatens to go too far.

'I'll stick to the shallows,' he says, waving to Reggie who's chortling as a big wave soaks his knees. 'This is the most fun I've had in a very long time. Come on, Tommy!'

Half an hour later, they're all standing on the firm sand gazing up into the narrower bay that shelters the hotel in Tommy's picture. To Lu's delight there's a wedding reception taking place today. Four tiny brides-maids in blue frothy dresses are hopping and skipping in the sand near the outdoor bar, and adult guests are just beginning to spill out onto the beach too, laughing and chattering, clutching brimming champagne glasses.

'Let's have a photo in the same spot that Tommy's was taken, before it gets even busier,' says Isaac. 'Although I

guess we don't have to get proof we've been here now that we've got him with us.'

'It'll still be good to have a record of everywhere we've been. We can make an album of our own when we get back.' Lu passes Isaac her phone and tries to get in the exact place where Tommy must have stood. She doesn't want to intrude on the wedding party so decides she's close enough here and smiles for the camera.

'Am I about right, Tommy?' she asks.

He nods approvingly. 'That was a bloody good day,' he reminisces, a broad smile on his face. 'Her name was Brenda, the woman in the picture with me. It was her cousin's wedding. I still get a Christmas card from her.'

Lucia beckons them all closer. 'Now one of us all,' she says, and they squeeze in together, beaming, as she stretches her arm out as far as possible to get everyone in the shot.

'Right, we should be getting back,' says Polly when they've got all the pictures Lu wants. She's been glancing anxiously at the sea for a while now.

'There's plenty of time yet, but we could do with finding the pub Tommy's booked us into before we all need a nap,' says Isaac. His eyes are heavy, but Lu hasn't seen him this relaxed for years. His hair is standing on end, and the faint shadow of stubble on his chin gives him a more casual look than his usual tidy image.

'Can you do a cartwheel, Poll?' he shouts, running down the beach in the direction of the town.

'I bet I can do a better one than you,' she yells back.

Lu and Peter plod along with the buggy as Polly and Isaac show off shamelessly to each other and Tommy takes action shots of them on his phone. *They're remembering how to be children again, even if only for a little while*, thinks Lu. She smiles. 'This is what they've been missing, Reg,' she says to the small boy, who's waving his arms in glee as he watches them, crowing to himself. 'In fact, I think this is what we all need.'

Back at the van, Lucia decides she'll drive this last few miles. The thrill of the open road is wearing off as tiredness sets in and she wonders with a sharp pang what Des is doing now, and if Nigel and Petunia have noticed they've gone yet. Lu gives herself a mental shake. It's early days, and this is a very good start for someone who has avoided anything remotely like an adventure for most of her life. An effervescent sense of anticipation is building up inside her. The compass is in its box by her side and the world is at her feet.

'I hope you didn't mind me taking over and choosing the next place for us to stay?' Tommy asks them all. 'I won't be so bossy usually, it's just that I've got such fabulous memories of Pengelly and I wanted to make sure we had the best base to see it properly.'

The others say they have no problem with this and neither does Lucia. Newquay is stunning but she has the strangest feeling that Pengelly is going to be even better.

124

Chapter Sixteen

Lucia turns to check on the others when she's pulled her overnight case and handbag out of the van and finds that Polly is just returning from another exploring mission, eyes shining. She's been a little way down the cobbled lane that they first saw in Tommy's photograph to see if it's navigable with the buggy.

'I saw the sea,' she says.

'You saw it at the last place, right close up,' says Isaac, arms full of a wriggling Reggie, and clearly mystified at her excitement.

'Yes, but this is . . . I don't know . . . different. It's such a beautiful view looking down Memory Lane towards the beach and the harbour. If I could paint, I'd set up and have a go.'

Tommy is coming back out of the pub now with Peter in tow. 'This place is even better than I remember it,' he says gleefully. 'I've checked us in, all except Isaac who wants to sleep in the van. We can have dinner here tonight and then you can fill me in on the longer-term plan. Lu said something about you all choosing a place to visit. Does that mean I get a go?'

Of course,' says Lucia, 'We haven't planned any further than Cornwall yet though.'

'So the sky's the limit. Although we probably need to pull in some places you've not seen yet, for variety,' Tommy says.

'That won't be hard. Our family isn't big on travelling, Uncle Tommy,' says Isaac. 'I thought you'd have twigged that by now.'

'Mine neither,' mutters Polly.

'Right. Well, it's never too late to see the world. Let's get your bags inside, have a pint and then go exploring before the evening chill sets in,' Tommy says. 'There's someone I'd like you to meet if she's still in the land of the living, and we've got another photograph to take, to add to our record of this epic road trip.'

They find their rooms, Polly settling Reggie's extensive luggage in the twin room she's sharing with Lucia, and then wander towards what seems to be the centre of Pengelly. There's a large shop, a village green that's only slightly smaller than the one at home and a magnificent village sign.

'I've got a photo of this too,' says Lucia, brandishing a second rather dog-eared picture.

'Pengelly's sign was renovated by the lady I want us to visit,' Tommy says, patting the brightly painted plaque fondly and peering at the photograph with interest.

Polly takes Lu's photograph standing in front of it. 'Is she the person in this picture?' she asks him.

He nods rather sadly. It's hard to tell much about the

woman in the frame, because she's half-turned towards Tommy and is being engulfed in one of his trademark bear hugs. Her hair is just visible, a fiery red, and she looks very thin.

'What would be really great,' Lucia says, 'is instead of Isaac and me, your old friend could be in the next picture, if she's still here. How cool would it be to get a photo of her with you in the same place?'

'That's just what I was thinking.'

'Did she live nearby? Shall we just turn up or ought we phone first? If she *is* still around, she might not want all of us to descend on her. How old is she anyway?'

Tommy blinks at all Polly's questions, but does his best to answer. 'Her house is just up the road, opposite a big place called Seagulls. If Angelina is still here, you can bet your bottom dollar she won't mind how many of us there are. And she'd be at least ninety by now.'

'Let's go a bit further and see if we can find it,' says Isaac, taking charge of the buggy.

Less than a hundred yards up the street on the left, Polly points to a rambling old house on the other side. 'That's Seagulls,' she says, 'so the one we want must be . . . right here.'

Sure enough, the painted wooden sign on the gate on their left says *The Willows* in large, colourful letters. They can hear loud rock music coming from the open window of a downstairs room.

'Isn't that Metallica?' asks Polly. Peter groans faintly. 'I think I can see someone in there.' As Polly speaks, the song ends and is replaced by 'Another One Bites The Dust'. 'A lady of varied tastes. Heavy metal, Queen . . . we should stick around and see what's next. A bit of opera? Kylie?'

'Or we could knock on the door?' Lu's suggestion is met with nods of approval.

Tommy hangs back as they manoeuvre Reggie down the narrow path and Isaac reaches out to the heavy brass knocker, but before he can bang it, the door swings open and a very thin semi-naked old lady stands in front of them holding a loaded brush. Her hair is an unfeasibly bright orange and she's got blue paint on her nose. She's wearing a loose linen shift with shoestring straps in a startling shade of green, and one of the straps has slid down over a bony shoulder leaving her in danger of losing the whole thing.

'Guests!' the lady cries happily. 'Wonderful! Come along in, don't stand out here on the step. You'll have a gin, of course?'

She turns and rushes back down the corridor, disappearing into a room at the back of the house. Lu exchanges doubtful looks with the others, shrugs, and they follow her in.

In the large kitchen they find the lady, who they've all recognised as a much older version of the Angelina in the photo, mixing a large pitcher of gin and tonic. As they watch, speechless, she deftly slices and throws in a whole lemon and a huge handful of ice from the freezer.

'I've only just discovered gin,' she says, 'but isn't it

absolutely marvellous? There are very many different kinds these days so you could never get tired of it. I made the change from Bacardi for the good of my health. The coca cola, you know, was upsetting my stomach. The small person is a little young for gin, I'm guessing?' she asks politely, bending down to get a closer look at Reggie, who is clutching Isaac's bluebird and looking at her with saucer-eyes.

'It's fine, I've got his drink here,' says Polly hastily.

Lu notices that Tommy is keeping out of sight, half-hidden behind Polly and bending to tie his shoelace. His face is pale, and she wonders if it's because Angelina has changed a lot since Tommy was here. He's certainly not keen to make himself known yet.

'Now then, tell me honestly, what did you think of them?' Angelina says, handing them each a brimming glass and peering at the group short-sightedly.

'Think of . . . what?' asks Isaac, taking a sip of his drink and almost choking at the strength.

'The paintings, dear. You're going to write about them for your newspaper, I'm told. I wasn't expecting quite so many of you but it's lovely that you've visited my exhibition *en famille,* as it were. She wobbles as she points vaguely in the direction of the village green and Isaac averts his gaze as the dress slips down and gives them an alarming view of most of her naked skinny body.

Lu swiftly pulls the straps up and helps Angelina to stand upright. 'I think you must have mistaken us for someone else,' she says gently.

'You're the reporters from *The Truro Chronicle*, aren't you?' For the first time, the elderly lady looks uncertain and a little baffled.

'No, we're just visitors from the Midlands.'

'But . . . so you haven't seen my paintings?'

Angelina's bottom lip wobbles and Tommy finally steps forward. 'If the paintings of which you speak are on display somewhere local, I'm quite sure we would love to go and look at the exhibition,' he says. 'Angelina – it's me, Tommy.'

'Tommy?' she repeats, stepping forward and grabbing his arm. '*My* Scrumptious Tommy Lemon-Drop?'

'Well, yes,' he answers. 'Or that's what you always used to call me anyway, Ange.' He grins at the others rather sheepishly as they try to hide their own smirks.

'I *knew* you'd come back eventually! Here, have a gin.'

They raise their glasses to each other, and Angelina takes a huge gulp from hers, swaying slightly.

'Have you eaten today, darling?' Tommy asks, frowning. 'I know how you used to forget about food when you were painting.'

The elderly lady wrinkles her brow. 'Ah. Probably not. I might have had an apple and some cheese last night. I just wanted to . . .'

'Yes, I'm sure you did, but you need to keep body and soul together. Look, I'll rustle you up a sandwich while my lovely touring companions finish their drinks, and then we'll go and see your pictures, how does that sound?'

'Oh well, I suppose I should eat, but you promise you'll go and look?'

Tommy heads for the kitchen, so Lucia takes over. 'Absolutely. Where will we find the exhibition?'

Angelina brightens immediately. 'In the village hall. It's only a little way up the road, you can't miss it. Right next to the church. Oh, I would so love to hear what you think. Will you come back later and tell me?'

'Definitely,' says Lu. 'But while we're here, can I just show you this photograph?'

She digs in her bag and pulls out the envelope with Tommy's pictures in it. Holding out the one featuring Angelina, she says 'I thought you'd like to see it. For old time's sake.'

Angelina takes the photograph with only a slight shake of the hand. She peers at it and blinks. 'Oh my goodness, that's the two of us, isn't it? I've got a copy somewhere too.' She looks around vaguely as if it might appear.

'We're on a sort of a mission to visit some of the places that we've chosen as part of our tour, and Pengelly's our second stop,' Lucia says, taking the photograph back when it looks as if Angelina's going to appropriate it to replace her own.

'Oh, I'm not surprised Tommy picked our village.'

'Actually, it was me . . .' Lucia begins, but Angelina is on a roll. 'That man was the life and soul of every party when he stayed here,' she tells the others. 'He came back year after year for a while. I think it was my fault he stopped coming.'

Really? Why was that?' Lu is fascinated by this butterfly of an old lady.

'I don't think there's any need to go into all that, Ange. How about eating now?' says Tommy, coming back from the kitchen with a hastily assembled and rather untidy sandwich.

'Oh, you surely don't mind me telling your friends what happened between us, all those years ago?'

'I guess not.' He hands over the sandwich and goes to lean against the windowsill, gazing out over the bay.

'It's no secret, there's no need to fuss. I was never very good at being faithful, that's all, and there were one or two other people involved.' She flicks a rather flirtatious glance at Peter, and he recoils slightly.

'Well, anyway, Tommy got offended, didn't you, my old sausage? But I'd always made it clear we weren't exclusive, so I don't know why he got so cross. It was just that he walked in at an unfortunate moment.' Angelina gives an unexpectedly girlish giggle and covers her mouth with a paint-smeared hand.

'Ooh. This is interesting,' says Polly. 'Tell us more.'

'Looking at Tommy's face, I think that's probably enough. Finish up your gin, all of you,' says Angelina. 'Then you can go and see my pictures and come back and tell me all about them, can't you? And if those journalist people are there, send them this way for a drink. There's plenty more in the fridge.'

Before long, Lucia and the others find themselves ambling rather unsteadily around a very smart village hall taking in a wide range of pictures. Some are so garish and ham-fisted as to be embarrassing. After a few moments Lucia mutters a warning to the others to be tactful in their comments about the exhibits because it's clear from overheard conversations that some of the artists are actually in the room. Other paintings are dainty and pretty, watercolours of birds and flowers. A few are portraits and these vary considerably in quality, the most entertaining being a Picasso-style affair entitled 'Susan' portraying a round person with several extra legs and four eyes.

'I wonder if Susan lives in the village,' murmurs Polly to Isaac. 'If she does, she'll be quite easy to spot.' They both glance around furtively before collapsing into uncontrollable mirth.

'Shhh,' says Lu. She's just hit pay dirt. On the far side of the long room, the whole end wall is dedicated to the most breathtakingly beautiful seascapes she has ever seen. They're all signed with a generous scrawl that looks like Angelina Moffatt and they make Lu want to cry.

'Are these pictures for sale?' she asks, catching hold of the sleeve of a man with a neat grey beard and well-worn cord blazer and trousers as he saunters past with a clipboard.

'They are indeed, I can put a sold sticker on any you take a shine to. I'm Tristram,' he says, holding out a hand. 'I lead the steering committee for the yearly art display and it's a thankless task, let me tell you. And you are . . .?'

'Lucia Lemon, just visiting, but we met Angelina earlier and I would just love to take home one of her pictures.'

Lu peers at the price tags on the nearest two paintings. Three hundred pounds? That's more than she can afford at the moment, even with what's left of her windfall. Who knows how she's going to fare for cash if Des never comes back? But there's a smaller one that's taken her fancy that's only priced at a hundred and seventy. It's a view of the beach and harbour and must have been painted from the top of Memory Lane, in more or less the exact spot where Polly stood and admired the scenery so much. On impulse, she follows Tristram to the desk by the door and buys the picture. She'll give it to Polly as a memento of this lovely trip. But what can she get for Isaac?

Looking round, Lu sees that the others have found a back room serving tea and cakes and have retreated there with Reggie. They wave to her and she mimes *see you in a minute.*

'Before I put my card away, do you have any paintings of food? I know that's a bit of a weird request, but my son's recently rediscovered his love of cooking, and I'd like to get him something to celebrate that. It's either that or more bird in a tree pictures, and I really think it's time he branched out.'

Tristram laughs. 'Oh, I like what you did there – tree, branch . . . very clever. Well, if you want paintings that look good enough to eat, you've come to the right man. I run the seafood restaurant in Pengelly and I dabble a little myself in watercolours. This is the first time I've been brave enough to put something in the exhibition, but there are one or two you might like.'

He leads her to a secluded corner where several pictures hang, framed in what looks like driftwood, all depicting stunning arrangements of food on rich dark blue and gold dishes. She points to a bowl of avocados, split open to reveal their creamy pale green middles and flanked by crusty bread and vibrantly yellow slices of lemon. The half-full goblet next to the plate is made of iridescent cobalt glass. In the background, a gilded cage with the door standing open houses a very fat blue parrot.

'I'll take this one,' Lu says. 'He'll love it. Blue's his favourite colour and as you may have guessed, he adores birds. Not a branch in sight either. Can I collect both of the pictures tomorrow?'

Tristram beams his approval and soon the paintings are being wrapped, while Lu goes to join the others.

They head back for Angelina's house and she is overwhelmed by their response to her paintings, happily agreeing to come outside with them to stand next to Tommy and be photographed. Polly manages to persuade her into sandals and a shawl and they eventually all hug her, Tommy with particular affection, and say goodbye.

'Just for the record, I was never unfaithful to you, Ange,' he whispers. He sees Lucia has overheard him, and she thinks that was probably intentional.

'Let's go and book dinner in the pub,' says Isaac as they walk back to The Eel and Lobster. 'When we've eaten we can all have an early night. I've got some work to catch up with.'

'I . . . erm . . . I need to just nip back and say something else to Angelina,' Tommy says suddenly. 'You go on ahead, I'll catch you up.'

'Okay. And tomorrow we'll explore properly. I want to go right down Memory Lane and along the shore to the harbour,' says Polly, her eyes shining.

'I'm going to have a long soak in the bath after dinner.' Lu's suddenly exhausted but the night's not over yet. 'You should too, Poll. We can put our 'jamas on after that and have a really good chat and a mug of hot chocolate.'

'Yes, that would be lovely,' says Polly, but her words don't match the tone of her voice.

Lu exchanges glances with Isaac and Peter as Polly goes ahead with the buggy. 'There's a mystery here,' she says, 'and I'm going to get to the bottom of it.'

'Oh Mum, please don't go there again. You'll only upset her.'

Peter nods. 'He's right you know, my dear. This is a delicate matter, in my opinion, and you'll need to tread very carefully if you go any further. Which of course, you will,' he adds, seeing Lu's expression.

'I'll be careful, I'm not completely insensitive,' she says. 'But sometimes a person needs to talk. Polly's got troubles. If there's any chance at all that she wants to share them, tonight's the night.'

Chapter Seventeen

Yawning, Lucia makes the promised hot chocolate from the hospitality tray in their room and gets into bed to wait for Polly to finish her bath. The gentle rhythm of Reggie's snores and the distant whoosh of the waves as the tide comes in over the pebbles at the top of the beach are the only disturbances, and both are such peaceful sounds that Lu feels herself drifting off to sleep. She sits bolt upright – mustn't miss this chance to see if Polly really does want to unburden herself. If not, she'll back off and leave well alone. As she rubs her eyes, stifling yawns, she hears a faint tap on the door.

'Lucia? Lu, darling? Are you in bed?' Tommy's voice is low but carries just enough for her to hear. Lu reluctantly leaves her warm nest under the duvet, tiptoes to the door and opens it a crack.

'What's up? Is something wrong?' she whispers. 'Don't wake Reggie, he's only just settled.'

'I need to talk to you.'

'What, *now*? Can't it wait until morning?'

Lu can see from Tommy's expression that it can't. Sighing, she props the door open with a slipper and slides out into the hallway. Tommy looks ruffled, as if he's been running his fingers through his already wild curls. There's a delicious waft of the familiar aftershave, light and crisp.

'Have you been speaking to Isaac?' Lu says, trying not to sound defensive. 'Has he told you to warn me off upsetting Polly? I'll be careful, honestly.'

He shakes his head. 'No, I haven't seen him. This is about something Angelina said. I went back to ask her advice. She guessed I was anxious, and she's made me realise a few home truths. I've known her for years. She's one of the few women I've ever been able to bare my soul too.'

'I gathered that.' Lucia can hear an unpleasant tone in her own voice. Waspish. What's all that about? Of course Tommy knows Angelina well. They're old friends.

Tommy starts to say something else and then seems to change his mind.

'I'm glad I gave you the compass,' he blurts out eventually.'

'Des and me, you mean.'

'Let's not pretend, I knew it would choose you. For reasons of his own, which we won't go into now, Des isn't the right one.'

Lucia's tired mind tries to think of the right question to ask but Tommy's brilliantly blue eyes are on hers and she can't think straight.

'Lu? What are you doing out there?' Polly's voice breaks the spell so brutally that they both flinch and take a step back.

Before Lu can think of an answer, Tommy's gone, raising an arm and striding away down the corridor with a spring in his step that belies his seventy years. She turns back into the bedroom and kicks the slipper away, catching the door just before it bangs. Polly is waiting, frowning slightly.

'Was that Tommy? What did he want?'

'Erm . . . nothing much. Just . . . stuff. Actually, I haven't got a clue what he wanted. Did you have a good bath?'

'Oh, it was blissful,' says Polly. 'My skin's all wrinkly now. I stayed in there so long I thought you'd be asleep already.'

'It was a close thing, my eyes kept closing, but I wanted to talk to you. And then Tommy turned up. Anyway, that doesn't matter now. We've got things we need to discuss.'

'Ah.' Polly sits on the edge of her bed to towel her hair dry. 'I thought we might have.'

Lucia takes a few deep breaths, willing herself to get her thoughts away from the compass and the disturbing encounter, back to the matter in hand. 'Look, Poll, if you really don't want to tell me about your past I understand, but sometimes you look so sad. Would it help to let some of it go, whatever it is that's troubling you?'

Polly goes to hang up her towel and begins to drag a brush through the long tangles of her hair. She looks very young in her short nightshirt and Lu's heart goes out to the troubled girl. She waits as patiently as she

139

can. Does Polly trust her enough to come clean about what's on her mind?

'I don't mind talking to *you*,' Polly says eventually, getting into bed and reaching for her mug, 'but you've got to promise not to pass any of this on to Isaac. I don't want him to feel sorry for me. We're friends, on equal footing. I need to know he likes me for myself, not because I'm some sort of tragic figure to be pitied.'

'I'm sure he wouldn't change the way he treats you. Polly, you must be able to tell that Isaac's getting very attached to you?'

'Is he? I hardly know him really. He hasn't . . . you know . . . made a move or anything.'

Lucia hesitates, loyalty to her son fighting with the desire to put Polly in the picture to save any future misunderstandings. 'Isaac's always been different to the other boys his age. My little brother was the same in a lot of ways. You remember I told you about Eddie dying when I was fifteen and he was twelve?'

'Yes, and I always wanted to know more about what happened but I didn't want to upset you. I think about him every time I look at that happy family photo. Your Eddie was like Isaac? How?'

'Well, they both tended to be obsessive about things when they were young. Of course, Eddie never had the chance to grow up so I've got no way of knowing if . . . if he'd . . .' Lucia blinks tears away and holds up a hand to stop Polly getting out of bed to hug her. 'No, don't be nice to me, I'm trying to say things I've never told anyone except Des.'

Polly settles down again, eyes large with sympathy.

'Isaac finds it hard to make friends,' Lu says quietly, in control again. 'Just like Eddie did. When he was younger, we tried to help him by asking other children round to play, but they didn't understand him. He couldn't cope with anyone but me in his room in case they disturbed his toy cars or his collection of bird books. He would lose his temper very quickly, shout and scream and then go and hide. Eventually, we gave up. It was upsetting him too much.'

'That's so sad,' Polly says. 'I know he's kind of quirky but I see it as a good thing. He's intuitive and clever. The way he's tackled inventing that new computer game . . . well, it kind of blows my mind, Lu.'

Lucia pauses. 'What did you say? New game?'

'Yes, I thought you knew. He's creating something really special. He's hoping one day he can leave his job and go out on his own, marketing his own stuff. I reckon he can do it.'

Lu's torn between pride in her son's talents and mortification that he hasn't confided his hopes for the future in her. Pride wins.

'I'll wait and let him tell me himself. He probably held back because of not wanting to go through a whole load of questions from his dad. Des would've wanted to know all the financial ins and outs and ignored the dreams, it's just the way his mind works. He's very practical and he doesn't get Isaac really. He thinks he needs to man up and throw himself into life more. But this *is* Isaac's life. He likes it this way.'

There's a long silence. 'Lu, how did Eddie die?' Polly asks eventually. 'Don't tell me if you don't want to,' she adds quickly.

'No, I want to talk about him tonight. There was a school trip to France. We were both meant to be going but I got glandular fever at the last minute. My mum and dad had only ever said Eddie could go if I was there to keep an eye on him. So they tried to cancel but the teachers said they couldn't have a refund and anyway, it wasn't fair on Eddie to spoil his fun.'

'I guess they were right, weren't they?'

'The ones going on the trip didn't know Eddie well. He was . . . dangerous. Oh, not to other people, but he just had no brakes, do you know what I mean? No common sense. Without me to rein him in, he was a loose cannon. Anyway, that's enough about Eddie.'

'But . . . how did he . . . I mean how did he actually die?'

Lucia tries hard but she can't get the words out. The lump in her throat is too big. She breathes in and out slowly, the way she's been told to do. A panic attack now wouldn't help at all. 'We'll come back to that another time. Tell me about you now, Pol,' she says, when she's sure she's back in control.

Polly reorganises the duvet over her raised knees and sighs. 'So . . . you promise this is just between us?'

'Of course it is, pet, if that's what you want.' Lu waits again. Reggie rolls over and grumbles to himself and they both glance over to the cot, but he's soon sound asleep again.

'Right. Here goes. I told you I had a sister. Her name was Alice.' Polly swallows hard. 'But I called her Owl.'

Lu smiles. 'That's a sweet nickname. Why?'

'She wore those little round glasses when we were growing up and she always had her nose in a book. And also, her favourite book character was Owl from *Winnie the Pooh*. She always called me Lark because I woke so early. Still do. Our mum was Pigeon because she's round and comforting and she clucks. We used to say we were like three birds on a branch.'

Nothing else seems to be forthcoming. Lucia perseveres. 'Did you and Alice look alike?'

'No, her hair was bright auburn, like our dad's was. Like Reggie's, although he hasn't got much of it yet.'

'Oh, so Reg takes after his aunty? That must be bittersweet. How old was Alice?'

'Nineteen.' The whisper is so faint that Lu can't be sure she heard it, but Polly's voice gains strength as she carries on. 'I'm so sorry about Eddie. I had a feeling you and me were on the same wavelength from the start but I had no idea why at the time.'

Polly puts her mug down and wraps her arms around her knees, hugging them tightly. Her face is turned away from Lu and her voice is so quiet when she speaks again that Lu can barely hear the muffled words.

'You're wrong about Reg looking like his aunty though,' says Polly, 'Reggie looks like his mum. He isn't mine. He was Alice's baby.'

The silence stretches between them for a long moment. Lu clears her throat and murmurs 'Oh, Poll.'

'It's okay, I want you to know about it. Alice died last September when Reg was a month old. She'd kept saying she wasn't coping, and she'd moved back home to live with Mum. I was in Spain, just kind of bumming around working in bars at the time, having some sort of pathetic *finding myself* experience.' She laughs bitterly. 'What a loser. I didn't come home even when Mum said how low my sister was. I'll never forgive myself.'

'But what happened? I don't mean to pry, but it might help to tell me everything now you've started.

'I doubt it. Thinking about her makes it worse. I'm sorry I bit your head off about the breastfeeding, Lu. It was just that Alice struggled so much with it, and Mum said it was the last straw for her when she had to give up. She thought it meant she was a failure as a mum.'

Polly angrily brushes away some of the tears that are pouring down her face and Lu hands her a tissue. She waits patiently until Polly takes a shuddering breath and carries on.

'One day Alice waited until Mum was out shopping, pretending she was going to have a lazy morning at home with Reg. Then she took him out to the local fishing lake. She walked into deep water with him in his pushchair.'

Lu feels frozen to the spot as the shock of this hits

her. After a moment or two she forces herself to get up and moves over to Polly's bed, pulling her into a hug. 'Oh, my love, that's awful. But go on, if you can. I think you need to get all of this off your chest.'

'Someone raised the alarm and they got them both out. Reggie was lucky. He survived but Alice didn't. She'd weighed herself down too thoroughly. The pushchair saved Reg. It bobbed up to the surface.'

Polly's sobbing now, a harsh, heart-breaking sound, and Lu holds her close, murmuring endearments into her hair. When the worst of the storm has subsided, she presses on, determined to release as much of this poison as possible from the girl's troubled mind.

'What happened with Reggie?'

'Our mum is his legal guardian and I came home as soon as I heard, but what use was that? It was too late. I should've got on a plane as soon as I knew Alice was struggling. Anyway, we managed to stagger on together for a little while but then Mum broke down completely. The pain was too much. Finally, I managed to persuade her to admit she needed help. My dad left when I was five, so she's been on her own. Alice and Mum never really got over it. I think the two of them are . . . were the same in a lot of ways.'

'How do you mean?'

'Fragile. Easily hurt. Volatile. Thin-skinned. All those things. Dad always seemed steadier somehow. He kept us all on an even keel. He was so funny. You couldn't be down for long when my dad was about. God, I miss him so much. I've spent years being furious with him for going but I think living with mum nearly drove him mad. She can be violent.'

The last four words, spoken in little more than a whisper, seem to sum up everything Polly's been saying. 'Where is your dad now?' she asks.

'Shropshire. He lives on a smallholding in the middle of nowhere with his new woman. She's a few years older than him, apparently, and she doesn't have any encumbrances except chickens and goats. He gets in touch every now and again. He came to Alice's funeral but Mum was so bitter and angry, she wouldn't even let him come inside the house, let alone the church.'

Even if there are reasons for Polly's dad leaving, Lu's heart goes out to this woman who was abandoned with two young children and now has to face such an awful bereavement and cope with a small motherless baby, not to mention a desperately grieving and guilt-ridden sister. 'I can see how terribly hard it's all been for you . . . and for your mum,' she says sadly, wishing she could think of something more useful to say.

'Mum's gone to stay with an old friend in Scotland for a while. I said I could look after Reggie for now, but it's not been easy. I didn't know anything about babies when Alice . . . died.' The last word is a croak, and Polly buries her face in Lu's shoulder.

'But what about Reggie's father? Didn't he want to be involved? You haven't mentioned him at all.'

Polly disentangles herself from Lu's arms and goes

into the bathroom. Lu can hear her splashing her face with water. She waits. Polly comes back in and goes over to the window, opening it a crack to let in the sea air.

'Reggie's dad?' prompts Lu, gently.

'Reggie's dad has no idea that he's a father at all. And for now, that's the way it's going to stay. Lu, thanks for listening but I've got a banging headache and I really need to sleep. I'm glad I told you though. You're such a lovely person. Coming to your house was the best thing that's happened to me for years.'

'You never did tell me why you ended up in Chandlebury.'

'Oh . . . well . . . it was a random choice, really.' Polly is still gazing out to sea and she doesn't look round. 'You know the sort of thing – stick a pin in the map and go where fate takes you?'

'I see.'

'Lu, I've changed my mind about this being a secret. Will you tell the others all this sometime? I'd like them to know, especially Isaac, but I can't face going over it all again.'

'Of course I will, love, if that's what you want.'

Lucia has a very strong feeling there was more to Polly's arrival in Chandlebury than coincidence, but now's not the time to dig any more. She tucks Polly into bed just as she used to settle her own son and smooths back her still-damp hair. 'You have a lovely big rest now and everything will seem better in the morning. Sleep tight, my love,' she says, using the words she's said so often when Isaac has been troubled.

Polly snuggles down, heaves a huge sigh and is asleep in seconds but Lu lies awake in the darkness as the hours pass. This journey is wonderful but she can't help her mind returning to the problem of her marriage. Des might return to their home at any moment. Bob can't be that enthralling, can he? And her husband has never strayed far from his family before. What will she say to him when they finally meet? And will she really be able to welcome him back and set to work to make everything right? What's more important, does she even want to?

Chapter Eighteen

The wide view of Pengelly bay calls Lucia as soon as her eyes are open and she's soon leaning on the windowsill, breathing in the exhilarating, early morning scent of the sea. It's only six o'clock, but already she's longing to be down there on the beach to clear her head and get a fresh perspective on what happened last night.

Polly's still sound asleep, with only the top of her head visible under the puffy duvet. This is the most comfortable bed Lu has ever slept in apart from her own, so she can understand why Polly might not be ready to get up for a while. She must have been exhausted last night after her emotional revelations and luckily Reggie looks just as cosy in his travel cot in the corner of the room.

Lu wonders if there's any way she can slip into her clothes without waking these two. As quietly as she can, she wriggles into underwear and jeans. Her T-shirt and socks have disappeared somewhere but as she rummages for them Reggie stirs and rolls over, so she gives up and pulls on her hoodie. The day doesn't look too chilly and she'll soon get warm when she's walking. Grabbing trainers and her bag she tiptoes from the bedroom, closing the door behind her with hardly a sound.

149

In five minutes, Lu is down on the sand and racing towards the sea. It's years since she ran for more than a hundred yards for a bus or after an escaping child and she's very soon out of breath, but her cheeks are glowing, and she's full of energy and hope. Thoughts of Des are far away. Today is for celebrating life. She spins around and around, letting out a wild cry of joy. The sound of an answering whoop takes her by surprise, frozen to the spot as a thin figure wavers towards her, trailing scarves and other flowing garments.

'Angelina,' Lu gasps, moving towards the elderly lady with her arms outstretched to intercept her if she trips.

'I thought it was you,' Angelina shouts when she's close enough. 'I saw you from my upstairs window, and thought I'd ask you in for coffee and a currant bun.'

Lu marvels at the way this person who must be ninety if she's a day can cover the ground at such speed and hardly be out of breath. Angelina reaches her and catches Lu by the hand.

'Tristram told me you bought one of my paintings,' she says, beaming. 'I wanted to say thank you. I don't get many visitors these days.'

For a moment, a look of intense sadness passes over the old lady's face and Lu has a vision of the loneliness that might be a problem for her even in the heart of a small village like Pengelly. The same issue crops up in Chandlebury, and Rowan often mentions it, wondering if there's something they could all do to make life better for their older residents.

'I'd love to come with you,' says Lu, who has been thinking she should really get back soon but can't resist the appeal in Angelina's eyes. 'I've got my phone with me. The others will text if they can't find me and they're worried.'

'Oh, those mobile telephones,' says Angelina with a sniff. 'I suppose they're useful at times, but I wouldn't be at all surprised if your family use yours to summon you back just as I pour the coffee and we start to talk about something really interesting. Pah!'

Lu laughs. 'They might try,' she says, 'but they can manage without me for a little while.'

Angelina takes Lucia by the arm and they walk back across the firm sand and over the shingle at the top of the beach. 'Is this your first visit to Pengelly?' she says. 'Fancy you knowing my Tommy.' She simpers a little and Lu has a sudden flashback to the skittish woman who'd appealed to Tommy.

They approach Angelina's house from the rear. The back door is wide open. 'We don't bother with locking up around here,' she says, seeing Lucia's raised eyebrows.

Angelina sheds a couple of scarves, settling Lucia in a wicker chair in the conservatory, surrounded by huge leafy plants and a host of orchids.

'This is a beautiful house, and a fantastic view,' says Lu, feeling any last shreds of tension drifting away.

'I've lived here all my life. Never married. Now, make yourself comfortable while I get the coffee organised. It won't take me long.'

Lucia leans back in her chair and gazes across the bay, watching a man throwing a ball for his two dogs. She thinks she recognises Tristram from the gallery but it's too far away to be sure. The thought of the two pictures she's bought makes her very happy. Polly and Isaac will be delighted with them.

'So, tell me more about yourself, Lucia,' says Angelina, coming back in rather unsteadily carrying a tray loaded with a coffee pot, tiny cups and a plate of buns. 'It's so good to see Tommy again, we had some good times and I'm intrigued by your quest. I hope you don't mind me asking, but how come you're all travelling together? If you don't mind my saying, you're a pretty mixed bunch.'

Lu sips the strong black coffee that's passed to her and wonders how much to divulge. Angelina is smiling at her so benevolently that she has an overwhelming urge to reveal everything – all about Des's desertion, her feelings of betrayal, her hopes for Isaac's future and her growing anxiety about Polly and Reg.

'Go on, dear. I'm listening,' says Angelina, pouring more coffee.

The words tumble out, slowly at first and then gathering speed. It's a much edited version of the story so far but even so, Angelina seems riveted. Eventually Lu runs out of steam.

'And Tommy gave Des and me a generous dollop of money, and . . .well . . .some other things . . . ,' she finishes. 'Now it's your turn. Tell me about you and Tommy. It's only fair.'

Angelina smiles as she looks out of the window, her gaze far away on the distant sands. 'We'd been lovers for a while,' she says quietly. 'When it ended, due to my stupidity I have to admit, Tommy was finding it hard to leave here, even though he must have known I was a bad bet.'

'He couldn't leave because he loved you too much?' The thought is unsettling, and she gives herself a mental shake. This was all a very long time ago, and anyway, how Tommy felt about Angelina is none of her business.

'Oh no. Nothing so romantic. Tommy Lemon is an honourable man. He thought he'd be letting me down because he'd more than half promised to help me set up a new business selling my paintings. He thought I couldn't, or more likely wouldn't do it, left to myself.'

'So you . . . kind of . . . set him free?'

The old lady nods. The sadness on her face transcends the years. 'He's an adventurer and a risk-taker, as you know. I sent him away because he couldn't do the deed himself. He's much younger than me and I knew he wasn't ready to settle down. He never has been . . . until now, perhaps.'

Lucia is about to follow up this last remark when her phone bleeps. 'Damn. They've twigged that I'm missing,' says Lu. 'My son and Polly, I mean. And I'm sure Peter and Tommy will be on the case too, by now. Even Reggie might have noticed I've gone. My five minders.'

'How nice to be wanted. I never had children. Too busy having fun, I suppose. Sometimes I wish . . . but

I wouldn't have had time to paint, would I? Listen, Lucia, before you go, I need to talk to you about the compass. I don't suppose you've got it with you, by any chance?'

'I . . . what did you say?'

'The *compass*, dear. Tommy told me you were the new owner. Is it here?'

Lucia looks down at the bag at her feet. Angelina's eyes follow hers and she claps her hands, with the glee of a small child spotting an ice cream van.

'You *have* got it! Let me see . . . please? It's been so long . . . is it still the same?'

'How do you mean, exactly?'

'Oh, Lucia – don't play dumb. Is it . . . helping?'

Frowning, Lucia reaches down and rummages for the leather case. Angelina's hands are clasped together tightly now, and she seems to be holding her breath.

'I can't help wondering how you know so much about this?' Lucia asks, as she opens the case, revealing the glowing colours of the enamelled face.

'That's an easy one to answer. I know about it because it was me who passed it on to Tommy. I've often wished I still had it, but in my heart I knew the moment was right. I was relying on it far too much. I wonder why Tommy felt it was time to give it to you? I don't suppose . . . would you let me hold it, just one more time?'

Lucia's head is reeling now. There's too much to take in here. Angelina's eyes are glittering and her cheeks are very pink. She reaches out a shaking hand towards the compass just as the phone bleeps again. Lucia snatches it up, so full of relief that she can barely breathe.

'I'd better go. They need me.'

The old lady closes her eyes for a moment and breathes deeply. When she opens them again she's back in control. 'Yes dear, you must go. Come again if you have time. We have a lot to discuss, I think. You could bring that charming older gentleman with you?' Angelina reaches out and hugs Lu. 'Tommy's friend seems very personable. Perhaps he'd like to come and stay here with me for a holiday sometime.'

Lucia puts the compass away safely and makes a non-committal reply, privately fearing for Peter's sanity if he risks such a visit. She walks back by the road rather than the beach, so pole-axed by this conversation that she even forgets to admire the view. She lets herself into the pub by the back door, locks up again and puts the key back in the bowl with hands that are still trembling. Creeping up the stairs, she meets Polly on the landing with Reggie on her hip.

'I was coming to look for you.' Polly says. 'We're ravenous. Peter and Tommy are talking about ordering a full English breakfast with extra sausages and black pudding.' She shudders. 'Are we having breakfast in the lounge?'

'Yes, let's go down there now, I smell bacon.'

'Yuck,' says Polly, but she follows quite happily. Lu's relieved that yesterday's traumas seem to have faded away for a while. Being only 25 has its benefits, resilience for one. She wishes she could say the same for herself. A tension headache is building up behind her eyes and the thought of food is making her stomach churn.

In the lounge, Isaac, Tommy and Peter are sitting near the window with a pot of coffee between them and a newspaper each. Isaac has already pulled a highchair for Reggie up to the table and Polly nods at him approvingly.

'I've just been to see Angelina,' Lucia tells them, avoiding meeting Tommy's clear gaze with difficulty.

'That's nice,' says Polly, 'How did she seem? I'm worried about how thin she is.'

'Oh, that's nothing new,' Tommy says. 'She's never been one for eating properly. Once she gets stuck into a painting, she exists on cheese and apples with the odd pasty from the shop.'

'We maybe could organise a regular shopping delivery for her if you think it'd help, but I'm not going to think about Angelina or anyone else but you lot for the moment,' Lu says. 'We're at the seaside now. Even better, we're in Cornwall. The landlord mentioned sea caves that you can reach at low tide. There are scones to eat and a beach to explore.'

Chapter Nineteen

Later, as they pick their way carefully down Memory Lane after a sudden shower of rain has made the cobbles slippery, Lu feels the morning's tension slipping away at last. There will be time enough later to think more about what Angelina has said. For now, a contentment she hasn't experienced for years washes over her and she shivers with pleasure. They pass what must have once been a long row of fishermen's cottages and eventually reach the shingle.

'We'll have to carry the buggy over this bit,' says Isaac, picking up the front bar as Polly takes the strain at the back. Peter is already taking his shoes off. Lucia hangs back to have a word with him as the others stride off down the beach.

'I think we should call it a day here,' she tells Peter, lowering her voice so Tommy can't catch what she's saying. Pengelly is wonderful, but putting distance between herself and Angelina seems like a good plan at the moment. She can't help feeling that the old lady will try to get her hands on the compass again at the first opportunity.

'Oh, that's a shame. I was just getting into the swing

157

of this paddling lark,' Peter says, wriggling his toes in the firm sand. 'Haven't had this much fun since . . . well, since I lost my wife.'

Peter shields his eyes against the glare from the sunlit sea and watches the rest of the party head for the shoreline. 'They're not going to want to leave here yet,' he says. 'But let's not forget who's the boss around here.' He grins down at her and Lucia's heart swells with affection. 'Where next then?' he asks.

'Can we talk about that all together when we're back at the pub? There's something I need to do first,' Lucia says.

'Absolutely. I've got a marvellous idea of my own but I'm not sure if it's practical or if anyone else would go for it. We'll discuss the matter in the fullness of time, my dear. Now I need to dip these aged toes in the water.'

Lucia looks down at the toes in question. Peter's feet look as if they've never before seen the light of day. The skin is brilliantly white and his ankles are thin and bony. She has a sudden pang of alarm at the thought that she hardly knows the man and yet she's dragged him away from the only home he's ever known and now she has not the slightest idea where they'll go next. When her eyes return to his face though, she's reassured. His smile is radiant and she can see he's itching to join the others.

'Off you go,' Lu says. 'I'm just going to sit here for a little while and get my breath back. It's been a crazy few days.'

Peter needs no further bidding and heads off down

the beach as Lucia sinks down onto the firm sand and opens her bag. Cross-legged, she fetches out the compass and takes a moment to admire the sheer beauty of its colours in the bright morning sunshine. Then she follows the now familiar ritual of holding it in the palm of her hands.

A deep sense of peace flows through Lu's body as, still for the first time today, she lets her mind rest. The sound of the gulls and Isaac's joyous laugh, something she's not heard for what seems like an age, permeate her soul, and the fresh sea breeze seems to be clearing out all unwelcome thoughts about the state of her marriage. The tang of salt in the air, the growing warmth of the sun and the barking of a distant dog as it leaps in and out of the waves are enough for a few moments, but then she remembers what she's meant to be doing before the others return.

The compass and the barometer have been busy while Lu's been daydreaming. The needles have already settled, with the compass indicating due south and the barometer clearly pointing to the word *variable*. Lu is relieved that they've left *cloudy* behind. That must have referred to Tommy's feeling, she thinks. Maybe the compass is still able to feel echoes of its previous owners emotions? That would make sense. She gives herself a little shake. Actually, none of this makes sense, it's suspending disbelief that's the thing here.

Taking a moment to reassess her own views about the compass, Lu realises that every time she reaches for it, she's becoming increasingly certain that it does have . . . powers. Even admitting this to herself makes her feel a bit silly but she can't deny the truth of it as it forms in her mind.

So, *variable* and *south*. What can it mean? Lu tries to conjure up an image of the layout of Cornwall. Feeling as if she's cheating, she pulls out her phone and Googles the question. It's quickly apparent that travelling due south from here they would end up somewhere in the Bay of Biscay. Lucia shivers. It's time she stopped pretending. The compass is telling her to go to France and that is something she never thought she'd be brave enough to do. It's almost as if Eddie is calling her, but can she do it? And will the others even want to go so far afield?

Back at base, the group sit around the largest table in the lounge and make short work of the most enormous platter of sandwiches they've ever seen.

'I'd like to stay here forever,' mumbles Polly through a mouthful of panini. 'This is bliss.'

'Ah. And that's what I wanted to talk to you all about.' Lucia meets Peter's steady gaze and feels heartened. 'I think it's time we moved again.'

A chorus of groans come from Polly, Isaac and Tommy but Lucia ploughs on.

'These last two places have been my choice but we can go anywhere you like next. Has anybody got any ideas?'

Silence falls. After a decent interval to give the others

chance to speak, Peter clears his throat. 'I'd like to make a suggestion, if I may,' he says. 'Why not, as we're so close to the channel, head on down into France?'

Lucia stares at him. Is he doing this for her, in some twisted way, to force her into facing her past? But Sir Peter's eyes are wet as he carries on. 'Frances and I spent many happy weeks travelling through northern France in our old Bluebird. It was a bit too sporty for that sort of job but having the top down and the wind in our hair . . . and the rain sometimes, if I'm honest . . . was sheer magic. I would dearly love to do it again once more, before . . . well . . .' his voice tails off and Tommy reaches over to pat his friend's hand.

'I'm game,' he says. 'I've got my passport. Never go anywhere without it.'

'Oh, so have I,' Peter agrees. 'Old habits die hard. "Be prepared", Frances always used to say. Sometimes even when we thought we were just visiting friends on the Sussex coast we'd wind up in Newhaven and on the ferry before you could say *au revoir*. But what about the rest of you?'

Isaac frowns. 'I don't even know where my passport is,' he says, rather too loudly. 'I only got one because there was an exchange trip planned at Uni but, I never needed it in the end.'

'It's here, I put mine and yours in just in case.' Lucia waits for Isaac to get even crosser at the prospect of being forced to step even further out of his comfort zone but Polly has moved closer to him and it seems as if her

161

presence is enough to reassure him, for the time being at least.

'You'll be fine, love,' Lu says. 'If I can do it, you can too. It depends what everyone else wants to do though. Polly, I know you've got your passport because I reminded you. Oh, but what about Reg! I hadn't thought of that. Of course he'll need a passport too. He'll have to go on yours. Never mind, it'll just mean we'll have to wait while you add him. We can probably do it at a post office.'

Polly's looking at her feet. 'No, we can't do that but it's not a problem. He's got a separate one. There were . . . reasons. And mine's still got five years to run.'

'Excellent. So what's holding us back? Is it a good plan?'

'Where would we go from? I don't know anything about getting across there.' Isaac says. Lucia thinks he sounds less resistant now and Polly's eyes are sparkling.

'I haven't really been anywhere abroad apart from a little bit of Spain,' she says. 'I'd love to see France.'

'Well, if Lucia and Isaac are happy to make northern France our next port of call, we can make some enquiries about ferries. We're not too far from Poole, are we? How do you all feel about a bit of a cruise to Cherbourg?'

Chapter Twenty

In the event, leaving Pengelly is easier than Lucia expected. They've all fallen in love with the place, but there's a definite sense of adventure in the air as they pack up the bus.

Isaac takes the wheel and Peter the front seat as they chug their way out of the village, with Polly chatting to Tommy in the back as Reggie closes tired eyes for a nap. Lucia sighs. The winding, cobbled streets down to the sea and the hotchpotch of cottages and grander houses strung out along The Level leading to the beautiful old church and the green seem to have sneaked right into her soul in the short time they've been here.

'I wish we could stay longer,' Polly says. 'It's gorgeous here and there's still so much to see, but I can't wait to see France.'

'Oh, me too,' says Tommy, craning his neck to get a last glimpse of the village as they head towards the road that will eventually lead them over Bodmin Moor. 'We can always come back,' he adds, hopefully. 'I think Angelina would like that. She asked Peter and me to stay with her next time, you know.'

Lucia exchanges a rather worried glance with Polly but

163

then thinks on reflection that a few days with Angelina might be a tonic for the two friends. The old lady is full of joyful optimism and she'll adore the company, so long as they bring copious supplies of gin with them.

Their enjoyment of the next part of the journey is hampered by the fact that the weather turns humid when the sun comes up properly, which will be wonderful when they reach a beach and can cool off in the sea, Isaac comments, but not so great for driving. At least Reggie's asleep for the first part, and when they stop for a much-needed break, Lucia is more than happy to get behind the wheel.

'I wish you'd have let me be put on the insurance,' says Tommy, not for the first time. 'I could have helped out. I'm not a bad driver, you know.'

'We're fine, I'd rather you just enjoyed the scenery and helped to entertain Reggie. I'm going to hand over to Polly or Isaac when we reach Poole though,' Lucia says. 'Getting onto the ferry isn't something I've ever tried. We might end up in the water.'

'I don't mind having a go,' says Tommy, eagerly. 'It won't matter that I'm not insured just for that bit, will it?'

'Well, it would definitely be an issue if you crashed into someone else's car or got wedged between two caravans. Just like I'm afraid I might do, Isaac.'

'Don't put yourself down, Mum. You'd be great, but that's fine. We don't mind, do we, Poll?'

Polly shakes her head, busy settling Reggie with a snack. 'Not at all. I'd love to do it,' she says. 'Bring it on.'

'You're in for a treat, my dear,' Peter says, leafing through the maps to find the one he needs. 'Ha, that's it – the Cherbourg peninsula. If I remember rightly there used to be a few campsites not far from the ferry port if we've had enough of being in the van. Either that or we can press on further south. What's the verdict?'

'Thank goodness you came with us.' says Polly, 'It's like having our own private travel guide. What with you, the Sat Nav and Tommy's maps, we can't go wrong.'

Peter beams at Polly. 'I can't help feeling as if I've not followed the rules with my choice of venue though,' he says. 'There's no one particular place I want to visit, it's just the area. I have such good memories of touring around here, even if the war graves and the landing beaches were a grim reminder of bad times.'

'That's fine, so long as you're not going to take a nose-dive into gloom when we get there.' Tommy's face is a picture of concern. 'This is meant to be a joyful trip. Not that I don't think we should be respectful of the past,' he adds hastily when he sees Polly frowning at him.

'No, I won't, Tommy, and that's a promise. This is the most fun I've had in years. I'm not about to spoil it for us all.'

'I know you're not really. We've all got the adventuring bug, haven't we? In different ways . . .' Tommy lapses into silence and concentrates on amusing Reggie.

Lucia thinks about the compass, tucked away in her travel bag. The thought of it is comforting. This is unfamiliar territory, even if she has got four minders. All these years of staying close to home have taken their toll on her confidence, and the thought of Eddie's last holiday still weighs heavily on her mind.

Eddie was always a strange mixture of bravado and fear, which meant there was no saying what he would do in any given situation. Looking back, it's amazing their parents ever dared to take him anywhere. Even the school visit to Alton Towers, the year before that fateful school holiday, had ended in disaster, with Eddie breaking not only his own wrist but damaging three of his friends. They had to close one of the rides down after that for investigations, but nobody could have expected him to . . . her mind shies away from the thought. Ed was a law unto himself, as Dad used to say.

Lucia remembers lying in bed as Eddie set off with her parents to board the coach. She'd been clammy and wobbly with the last traces of glandular fever, but she'd known deep down that her mother had thought she was exaggerating her symptoms because she didn't want to go on the trip and be Eddie's keeper.

Was it true? Could she have gone? Lucia will never forget the feeling of unutterable weakness that took a long time to shift. If she'd have dosed herself up with paracetamol, she might just have managed to get on the coach, but in her heart Lu knows she'd not have been much good to Eddie feeling so awful.

For the first time, Lu wonders why Des has never pointed all this out to her when she's agonised over her part in Eddie's death. He must have been able to see some of the things she's only just facing, being at something of a distance from the painful memories? An uncomfortable thought crosses her mind. Surely Des didn't encourage her reluctance to travel for his own ends? That would be really mean, wouldn't it? But he's never wanted to go anywhere either, and he hasn't got the excuse of Lu's terrible paranoia about accidents. So what exactly is Des afraid of?

The miles trundle by as Lucia mulls over the past, and she pays only vague attention to the discussion that's going on about their next steps. In the end, the general opinion is that by the time they've crossed into France, Polly, Isaac and Lucia will have done enough driving, even if they do keep taking turns.

'I'll Google one of the campsites we looked at last night and book ahead,' says Polly, 'That one on the coast looked amazing. You can stroll through the dunes and you're right on the beach. It's all flat sand, perfect for paddling.'

The ferry crossing is uneventful apart from Reggie being violently sick on Polly's shoes, but by the time the van rolls off the boat in Cherbourg, he's perked up again and is burbling happily as they all sing along to the holiday mix that Isaac has surprised them with. It's full of Isaac's favourite up-beat summertime tracks. Winding their way along the coast road to the first site, Lucia's heart feels light, and again she ponders on why she hasn't made herself take this big step sooner.

When they reach the place Polly's booked, Tommy

starts rummaging in his bag for a phrasebook. 'What are we going to have for dinner?' he says excitedly. 'Can I order? I'm fine if I plan what I'm going to say. It's just that I don't always understand the answer if they talk too fast.'

'Look, can we leave talking about dinner until we've found a pitch? I'm hot and tired and I need a beer.' Isaac pulls up outside the camp office. 'And who's best at speaking the language *without* the aid of a book? I only got as far as asking for croissants and coffee when we did French at school.'

Tommy doesn't reply to this question. Peter scratches his head. 'I don't mind having a try, if you're stuck,' he says. 'I used to be able to make myself understood pretty well. I'm a bit rusty though.'

'No, it's fine,' Lu says, plucking up her courage. 'I need to stretch my legs and at least have a go at communicating.'

Climbing stiffly out of the van, she heads for the wooden shack marked *La réception*. Inside, the only person she can see is a very old man with a ledger. He's reaching for a huge bunch of keys. Pointing to a sign that says *Closed* in several languages, he shrugs.

'Bonjour,' says Lucia, her mind emptying itself of any useful French phrases as she pastes on her best smile and tries to sound confident. 'Erm . . . vous avez . . . un . . . une . . . anyway vous avez a reservation. For two nights,' she adds.

The man frowns and points at the sign again. He shakes his head firmly.

'But look, we've been driving for hours, we've got a baby who needs to have a nap, we've got to go and find either a restaurant or a supermarket to buy food or preferably both,' Lu gabbles, giving up on her schoolgirl French. 'We don't need you to do anything, just send us to a pitch.'

The old man wipes his nose on his sleeve and coughs alarmingly, shaking his thin frame until his eyes water. Beginning to despair, Lucia looks around for a saviour and finds her in the back room, puffing on a cigarette and reading a paperback novel with a very gaudy cover. In the picture, a couple are becoming very friendly up against what looks like a barn. A sheep looks on worriedly.

'Excusé moi,' Lu bleats, dredging up the only other couple of words she can remember. 'Can you help me?'

The young woman sighs heavily, puts her book on the table face downwards and ambles into the outer office, flicking the dog end of her cigarette into a tin bucket on the way.

'Yeah?' she says. 'What seems to be the problem?'

'Oh, you speak English. Thank goodness. My French is rubbish.'

'It is,' the woman nods. 'I suppose you want a pitch?'

Lu decides there's no point in taking offence at the attitude on display here. 'Yes please,' she says. 'That's all I need. We can do the paperwork later if you like. Only there's a baby . . .'

'There's always a baby. Or a toddler. Or an old mother.

I don't know why you people bother. Why not stay at home and save yourselves the effort?'

'Oh. You're not French then.' Lucia struggles to adjust to this Australian version of what she imagined to be the youth of France.

'You've got to be kidding me. If I was, I'd be having my siesta, like Janis here should be doing. I'm Naomi, by the way.'

She pronounces the old man's name Yanis, and at the sound of it he looks up and curls his lip at Lucia. She glowers back, completely out of patience. What's wrong with these two? How hard would it be to give a bit of a welcome to a weary traveller?

'So hit me with it, you're miles from Blighty, you've a tent to pitch, you've not brought any food with you and even worse, you've got no beer?' Naomi easily manages to make the whole venture sound ridiculous and Lucia has a profound longing for home, with her own shady garden and swinging seat.

She nods, suddenly realising how exhausted she is. 'A tent, an awning and a motorhome. We could do with some shade, if that's possible, for . . .'

'The baby . . . I get it. Right, follow me. You can put your unit on one of the enclosures near the sea if you like, under the trees. The site shop opens again at three o'clock and the bar's over there if you need a cold beer later on. We do food after six. It's basic but it tastes just great. *Moules et frites*? *Steak haché*? Any good? I'm the cook so you'll get a good feed at least. And I'm the

170

cleaner. Oh, and the site manager when old Janis is in a bad mood.' The woman holds out a hand and Lu shakes it, holding on as if to a lifeline.

'Any good? Are you kidding? It sounds like heaven. Just show us where to go.'

Chapter Twenty-One

The two women leave the reception area as the old man subsides into a lounger and closes his eyes. Lu waves to the others to follow as she walks behind Naomi to a pitch, as promised, right on the edge of the site, a stone's throw from the beach.

'I think you made a fabulous choice here, Poll,' she says, as the others pile out of the van. 'Two nights of peace, the sound of the sea, and some stupendous, home-cooked bar food. I think I've died and gone to heaven.'

Peter laughs. 'You and me both,' he says happily.

They soon make camp, and Lucia looks round proudly at the sheltered pitch, now filled to bursting point with the van, the large green and cream awning and Isaac's little khaki tent. There's just room for a picnic rug and the four folding chairs donated by Peter. Isaac subsides onto the grass with Reggie, spreading the rug for them both and lying down on his back with the little boy on his chest. Reggie murmurs contentedly and sucks his fist.

'These chairs are a bit shabby but that's because they've seen a fair few journeys in their time,' Peter says, brushing the seats down before lowering himself into the sturdiest looking one.

'Four? Who used to sit in the others then?' asks Isaac.

Lucia winces, imagining as Tommy had done that Peter's holiday memories might make him melancholy after all these years, but he smiles. 'My wife, Frances, and our best friends, Cecil and Fenella. Oh, we had some good times, travelling through France and Italy. Fabulous food, delicious local wine and good company. Cecil and I each took our own car so we had some space away from each other with our wives and we usually stayed in family run hotels or camped. What more could a person ask for?'

Tommy hands Peter a small bottle of beer with condensation running down the sides and the older man gasps. 'Where did you get this, my friend? It's freezing cold. How heavenly.'

'The shop finally opened,' Tommy says.

Isaac strokes Reggie's back as he snuggles into his favourite position. 'So what happened?'

'How do you mean?'

'What happened to Frances?'

'Don't tell us if it's too upsetting,' Polly says quickly, joining them and settling down with Reggie on her lap.

Lucia holds her breath. Peter doesn't seem fazed by Isaac's clumsy question but he leans back in the creaking chair and swallows half his beer in one go before replying.

'Not at all. It's a very long time ago now. Frances and I began our travels abroad when we first met and carried on until our son was born. After that we tended to stick to Wales because my wife had relatives there and they

173

wanted to see the boy as often as possible, naturally enough. We both loved Wales. We toured there often.'

Lucia waits, sensing sadness in the air. She doesn't know if she really wants to hear the rest of this story but the warmth of the afternoon, the roar of the waves just beyond the dunes and the sound of Peter's wonderfully plummy accent are soothing. His voice reminds Lu of the old BBC announcers she's seen in black and white documentaries.

'I was just forty when Frances . . . was killed. We had our boy, Miles, when we were first married and he was at university in Plymouth when his mother passed away. He was . . . is . . . a complicated person, and I think he blamed me for the accident. In fact, I know he did. And still does.'

There's a long silence, punctuated by Reggie's sleepy snuffles as he drinks his milk. Seagulls cry to each other and wheel overhead. The sound is mournful and makes Lucia want to weep for Peter, for his wife, for all that they lost. She waits to see if he will tell them more about Frances.

'As I was saying,' he continues eventually, when Lu has almost given up hope, 'my darling girl was involved in a terrible accident. She was running for the bus and she tripped and fell in front of a car. She always wore the most impractical high heels. The car was speeding, and the driver had been drinking. She didn't stand a chance.'

'That's awful. But how could that have been your fault? Why did your son blame you?'

'That's easy. It was because I could have given her a lift into town that day but I was impatient when she took so long getting ready and dashed off to work without waiting for her. She had a lot of good traits, but keeping to a timetable and hurrying up . . . well, that wasn't one of them.'

His expression is bleak, and Lucia is tempted to change the subject as soon as she decently can, but they've come too far now. Her own guilt at the memory of her part in Eddie's death forces her on.

'Peter, you might not want to answer this now, but was timekeeping important in your job?'

'How do you mean? What's that got to do with anything?'

Lucia struggles with how to phrase her next question tactfully but decides she's said enough. Unfortunately Isaac doesn't have his mother's knack for leaving well alone. He ploughs on.

'Did Frances know how much you needed to be at work on time, Peter?'

'Oh, I see. Well, yes of course. I was an accountant. It was in the days when my father was hale and hearty so he was running the estate and we lived in the west wing. It took me a good forty-five minutes to drive into the city and the traffic was hellish at that time of day.'

He falls silent, deep in thought. Eventually, he stirs himself. 'I think what you're both trying to say is that Frances should have known better than to be so slow in getting ready when she knew I was on a tight schedule?'

Lucia says nothing. Her heart is aching for the proud

old man. The pain in his eyes is plain to see, but maybe this will help to loosen the tight bands of blame, even a little bit.

Peter clears his throat. 'I have thought about that point. It was always a bone of contention between us. Frances was terribly disorganised when it came to doing anything in a hurry. A wonderful wife and an excellent mother, but . . . somewhat dizzy about timing. It caused quite a few rows, and we had one that very morning before I stormed off. I had a meeting with a very important new client and I really couldn't risk getting caught in the rush hour.'

There is silence again, apart from the sound of the gulls and the gentle murmur of the sea on the other side of the dunes. Lucia waits, hoping she won't need to say more, but Isaac is on a roll now.

'So, I reckon what Mum's getting at,' he says, 'is that your Frances should have got her act together sooner when she knew you were in a rush.'

'That's a bit harsh, Isaac,' says Polly. 'There were lots of other factors too. Sometimes an accident is . . . well, just that. Circumstances coming together and bad stuff happening.'

'And a drunken driver in the mix too,' adds Lucia, wanting to gag her son. Why did he always have to be so black and white?

'Yeah, I guess,' Isaac acknowledges, 'but I'd have stormed off too, if I was Peter. Frances should have had more sense. Bloody annoying woman.'

Everyone stares at Isaac for a moment, shocked at what he's just said, but Peter begins to laugh, and they all smile nervously. He rocks in his chair with mounting hysteria and gasps for breath, tears trickling down his cheeks. The others look at him warily. Is the old man laughing or crying? Maybe both? Lucia wonders if all this soul-searching has been too much for Peter but he pats her arm reassuringly.

'I love your refreshing honesty, Isaac,' he says, when the wave of laughter has waned. He gets out another of his trademark snowy handkerchiefs and wipes his eyes, taking the beer and downing half of it in an enthusiastic gulp. 'If only it were so easy to shift the blame.'

'I wasn't trying to make Frances sound like the bad guy exactly,' Isaac says, glancing at his mother's forbidding expression. 'It's just something to think about, you know?'

'Or *not* think about,' says Polly. 'Why would Peter want to feel worse than he already does? He doesn't want Frances to be blamed.'

'But it was her fault,' says Isaac, looking round at the others, a bewildered expression on his face.

'There's always more than one side to a story, lad,' says Tommy. 'Nothing's ever that straightforward.'

'But . . .'

Peter smiles rather wearily. 'You're quite right, Isaac. Frances *should* have hurried herself up. And in fairness, I knew there was always someone around at Meadowthorpe Manor to give her a lift into town later.'

'Absolutely. You wouldn't have left her stranded,' says Lucia.

'No indeed. It was just unfortunate that the estate worker she chose to ask could only take her part way on that particular morning. And because she still wasn't ready on time for him, he hadn't got time to take her all the way, so she had to run for the bus when he dropped her off on the edge of the city. And that's how her story ended. Way too soon.'

'There you go then.' Isaac glances around at the rest of the group as if daring anyone to argue with him again.

'I hear what you're saying, but I've carried this guilt for a long time. I'll give your idea about letting Frances share the responsibility some thought though. And thank you, Isaac. Your clear-eyed view is a breath of fresh air.' Peter blinks back more tears.

'So, moving on from all that, how did you cope?' Lu asks, reaching for his hand.

Peter makes a wry face. 'In the only way I knew. I worked even harder than before, drank too much vintage cognac in the evenings when I finally got home, ate barely enough to keep myself alive and avoided talking to anyone as much as possible. What a charmer I was, eh?'

'But if Miles thought it was your fault, you must have found that even harder? Don't beat yourself up. You were grieving. It affects everyone in different ways at different times,' says Polly.

'Yes, one tends to be able to recognise the look on the

face of fellow sufferers,' Peter says quietly, looking at Polly and Lu. They both gaze back.

'We're on a mission to offload some of this guilt we've been carrying around,' says Lu. 'It's very heavy and it's not going to be easy, but we're part of the way there. Let's keep going. We're in this together now.'

Chapter Twenty-Two

The next morning passes peacefully. They're all tired, and Isaac can see that his mum, Tommy and Peter are in need of some time off, so he and Polly disengage the awning with some difficulty and take Reggie into the nearest town to stock up on food. The motorhome rumbles along the lanes picking up even more dust and tiny flies on its windscreen and Reggie hums quietly to himself as they pass lush green fields and woodland paths that wind away temptingly.

Shopping with Polly is unlike anything Isaac has ever experienced. Used to hurrying so that Reggie doesn't get bored, Polly completes the job at top speed but still attempts to read all the labels.

'It's difficult enough making sure I get the right stuff for Reggie when the contents are in English, let alone French,' she says despairingly, throwing a packet of porridge oats into the trolley.

'Surely cereal's the same wherever you are?'

'It's okay for you to be so blasé, Isaac, but I'm completely responsible for this small person. I've got to get it right.'

Isaac starts to formulate his next question, which is

180

going to be about why she's doing the job all alone, but Polly's already heading for the checkout. Never mind. There'll be time to find out more later, with luck. They drive back in companionable silence, with all the windows open and the warm breeze blowing Polly's hair around crazily. Her eyes are closed and she looks more relaxed than Isaac's ever seen her. Smiling across at her, Isaac is suddenly glad that he didn't pry. What does the past matter? She's here now, with him. He must try his best to get this right.

Later, when they've had lunch, Lucia announces that she's still shattered and she's going to have an hour reading in the shade. 'And if I were you, Poll, I'd put Reggie down in his cot for a sleep too. I'll keep an eye on him. Then you two can go off and explore if you like?'

Would Isaac like? Is she kidding? He sneaks a look at Polly to try and guess if she wants to be with him or not but she's busy lacing her trainers more tightly. It seems to take her ages. When she finally looks up, she's pink in the face. Must be because she's been bending down.

'D'you want to go for a walk with me, Isaac?' she says.

He shrugs, worried about scaring her off by shouting 'YES! I bloody do!' She looks a bit crestfallen when there's no immediate reply and Lucia steps in.

'Of course he does,' she says. 'Isaac, you really do need to work on your manners.'

Isaac's not sure what she means but he has another go. 'Yes please, that'd be great,' he says, and relief floods his whole body making him tingle all over as Polly smiles up at him.

Ten minutes later, Reggie's snuggled down in his travel cot talking to his fluffy blanket and Polly's at Isaac's side walking towards the gap in the dunes.

'Which way do you want to go?' she says. 'Left or right?'

He'd like to say *anywhere with you would be the most amazing place ever*, but he thinks that might sound a bit cheesy, so he suggests they make their way towards a row of tall pine trees in the far distance.

They take their trainers off and tie their shoelaces together so they can string them around their necks. The sand is cool and firm under Isaac's bare feet and the sun's shining again. He can't remember ever feeling this happy in his entire life, even when he was very young. The sun is warm on his face, the sound of the gulls is emotive and the urge to make a sandcastle is strong. It would be like the ones he made in his sand pit at home after a long day at school. The feeling of relief at being safely home again was always wonderful.

'Did you like being at school?' he asks Polly, following his own train of thought.

She looks surprised and doesn't answer straight away. 'Erm . . . not much,' she says eventually. 'Did you?'

'No, I hated it.'

'Why?'

'I just didn't seem to be able to find any real friends.' Isaac feels her slip her hand into his. He looks down, terrified of spoiling this perfection. 'You haven't got many friends even now, have you?' she asks.

He thinks about this for a moment. He knows it's true, but it's kind of embarrassing to admit it all the same. It's no good. His mind's gone blank.

'Did you not make any friends at uni? You were at Leeds, weren't you?'

'Who told you that?'

'Your mum. Why, is it a secret?'

They've reached a low sand bank now and stop to take in the view. The beach stretches out to either side of them. He can feel tiny shells between his toes and smell the wild, joyful aroma of salt and seaweed. There is nobody else in sight.

Acting on impulse for once in his life, Isaac lifts Polly's hand to his lips and kisses the palm of it, then turns it over and kisses each knuckle. He's never done anything remotely like this before and it feels as if it's happening in slow motion and they're in a film, the camera panning in to focus on Polly's small pink fingernails, bitten to the quick. He drops her hand, feeling foolish. She's standing very still, and he thinks she's holding her breath.

'Isaac,' she whispers, and wraps her arms around his waist. He holds her close, the rose-petal scent of her hair making him giddy. She fits just underneath his chin, as if she belongs there. They stay like that for what seems like a long time but probably isn't. Isaac doesn't look at his watch to see because he's pretty sure that would be a bad idea.

She moves away slightly to look up and Isaac wonders what he should do next. Should he kiss her properly? Does she want him to? Her eyes seem to be saying she wouldn't mind, so he bends and brushes his lips against hers, gently at first as a try-out. She seems to be enjoying it, so Isaac gives up any idea of knowing what to do for the best and just goes for it. They cling together and kiss for so long that he thinks he might fly right up into the sky like a balloon full of helium.

Finally, they break apart and blink at each other, smiling. That's when it all goes wrong. 'I love you,' Isaac says, before he can stop himself. Polly flinches.

'No, you don't,' she says. 'And you shouldn't say things like that if you don't mean them.'

'But I do mean it,' Isaac stammers, 'I . . .'

'You don't really know me so how can you say you love me?' They stare at each other. Isaac has no idea what to do next.

'What if I want to get to know you better, then?' he asks after a while. 'Can't we make a start today?'

Polly's eyes are flashing fire now. Isaac flinches. What did he do wrong this time?

'It's not as simple as that. There's so much you don't understand about me, Isaac,' she says, 'and I haven't got the slightest idea where we should begin.'

'Pretend I didn't say anything for now, if you like, Poll. Let's go and look at those trees first and we might do the serious stuff later,' Isaac says, and he can tell he's said the right thing this time by the way the tension leaves her shoulders and her eyes light up. There's a lot in this body language business, he tells himself, glad he's been making the effort to watch people more carefully to judge their feelings. It's hard work and you can't always tell, but it's getting a bit easier. Just a little bit.

They hold hands again as they walk along the beach and it feels even more natural this time. Maybe they're already learning about each other? Isaac hopes so with all his heart. When they reach the edge of the pine forest, he leads Polly into the shelter of the towering branches, one step at a time and her fingers grip his more tightly. This is turning out to be absolutely the best day of Isaac's life.

Chapter Twenty-Three

With the younger members of the party away and Reggie and Peter tucked up in the van for a sleep, it occurs to Lucia that she's accidentally left herself wide open for Tommy to talk to her about the compass again. Their brief encounter in the pub corridor is still on her mind and she's not at all sure she wants to repeat the experience.

'So, lovely Lu, what's next? Are you really going to have a nap or are we going to have a good old chat?' he says, moving two of the chairs to the farthest corner of their pitch in the shade of an ancient beech tree.

The afternoon sun is strong and she's glad of the cool refuge, but as she sinks into the chair, Lu's heart is racing. Is Tommy going to ask her for the compass back? Perhaps now his future isn't so settled, he'll want its guidance.

Tommy leaves her for a moment to fetch a bottle of water for each of them from the cool box, and then sits down. He stretches out his legs, and Lu rubs her bleary eyes. She's so sleepy that she can hardly keep them open but she can tell something important is coming, so she chugs half of her water and tries to concentrate.

A lazy bee buzzing around his head distracts Tommy briefly but when it's gone on its way to the nearby honeysuckle, he leans forward and takes her hand.

'I wanted to clear a few things up between us. I know you're in a strange place right now, with Des being such a prat. Sorry, I know I shouldn't bad mouth him, he's family when all's said and done, but my life, why would anyone leave *you*, darling?'

Lucia doesn't answer. Tommy's warm affection for her is immensely soothing and she doesn't mind how much he chunters about Des. It smarts that her husband has only been in touch to ask for a clothes parcel and still no thanks for it.

'Anyway, what I wanted to say, apart from you looking absolutely beautiful, as always . . .'

Lu rolls her eyes and he laughs. 'I know you think I'm full of flannel but this holiday is really doing you good. You're getting a bit of a tan already, and you look more relaxed than I've ever seen you.'

He laughs out loud at her imperiously raised eyebrows and she shushes him, gesturing to the sleeping baby in his cot. The side door of the motorhome is open and Lu can just see Reggie's bare toes wiggling. She gestures to Tommy to keep his voice down, finger to her lips.

'Sorry, I'll be careful not to wake him but that look reminded me of my mother when I'd done something really bad. I wanted to say that you have no need to worry about the compass. I'm not about to try and get it back just because my life has gone a bit pear-shaped, if that's what you were thinking?'

'I did wonder. You've got a lot of thinking to do, haven't you Tommy?'

'Yes, I have indeed. I'm looking at the big picture for once though. Can I tell you a little bit about my life, while we're alone, Lu? Don't worry, it won't take long. I'll summarise and then you'll still have time for your book.'

Lucia can't help smiling at this image of a gallop through Tommy's past, and there are areas of his life she's always been curious about.

'Go on then,' she says.

'I guess that's the most enthusiasm I'm going to get from you, so here goes. I'll admit I was a terrible flirt throughout my teens and at university. I thought I was God's gift to women.'

He raises a hand. 'No, darling, don't pull that face, it's a fact. Anyway, I saw how happy you were making Des in the early days, him having been hitherto a grumpy sod . . . so-and-so.' He hastily corrects himself. 'I decided to try and find a Lucia of my own. I worked hard at it for years.'

Lu's soft chuckle at this statement makes Tommy grin too. He leans forward and takes both her hands in his. 'I loved my teaching career and I enjoyed travelling in the school holidays even more but I've never met a woman who could hold a candle to you, darling.'

Tommy's hands feel warm in Lucia's. His strong fingers entwine with her own. This is turning into one of the most difficult conversations Lu has ever had. Here she is with a man who feels half stranger, half much-loved friend, feeling totally out of her depth. What's he trying to say?

'I tell you what,' he says, 'this is getting awkward. Let's ask the compass to help us.'

'What are you talking about? What are you going to ask?'

Tommy creeps into the motorhome, taking great care not to disturb Reggie and Peter. He comes back clutching the leather case. Opening it, he lifts out the instrument, cradling it like a new born chick.

'Here you are. Ask away,' he says, passing the cool marble object to Lucia.

Still mystified, Lucia takes the compass in both hands and settles it on her lap. The jade and azure patterns and the gold filigree glint in the dappled sunlight and she tilts it this way and that, wondering what Tommy's expecting her to do with it. He doesn't comment, just sits back in his own chair and nods encouragingly.

Breathing slowly, Lucia works hard to empty her mind of the current turmoil of thoughts. The compass has helped her before but she's never tried to ask it a direct question, hadn't even thought it was possible until now. Gradually, the quiet of the sleepy French afternoon, the warmth of the sun filtering through ancient branches and the sound of the gulls wheeling and crying over the dunes brings a peace that she hasn't felt for a very long time. The needles still until the barometer one is left pointing upwards in the central position to the word *change*. The compass is still set to *south*.

Lucia closes her eyes and lets a picture of Tommy come to the forefront of her mind. She lets herself relax into her chair, and waits. For what seems like an age, all she can feel is a deep contentment, but then shiver by shiver, the calm of the mood is ruffled by the beginnings of a wild excitement that floods her veins, like ice cold waves on sun-warmed skin. She gasps, and the bubble bursts.

'What?' Tommy asks eagerly, reaching for her hand and entwining his fingers with hers. 'What is it telling you?'

'I don't know. I was trying to let my subconscious take over and tell me what to do next. I felt completely lost.'

Tommy is still waiting for her to carry on. 'And?'

'Change is on the way. In fact, it's already here, isn't it? Look at us. Who could have imagined that you and I would be lounging in the sunshine together on a French campsite by the sea. And I think the message I'm getting, whether it's from my subconscious or somehow from this beautiful thing, is that we both have a lot more adventuring to do. There's a kind of dangerous feeling in the air though. I can't explain it any better than that.'

'Dangerous? I'm not sure what to say about that.'

'No, me neither. Tommy, I've always avoided anything even vaguely disturbing, whether it's good or bad. It isn't possible to change now.'

'Oh, but that's where you're wrong.'

Reggie starts his revving-up burble, signifying that he'll soon be demanding someone's full attention. Tommy smiles.

'I wish I'd had kids, Lu. I almost settled down once or twice, just to be a family man but it wouldn't have been fair.'

'Why not? You'd have made a great dad.'

'But the person you're with has to be the right one for that to be a good idea, surely?'

They look each other full in the eye for a long moment. Their fingers are still linked.

'Isn't it time to take a few calculated risks, Lu? I can be your safety net if you need one.'

Tommy's voice is like warm honey and the sparkling blue eyes are burning into Lu's soul. Could she? Then Reggie starts to shout and bang his wooden bluebird on the side of the van and she's jolted back into the real world.

Lucia puts the compass back in its case, still not sure what part it's played in this afternoon's events. 'I'm going to think more about this later, Tommy. It might be that the compass is trying to push me towards biting the bullet and facing my worst demons. We're in France. I don't know how much you know about what happened to my brother Eddie and how he died but the place isn't too far from here. I think that must be the danger.'

'There are risks in everything we do, Lu, and mountains to climb. I guess you could be getting confused between fear and excitement for what could happen next.

191

The compass could be focusing on your own future. Are you absolutely sure it's all about Eddie?'

Lucia doesn't answer. She isn't sure of anything anymore.

Chapter Twenty-Four

'Couldn't we stay here another day or two?' Isaac asks the others on the second morning, when the thought of packing up and moving on is almost too much to bear.

He's already told Lu that he loves the campsite by the sea more with every passing hour. To be able to wander through the spiky grass of the dunes to the shoreline any time he likes, to feel the sand between his toes and swim in the calm sea. Most of all, to do these things with Polly and Reggie fills him with a contentment he's never known before, at least not when he's been away from his own room.

Peter smiles. 'There are more places to see, far more. Don't you want to explore Normandy? We could visit one of the landing beaches. I'd like to pay my respects to the brave men who didn't make it home. My father was one of the lucky ones but many of his friends weren't so fortunate.'

Isaac looks dubious, but Lu thinks this is a great plan. 'We could see the Bayeux tapestry,' she says, clapping her hands together. 'I've always wanted to do that.'

'Oh, deep joy. A big piece of sewing and a long queue,'

Isaac mutters, grinning at Polly. Lu thinks the younger woman probably agrees with him but she's more tactful and keeps her own counsel.

In the end, they have a group meeting and decide to stay on the site for two more nights. Isaac is ridiculously grateful for this and makes a big effort with dinner later, having already bought the makings of a largely meat-free barbecue. Together with Polly, he marinades, slices and chops to his heart's content, and they eat the resulting feast on the beach.

As the sun goes down and the lights from the nearby houses along the shore begin to twinkle in the dusk, Lucia gives in to the peace of the evening and lies down on the sand, making a pillow with her sweater. As she closes her eyes she sees Isaac slip an arm around Polly's waist.

Tommy has wandered down to the water's edge and Isaac and Polly are sitting a little apart from Peter, with Reggie dozing across their knees. Polly leans against Isaac, and as a gentle evening breeze picks up Lucia catches the scent of Polly's fresh, spring-like cologne, faintly floral and spicy, like a herb garden in the sunshine.

Lu wishes she had thought to move further away from them but it's too late to get up now because they've started talking and they seem totally absorbed in each other. She tries not to listen but the same breeze is carrying their words to her and it's hard to resist eavesdropping even though the thought of it makes her cringe.

'Will you be ready to move on to the next place?' Isaac

says. 'Because I won't. I wish I could stay here with you and Reg forever.'

Polly doesn't answer for a moment and, but at last she says, 'I feel just the same actually, but I reckon it'll be good for us all to spread our wings and see some different places.'

'Will it? Why?'

Polly lowers her voice and Lucia only just catches the next words. 'I've been thinking about what your mum and Peter were talking about, Isaac. The three of us – I'm including myself with them in this – we've got what a shrink would probably call survivor's guilt. I've read a bit about it before but it didn't really help. I still felt just as crappy. None of us have been able to move on and start dealing with our sadness because to do that, we'd have to let at least some of the guilt go.'

'Yes, I suppose Mum has always had an obsession with her brother.'

Lucia opens her eyes slightly, willing her gauche son to backtrack and take back the clumsy words. Polly has moved slightly away from Isaac to look at him better. Ouch. *Cut him some slack, Pol,* Lu thinks, *he doesn't mean any harm, he just doesn't always get how to say things.*

'Obsession?' Polly snaps. 'It's hardly that. She loved him so much and she feels as if she should have been there to protect him.'

'Yes, but . . .'

'Peter's the same,' Polly continues, ignoring Isaac's attempt to speak. 'He's always seen himself as the one who caused his wife's accident. And he wasn't. It was just a bad set of circumstances, the same as Eddie's death. He's only just starting to heal.'

'I know, but . . .'

'And then there's me.' she carries on. 'I keep going over and over in my mind how I could have stopped my sister going into the water that day. I'm glad your mum told you about it, it feels right that you know. Maybe I couldn't have prevented what happened, whatever I did. Maybe that's just what she had to do?'

Polly runs out of steam at last and leans into Isaac again. Lu breathes a sigh of relief and closes her eyes tightly again.

'Er, yes, there's a lot to think about for all of you, isn't there?' Isaac hazards.

'There is, and this is only the beginning,' she says. 'Peter bringing all of his pain out into the open has started the ball rolling for us all. I'm nowhere near being in the right place to forgive myself yet, I know that, but I'm ready to work on it, which I definitely wasn't before I met all of you.'

'So . . . that's good?'

Polly laughs, a warm, comfortable sound that even at a distance, Lu can tell means it's okay. 'Yes, my friend, that is very, very good,' she says.

The next day is warm and sunny and they all spend it lazily, enjoying the beach, taking turns to have long naps in the shade and talking in short, desultory bursts. The hours seem to pass more slowly than usual, as if time is allowing them all to wind right down and enjoy being in the moment, as Polly puts it when they reconvene for dinner.

'It's all about mindfulness,' she says. 'We dash from place to place and we never stop to appreciate what's going on under our noses. I've just spent half an hour looking at a patch of marram grass and watching a load of insects get on with their lives. Imagine doing that at home.'

Lucia is about to scoff at this. She was forced into a mindfulness session on a training day at school once, and found it tedious to say the least. A week's course seemed to have been crammed into one day with a hard-core staff meeting tagged on the end, and she'd got home feeling even less relaxed than usual, full of dissatisfaction about how busy her life was. Now though, Polly's words make more sense.

'It's true,' says Tommy. 'While Polly was going all David Attenborough in the dunes, I took Reg down to the sea and we sat down a little way from the shoreline seeing how long it took the waves to reach our toes. It made him properly chortle. I haven't sat still that long for ages and I bet Reggie never has.'

Peter nods. 'And the best part was knowing you'd all still be here when I'd finished walking along the sand listening to the sound of the waves. When I turned to come back to camp, I'll be honest with you, I felt like singing.'

Isaac says nothing, but Lucia can see all these words have touched him. She smiles at her son and he grins back.

'What did you do, love?' she asks him.

'I washed the dishes from breakfast and lunch,' he says, 'but I did it really, really mindfully.'

Polly throws the end of a baguette at his head. Isaac catches it neatly and lobs it back, still grinning, and Lucia hugs herself and rejoices in the way he's gradually learning to interact with everyone. It's been a long time coming. She hopes so much that can keep the easy communication between them all when they get home. Isaac needs this so badly.

The following day is cooler, and Polly takes Reg for a walk in his buggy while the rest of the group set off on foot to a small local shop to stock up with a few basics for the next stop. Isaac phones Rowan to check on the pets and Lucia is relieved to hear they're eating well and behaving themselves. Petula's even managed to catch a mouse, something she hasn't bothered to do for years, and Nigel's fallen in love with the Dachshund that's just arrived at number eight.

Lucia examines her feelings after Isaac ends the call. Has all this talk of pets and the house made her homesick? She's delighted to find it hasn't, in fact it's had quite the opposite effect. Knowing that all's well has made her feel more adventurous, as if she's ticked yet another box on the essential holiday itinerary check list. Animals – fine. House – safe. Time to move further on the journey.

After yet another planning meeting, which Lucia is enjoying almost as much as the trip itself for the warm atmosphere that's building up between them all, they've decided to press on to Gold Beach and call in at Bayeux on the way to satisfy both Lucia's longing to see the historic tapestry and Peter's need to pay his respects.

'Have you got the maps ready for the next leg, Peter? This is still your choice, you haven't finished your turn just because you've got us across the channel, you know,' Isaac says.

'I think I'm organised now,' Peter says. 'I'm really looking forward to the war graves. In a sad sort of way, of course. It's something I need to do. The rest of you don't have to come to the cemetery with me, you know. It's a personal thing.'

'We'll all see how it goes,' says Lucia. Sudden terror at the thought of all that emotion in store makes her feel sick, but she sees Polly coming back with the buggy and tells herself that Polly must be feeling even more vulnerable, and Isaac has always had a mistrust of anything to do with graveyards. Lu's job today is to protect them if necessary. Maybe Polly won't want to see the graves. She's probably had enough of thinking about death. Lu hopes so.

The departure from the campsite is a relaxed affair. It's only a couple of hours drive to the next site and on the way they plan to have a picnic, see the tapestry and pull in one of the war cemeteries. Isaac sits in the back with Lucia and Reg, while Peter, in his element, navigates for Polly. Under cover of Reggie's singing and Peter's detailed instructions, Isaac leans towards his mum.

'Are you feeling okay?' he whispers.

She looks at him in astonishment, as if he's grown an extra head. 'Erm, yes, I think so,' she says. 'Why?'

'Well, everybody's been saying stuff about . . . grieving . . . I just wondered.'

Lucia laughs and ruffles his hair and she can tell he's trying hard not to pull away. 'Isaac, my heart's been torn in two ever since we had the call to say my brother wasn't ever coming home.'

'But why didn't I know how bad you felt? Still feel, by the sound of it?' he asks, holding Reggie closer for comfort.

'You're not exactly the world's most intuitive guy, are you? I'm not being horrible,' she adds, seeing his face fall, 'just honest – and anyway, it's not your fault that you don't . . . can't pick up on people's feelings.'

'I think I'm getting a bit better at it though, Mum.'

'Yes, I really think you are. And that's totally amazing. I can tell how hard you're working at understanding what makes the rest of us tick. Don't worry too much though, my love. We appreciate you just the way you are.'

'But is that enough?'

'Enough for what?' Lucia is playing pat-a-cake with Reg now, confused by all this unfamiliar sympathy from her son. Isaac lowers his voice even more.

'Enough for Polly. Will she get tired of me being so . . . so . . .'

'Emotionally complicated? Not if you love her as much as I think you do. Even someone with well-developed antennae can completely mess up sometimes with people they're supposed to care about.'

200

The bitterness is strong in Lucia's voice now and Isaac picks up on it and winces. 'So you still haven't heard from Dad since you sent his stuff?'

She shakes her head.

'Maybe there'll be a letter waiting when we get home.'

'And maybe I'll grow my hair long again and take up burlesque dancing. I'm joking, Isaac,' she adds, seeing his expression.

'And what are we going to do after Bayeux and the war graves, Mum? I can't help feeling you've got another reason for coming this way. I've never known you to be mad keen on medieval art before.'

Lucia looks at him for a moment. 'You really are getting better at seeing undercurrents, aren't you?'

The sudden silence drags on for far too long. 'It's not far from here,' Lucia says eventually, when Isaac seems to have almost given up hope of any more information.

'Erm . . . what isn't?'

'The place where Eddie died. The cliffs.'

They gaze at each other, and Lucia can see a shadow of her own terror reflected in Isaac's eyes.

'You don't mean . . . you can't be saying you want to go there?' Lucia nods.

'But Mum . . . it's going to be horrible for you. Why do you have to do a thing like that?'

She sighs. 'I've been going over and over this in my head and I don't think there's any way around it. Unless I see where it happened, I'll never really be able to say goodbye to Eddie properly.'

Isaac swallows hard but says nothing.

'Will you tell the others for me, please Isaac?' Lucia says. 'It won't be far out of our way if we drive to the Channel Tunnel instead of taking the ferry. We'll get to see some different places on the way and we can camp for a night near Calais before we go back to England if you like?'

'Okay. I suppose if you've made your mind up I haven't got a choice. Mum, I don't like you doing this but it's a really brave thing to do. The rest of us will just have to support you, if you're absolutely sure?'

'I'm sure. I think it's the only way I can move on,' Lucia says, trying to quell the unwelcome thoughts. The words *a brave thing to do* echo around her head. Brave, or completely insane?

Chapter Twenty-Five

Bayeux turns out to be mostly very beautiful and mediaeval. While Peter, Tommy and Lucia file into the tapestry building, Isaac quickly suggests a wander around the town with Polly and Reg. They amble along, crossing little bridges over the river with no particular focus until they come to a waterside café with big striped umbrellas outside.

'Beer?' they say in unison but then realise that one of them will be driving soon, as Lucia has already had her turn today. Instead, they order coffee and sticky pastries, laughing as Reggie's eyes light up.

'My last boyfriend had a thing about pain-au-chocolat too,' says Polly through a mouthful of buttery flakes of pastry.

'Oh. Did he?' says Isaac. He tries to sound casual but his stomach hurts even at the thought of Polly with someone else. 'And . . . when was that, exactly?'

'When was what?'

'Well, how long is it since you were together? How long did you know him? Was it serious? Did you . . .'

Polly holds up a hand. 'Hey, hang on, Isaac, what is this? The Spanish Inquisition?'

Isaac wants to reply, as his dad always does, 'Nobody expects the Spanish Inquisition,' but he doesn't know if Polly grew up on a diet of Monty Python or if she'll just think he's odd.

'Sorry. It's just that you've never mentioned this boyfriend. What am I supposed to think when you drop him into the conversation as if he doesn't matter?'

'Isaac, that's just why. Because he really *doesn't* matter. Chas is in the past. He's my ex. We split up well before my sister died. It's a good job we did because he was useless if I ever showed the slightest sign of crying and after we lost her, I cried for weeks.'

They look at each other for a long moment. Polly smiles. 'Well, at least we've made some sort of progress today.'

'We have?' Isaac isn't so sure. He seems to have well and truly trampled on Polly's feelings again.

'Yes, we definitely have. Look at me.'

Isaac dutifully looks. It's no hardship, she's stunning, he thinks, gazing at her long dark hair. Polly's eyes are the mossy green of spring woodlands, mesmerising in their power to look right inside his heart. The sunshine of the last few days has given her extra freckles and her face and arms are lightly tanned.

'Well?'

'I'm sorry, I don't know what I'm supposed to say, except you're beautiful,' he says humbly, overcome with the embarrassing floweriness of his thoughts.

Polly laughs. 'That's lovely, but what you're meant to

see is that I'm not crying today. I talked about my sister, I even said the word *died*, and there were no tears, Isaac. I usually have to make an excuse and go in another room for a little while or pretend to be asleep or at least dry my eyes when I mention her. Do you see now?'

Isaac smiles at her delight, equally thrilled. 'So you're getting better?' he says.

'Yes. I don't know how much better but it's progress, do you see?'

He nods and reaches for her hands, brushing the last crumbs from her fingers. Reggie's dozing now, mouth half open and a chocolate smear across his cheek. They both look down at the sleeping child and then back at each other.

'I wish he was mine,' Isaac blurts out, and immediately wants to take the words back.

'Do you, Isaac? Do you really?'

Isaac can't read Polly's expression, it's too complicated. Is she angry? Why is she looking at him like that?

She stands up before he's had chance to work out his response. 'Come on,' she says, 'It's time to meet the others.'

They walk back the way they came, more quickly this time. There's a touch of frost in the air, and it's nothing to do with the weather.

When the rest of the party reappear, they're all soon back in the van and off to the next stop.

'Where next?' asks Tommy. 'I don't mind so long as there's food there. You choose and I'll direct you with the map.'

'We should see one of the landing beaches now.' Lucia is looking through the Normandy photograph album as Polly drives. The particular snapshot she settles on could have been taken at any of the beaches and Isaac reflects aloud that it's a good job they've got Tommy with them, or it would have been very hard to decide where to start looking for this place.

'Do you want to tell us about the picture?' Lu asks Tommy, as they park the van.

He hesitates for a moment as the others look down at the photo in her hand. Isaac can see it's a picture of some sort of D-Day commemoration judging by the flags and banners. There are a few elderly servicemen in the background and a TV company's truck is setting up, ready for what looks like an interview. In the forefront, Tommy has linked arms with a very old soldier and he's pointing at the man's medals, beaming. The soldier is staring straight into the camera and his expression is sombre.

'We're at Gold Beach. It was a very special day for me,' says Tommy. 'I think we need to be standing on the shoreline for you to understand why that is.'

They walk along the gravel path towards the shore. Tommy is pushing the buggy today and Isaac and Polly are either side of Peter. It's a moment or two before Isaac notices Lucia has stopped walking. He leaves Polly and comes back to join her.

'Come on, Mum, the others are leaving you behind. What's up?' he asks.

She sighs. 'All these years I've been watching war films with your dad and services at the Cenotaph and so on, never realising how they must all be feeling. I must be really dim.'

Isaac's still mystified, so Lu continues.

'You watch the various armed forces lining up to pay their respects, shoulders back, eyes forward, and you think, wow, they were lucky, they came home from the war. But are they? Every day they carry the guilt that their friends lost their lives. How can they ever reconcile themselves to that?'

'But surely at least some of them must be just grateful and happy not to have been killed? To still have some sort of life left to live. Not everybody thinks like you, Mum.'

The others have also paused now to see why Isaac and Lu are being so slow. Isaac waves encouragingly, hoping they'll get the hint and walk on. His mum obviously needs to get this out of her system. He sees Peter bend his head to say something to Polly and then they both carry on walking.

'I know not everyone has this problem, but a lot of people must do, surely?' Lucia says, when the others are out of earshot. 'Some of us just carry it nearer to the surface. A lot bury it deeply so they don't have to feel the pain.'

Isaac shakes his head. 'I don't know what the answer is, then,' he says. 'Are you always going to feel this sad? Is Peter? And . . . and Polly?'

'No. We're not going to let the sadness win. We're fighting back now, Isaac,' she says, taking hold of his arm as they walk. He lets her hold onto him. It's a work in progress but it's getting easier, this spontaneous physical contact business.

Isaac ponders this new idea some more as they stand in a line just out of reach of the breakers. It feels like their own tribute to the fallen soldiers. There's no need to speak, they're in complete accord. Even Reggie is silent, perched on Polly's hip, sucking his fingers happily and watching the dancing waves.

A small girl kicking a football canons into Peter just as Reggie's starting to get restless, and with the mood broken, a wild feeling of abandonment seems to grab them simultaneously.

'So there's no need for me to tell you any more about my last visit here?' asks Tommy.

'No, my friend, sometimes we don't need to complicate matters with words. Let's leave the war cemetery visit for tomorrow,' says Peter. 'We've done enough deep thinking for one day. I vote we go and find a supermarket, make camp and have the most splendid barbecue ever!'

'Seconded,' says Polly. 'Come on, I'm starving already.'

Chapter Twenty-Six

The next day, fully refreshed from a night in their now familiar holiday beds, Isaac climbs into the driving seat for the short trip to the war graves. It seems Peter has his own agenda for this outing, and it's no random choice of destination. His father's best friend George is buried here.

'There are registers where you can look up names so you can go straight to the right place. It should be fairly straightforward to find George's headstone,' says Lucia. Peter is in the passenger seat with his map of the day. He's insisted that the Sat Nav be switched off again so they can do this the traditional way.

When they reach the parking area, it takes a few moments to decide who's going where. Isaac watches his mum and Peter walk through the archway that leads to the reception area of the cemetery, where the books of remembrance and the registers of names are stored. The gates are vast and impressive, and the two of them look very small as they go through.

'I'm glad we decided to miss out on this one, Poll,' he says. 'I reckon you've had enough sadness for one holiday already, what with all this talk of people dying. Looking at graves isn't going to help you feel better.'

209

'This is a beautiful place though, even if it's all so sad. Look at the way the headstones are brilliantly white in the sunshine and everywhere is so neat and tidy.'

They peep through the gateway and see the headstones marching away in long, regimented rows as far as the eye can see. It's tidy, but not grim, Isaac thinks. That must be a difficult thing to achieve. He looks at some of the graves near them and notices that they all have small bushes or flowers around them. A feeling of peace overwhelms him, far from the gloom he'd expected to be experiencing by now. He's never been very good at looking at death head-on.

'Shall we change our minds and go in after all?' he asks Polly. 'Reggie's asleep.'

They look down at the sleeping child in the buggy. Damp wisps of auburn hair cling to his forehead. His eyelashes are long and dark brown, shadowing his cheeks in two perfect semi-circles. One thumb is in his mouth and he's clutching Isaac's bluebird to his chest with the other hand.

'Oh Poll, he's such a lovely boy,' Isaac says.

'He is, isn't he? Funny how he loves that bird. It's got so many hard edges. You'd think he'd want his fluffy rabbit at nap time, wouldn't you?'

'I suppose so, but The Bluebird of Happiness is really important. Have you read the play? The Maeterlinck one?

'No, my mum wasn't big on stories. Will you tell it to me?'

'Last chance to change your mind. Consider your choice carefully – the bluebird or war graves?'

'Would it be very bad not to go in there, Isaac? We can still think of them out here and pay our respects. Let's go and sit at that picnic bench in the shade. There's some apple juice in the cool box. Tell me a story.'

Isaac clears his throat and focuses on the essence of the bluebird tale. It's stayed in his mind ever since his mum bought the simplified version as a board book. Later, they read the play together, and took turns to act out the parts. Isaac loved being Tyltyl best, or the Machiavellian Cat. Lucia had excelled as the Fairy Berylune and Light. Sometimes, his dad would join in as Dog, bouncing around and yapping, making Isaac and his mum laugh until they cried. Between them, they created something almost magical.

As he begins to tell his much-shortened version of the search for the Bluebird of Happiness, Polly's eyes widen and she leans forward slightly, keen to catch every word. Soon, Isaac gets into his stride, weaving the magical, sometimes macabre threads together.

'The two children, Mytyl and Tytyl live in the wood-cutter's cottage and they're very poor and hungry. It's Christmas Eve, and they can see the rich children in the house opposite having loads of fun and eating fancy food. They're just wishing they could join them when a hideous old woman, who they guess is a fairy . . .'

'Why?' Polly interrupts.

'Why what?'

211

'Why do they assume she's a fairy? She could just be a random old lady.'

Isaac sighs. 'Look, Poll, if you're going to keep butting in this is going to take forever. I'll lend you my old copy of the play to read when we get back but let's accept she's a fairy, okay?'

Polly grins. 'As you wish, oh master.'

He rolls his eyes. 'So, anyway, the fairy tells them they have to go with her on a quest to find the bluebird, and that'll save her little girl, who's very ill.' Isaac sees Polly open her mouth again and holds up a hand. 'Look, if you're going to ask what's wrong with her daughter, I don't know. I think it was her nerves, or something. Let me just get on with it.'

'Right. Sorry.'

'She lures them in with promises that she'll take them to the Land of Memory to see their dead brothers and sisters and grandparents again.'

'What? Is this meant to be a children's story? It's a bit grim.'

'Well, they weren't so protective in those days, I guess. Do you want to hear this story or not?'

Polly opens her eyes wide and gives Isaac her best smile – the one with the dimples and sparkly eyes. His heart flips and he takes a deep breath.

'So, then all the inanimate objects in the cottage come to life, like the loaf of bread and . . . and the milk jug and the woman with barley sugar fingers and fire and so on, and suddenly the dog and cat can talk.' He sees

Polly's expression. 'Don't look at me like that, it's no weirder that *Harry Potter*, is it?'

'I s'pose not. Carry on.'

Isaac glances at his watch. 'I'd better hurry up or the others will be back before I'm done. So they carry on through this crazy hidden world until they get to the Palace of Night and the Forest, which are pretty scary.'

'It's a wonder you didn't have nightmares. What was your mum thinking?'

'I loved it. My mind was already full of scary thoughts. This story just made me feel as if it was normal to have them.'

'Hmm.' Polly doesn't sound convinced but Isaac presses on.

'There's a wonderful part where the place is full of light. They're people of the future. Very sci-fi.'

Reggie begins to stir so Isaac speeds up. 'The gist of the story is that they actually find that the bluebird was back at home and it does cure the little girl but then it flies away.'

'Oh. So what's the point of the whole thing?'

'I think it's that you can go searching for happiness but quite often it's already there at home if you know how to find it. And the children give happiness to the little girl in the end, so it's about that too. Sharing the love. Sorry, I sound really creepy now, don't I?'

Polly claps her hands together and Reggie wakes up properly, opening his eyes and blinking at the wooden bluebird in his arms.

'No you don't, not at all. It's a bit dark but it's a great story,' she says. 'So the life you've been looking for was there all the time?'

'Yes. And that's what my computer game's about. I think it's going to be good, Polly. I've been working on it for ages and it's pretty near finished. All I need is someone to help me market it.'

Polly's eyes are sparkling now. 'And then what?'

'How do you mean?'

She sighs. 'You told me about the game before but not how high you're aiming. Is this a long-term career move? Will you leave your job?'

'Oh.' Isaac shrugs. 'I don't suppose it'll be that good.'

'Isaac, don't be so bloody defeatist. Why shouldn't it be? Have you got any contacts who could give you an idea if it's got legs?'

'Yes, I know a bloke who's in the business. He goes in the local pub sometimes. He's not exactly a friend but we've talked about gaming and stuff. I call in for a pint after work sometimes. Mum doesn't know.'

'Why not?'

'Huh?'

'I mean, why don't you want your mum to know you go to the pub now and again? It's not a crime, is it?'

'N . . . no, it's just, my mum and dad have this thing about me not socialising. If they knew I was making more of an effort, they'd go on and on about it, as if it was a really big deal. Encouraging me. Saying how good it is that I'm coming out of my shell.' He sighs. 'It's just a pint, Poll.'

'Well then. Go and find him as soon as we get back and pitch it to him. Or better still, have you got his email address? Prime him now, ready for the hard sell later. You say it's along the lines of the story you just told me?'

'Kind of. I've got the same sort of theme, but I haven't ripped anything off.'

'I can't wait to tell Reg all about the Bluebird of Happiness when he's old enough. I hope I can remember all the details.'

'We've still got the board book somewhere at home, I think,' says Isaac. 'It's really tatty but you can borrow it. I'd like to be the one to introduce him to the story properly though – pass it down to the next generation.'

'That'd be great, but it's going to be ages before he's ready, and who knows where we'll be by then?'

The words hang between them, and Isaac sighs. He watches Polly lift the baby out of his buggy and give him a feeder cup of juice. There's a strange pain some- where around his heart. After a moment he says, 'Is there any reason why you can't stay with us? I want to see Reggie grow up. Nobody does the voice of the cat like me, Poll, I'll tell you that for nothing. I can be evil and yet strangely compelling.'

She laughs, but her eyes are sad. 'That's sweet of you.'

'Not *sweet*. You make me sound like a puppy.'

'Cat or dog? Make your mind up.'

Reggie flaps his hands around and clonks Polly over the head with the wooden bird. Isaac reaches for him and stands up. 'Let's go and meet the others,' he says.

'We don't have to go all round the cemetery. We can just see the entrance and the bit beyond. You bring the buggy.'

He hoists Reggie up to one of his favourite places, on Isaac's shoulders. The little boy crows with delight and leans his cheek on the top of Isaac's head. Polly's expression is once again unreadable as she gazes up at the two faces so close together.

'Isaac, I'm not letting you wriggle out of this,' she says after a moment or two. 'It's time for a change. If you can make a go of this game, you could leave that boring job and branch out into something you're good at. That's the sort of thing Tommy gave you the money to do. Talk to him about your idea. This is your time to shine.'

Isaac's heart is too full to let him answer. They walk side by side through the giant archway and see the other three heading towards them, with faces that somehow manage to be solemn but not sad.

'Oh, Isaac, Polly, that was so moving,' Lucia says as they draw nearer. 'We found the one we were looking for. George has a lavender bush next to his grave and there were birds singing all around him. It's such a beautiful, peaceful place. I've always loved ancient village graveyards at home but this is something else. The scale of it is just mind-blowing. And it's only one of so many.'

Peter looks every inch the aristocrat as he nods to Isaac and Polly. 'Lucia's quite right,' he says. 'My father should have come here himself. He kept putting it off until it was too late for him to travel. It's a fine example of why we should seize the day. I won't give you the Latin for that, because it reminds me too much of my boarding school.' He shudders. 'How about you, Tommy?'

'You're joking, aren't you? I was a Secondary Modern lad. I messed about too much to pass the Eleven Plus. It was only later I managed to claw it back enough to get to teacher training college.'

'I didn't mean . . .'

Tommy laughs, and slaps Peter on the back. 'I know you didn't. I'm not touchy about my roots, I got there in the end. I can't stop thinking about all those young men who never had my chances though.'

They stroll back to the van, Reggie beating time to their steps with his palms on Isaac's head.

'Where now?' asks Peter, climbing in rather stiffly. 'That was so perfect, I hardly know how we can follow it.'

Isaac frowns up at the sky. The clouds have rolled over the sun and are moving swiftly in the chilly breeze. 'It's good driving weather,' he says. 'We've already talked about Mum's plan for the next part of the trip. Let's just go there now, shall we?'

'Now?' Lucia's voice is trembling. 'Oh . . . well . . . I thought you wanted to go further up the coast first?'

'Have you changed your mind, Lu?' ask Tommy, putting a hand on her shoulder. 'We can easily go somewhere else. It's going to be very hard for you, darling.'

Isaac cheers inwardly as his mum squares her shoulders and sticks her chin out. He knows that look of old and she's not going to bottle out of this.

'No, I'm still sure,' she says. 'I asked an expert. The verdict was that I should go for it.'

Isaac sees his mother exchange glances with Tommy and wonders what that was all about. Since when has Tommy been an expert?

'Come on, gang,' Lucia says. 'It's time for action. We've said before, we're in this together, and there's nothing, absolutely nothing that we can't do.'

Chapter Twenty-Seven

The first leg of the journey through Normandy passes quickly. Lucia can tell Isaac's in the mood for a drive and Peter volunteers to sit up front and navigate, which translates as looking at the map and arguing with the lady inside the Sat Nav.

Reggie's happy to look out of the window for the first few miles, chewing on a rusk and burbling unintelligible words followed by the triumphant blowing of a raspberry, his latest trick. This makes him chortle and kick his legs. Tommy sings nursery rhymes to him as the miles tick away and eventually the baby is lulled by the regular hum of the engine as they join the main road and the van picks up speed. His eyes close and his sticky little hand clutches Tommy's as his breathing regulates and he slides into sleep, closely followed by Tommy.

'He's so gorgeous, Polly. You're doing a great thing here, you know,' whispers Lu.

'I hope so. Alice would have done it better though.' Polly's voice is even quieter than Lu's, and she casts a quick glance at Isaac. Lu nods her understanding and carries on.

'I'm not so sure about that. I don't see how anyone

219

could look after Reggie and love him any better than you do.'

Polly shrugs. 'It's the best of a bad job. They say a mother's love is stronger than any other kind, don't they? I can never make up for that.'

'You don't have to make up for it though, do you? It's not your fault Alice chose to do what she did. All you need to do is love him the very best you can, and that's what's happening now. He's such a happy little soul. Your mum must absolutely dote on him too.'

'Yes, she does, but he makes her sad. Reg looks so much like the baby photos of my sister, you see.'

'Oh yes, that's got to be so hard for her. He must have something of his father in him though.'

The question hangs in the air and eventually Lucia gives up hope of any further comment from Polly and lets herself drift off to sleep, head cushioned on a pillow, listening to the soft sound of Fleetwood Mac from the current playlist. Isaac's humming along to 'Songbird', one of his old favourites, and Peter is smiling dreamily and gazing out of the window.

When Lucia rouses from her impromptu nap, she finds they've covered many more miles than she expected and it's almost time to leave the main road and start heading for the camp site they've booked. They pull up at a garage and café to refuel and then park behind it on a patch of grass, climbing out to stretch their legs and yawn. The crisp late-afternoon air is blissfully refreshing.

'Do you ever feel as if you could keep on driving

forever?' asks Isaac, drinking black coffee from a huge paper cup and biting into a croissant as if he hasn't eaten for weeks.

Lucia finishes her bottle of water and nods. 'Where are we?' she asks.

'Not far from Dieppe. I think the site's about an hour away. Let's just stretch our legs and then keep driving, if you're happy to take over for a bit, Mum. How are you feeling, Peter? Tommy?'

'I've not felt this well in years,' says Peter, flexing his shoulders and yawning widely.

Tommy glances across at his old friend. 'You certainly look better for the fresh air and good company,' he says, 'although by the sound of your creaking joints, we might need to glue bits of you back on fairly soon.'

Peter cuffs Tommy around the head and the two tussle like teenagers until Reggie sets up a wail of protest. 'That's enough, boys,' Polly says, laughing. 'You're turning into a bad influence. I want Reggie to grow up in a non-violent environment. You two are still reprobates at heart.'

'We wish,' says Tommy, looking across at Lu, who pretends not to have heard.

When they've all had a brief walk around, Lucia climbs into the driving seat with a shiver that could be excitement but is far more likely to be fear.

'I booked us in at the next campsite for two nights. We can extend it if we want to stay longer, they're not busy at the moment, but I don't think we'll want to hang around,' Lu says.

Isaac keys the number into the Sat Nav because although Peter has every map they could possibly need, he looks set for a snooze in the back. The van runs smoothly and reasonably quietly as Lu settles into the role of both driver and navigator. Tommy, Peter and Isaac are dozing within ten minutes of setting off, and Polly only waits to see the little boy is properly snuggled down before she reaches for a pillow and props her head against the window. Her gentle snores and Isaac's slightly louder ones punctuate the drive as Lucia bowls along wide, underpopulated roads. She reflects that if this was Britain, she'd have probably hit traffic by now, but so far they're making good progress.

One hand firmly on the wheel as they get to a long straight stretch of road, Lucia reaches for the CD pile she quickly selected before they left home. Picking one at random and keeping the volume low, she inserts it into the player. It's an old Wings album, and the sound of McCartney singing down the years brings back poignant memories of listening to *Band on the Run* on vinyl over and over again in her room. Her mother had bought the record for her dad's birthday but he hadn't appreciated the gesture. As a die-hard Beatles fan, he'd found all of the four's later recordings disappointing.

Lucia glances over her shoulder at her sleeping companions and risks turning the volume up slightly as she rolls on. The light outside is slightly eerie as the day slips further and further into dusk, and the roads are getting narrower. The album of well-known songs is sliding into her absolute favourite track – 'Bluebird'. Isaac stirs in his sleep as the opening words flow through the van. Lucia is worried that he'll wake, but as the song goes on, he just murmurs his favourite of all the gentle lyrics under his breath.

Lucia hears Isaac croon about *breeze* and *flying*, and blinks away sudden tears as she remembers long evenings cuddling her small, angry son when sleep wouldn't come and he was so very unhappy. She'd told him stories of the host of happy birds who lived above the clouds and spent their time sending down sweet dreams for the little children who most needed them.

'Make 'em send the dreams quick, Mummy, I'm sad,' he'd said, over and over again.

In the beginning, Lucia and Des had never been able to work out what made their son so vulnerable. The eventual diagnosis that he was Autistic made everything clearer, and Lucia could even begin to see some parallels with her brother Eddie's behaviour, but Isaac's struggles with school were painful to witness.

The slightest hiccup in the daytime could make his nights tortuous. As the van eats up the long miles, she thinks about Isaac's various passions over the years. The love of birds that she first noticed when he was only a toddler has never left him. Lu remembers one terrible spring morning when, before she could divert him, 3-year-old Isaac had found four dead baby sparrows that had fallen from their nest in the lilac tree. He sobbed for hours and nothing could comfort him. It was around that time Tommy had sent him the wooden bluebird, a present from a trip to Switzerland. After that, calming him had been easier, but some days nothing helped.

The song comes to an end. Reggie murmurs in his sleep, and Lu quickly chooses another CD for background noise. This one is a home-made mixture, and as the first track begins to play, Lu recognises it with a shock. Nora Jones. She's singing about her heart being drenched in wine. This is another of Lucia's all-time favourite songs. The CD was a present from Tommy for her birthday one year, when she'd briefly taken up yoga.

'You'll be needing some gentle music for while you're meditating,' he'd written on the card that accompanied it. 'I'm in Istanbul right now, but when I come home I want to see you doing a headstand.'

Lu hadn't thought it was odd at the time that Isaac's godfather should go to the trouble of recording a special mix for her. Tommy has always been thoughtful and although when Isaac was born he made it clear that his lavish gifts would now be all for the boy, he never failed to send a small token on Des's and Lucia's birthdays. The moments they recently spent in the sunshine by the caravan spring into her mind. Tommy holding her hands in his and telling her she was beautiful, the warmth flowing between them, the underlying message in his words. The way he says he tried to find a Lucia of his own . . .

Could this collection be a perfect, extended love letter?

Surely not. Up until recently Tommy has never been anything but casually friendly towards her, like an older brother, only much better. Their age difference hasn't seemed noticeable. Tommy is the sort of person who appears ageless. He's crazy and energetic and . . . with a jolt, Lucia finds she's thinking of Tommy as a man, rather than just an affectionate member of her family.

Stop it, she tells herself sternly, *you're letting your imagination run away with you. What a massive ego you must have if you think you're the sort of woman to inspire a man to this sort of gesture.*

Lucia reaches out to turn the music off but as she does so, the next track comes on. Now her suspicions have been aroused, she listens to the words much more carefully. It's 'Me and Mrs Jones'. She chuckles to herself when she imagines what the song would sound like if *Lemon* was substituted for *Jones*. Not nearly so romantic. But as the track continues, the aching longing in the words makes her heart feel as if it's being squeezed, and the urge to giggle disappears. This isn't funny. She owes it to Tommy to listen to the whole thing.

Lucia's beginning to flag slightly now, even with the supply of humbugs and barley sugar sweets she's got to hand. Driving nearer and nearer to the place she dreads visiting and yet longs to see is frightening, but this amazing soundtrack is pure romance, even if she might be jumping to the wrong conclusions. As song after song plays, Lucia absorbs every lyric. Some are old tunes, others are more recent. Tommy has always had an eclectic

225

taste in music. The final track is the melancholy 'If You're Not The One', by Daniel Bedingfield.

As the last line echoes away, eerie and mournful, Lucia shivers. Exhaustion overwhelms her. What is she going to do? What will Des say if she tells him she suspects Tommy has always had a thing for her? He'll either laugh at her conceit, or alternatively be overwhelmed with fury. She's sure he'll be back soon, if he's not at home waiting for her already.

Holding onto the steering wheel with every ounce of her strength, Lucia sees a road junction ahead. The sign for the campsite appears just as the Sat Nav bursts into life and tells her to turn right immediately.

Lucia bumps the van gingerly over the humps in the shadowy lane leading to a farm and a large meadow. She's never felt so tired in her life but somewhere along the way, a decision has been made. It's time to face the past head on. Eddie, ever present in her head, is approving. There's only one place she can do it.

'Wake up, guys, we've arrived,' she croaks, 'and if we don't hurry up and make camp I'll just have to sleep right here.'

In the rear-view mirror, she sees Tommy's eyes are already wide open. He stretches out his arms as far as he can in the cramped seat before he gently shakes Peter awake. Isaac lifts Reggie from his seat and with a gesture to Lucia to say where she's going, Polly heads off towards the site office, where luckily a light still burns.

'Goodness me, what a long way you've driven, my

dear,' Peter says as he climbs stiffly from the van. 'It must have been quite shattering for you, and all we've done is snore.'

'Oh it wasn't so bad. I had company of a sort,' Lucia says, reaching for her overnight bag.

She sees Tommy looking at her, and blushes. What on earth is she going to do now? 'I'm glad you liked it, darling,' is all he says.

Chapter Twenty-Eight

Fresh from one of the best showers he's ever had in his life, Isaac walks back across the field, still towelling his hair dry. He sees Polly and Tommy sitting with the baby on the tartan rug outside the van, carefully building a tower of bricks. As Polly puts the last one in place, Reggie swings his arm round and dashes them all to the ground, gurgling with joy. Peter emerges from the awning, stretching mightily.

'Good morning, campers,' he says. 'Have you seen Lucia? I thought I'd take us all for breakfast in that little café by the farmhouse when you're ready.'

'She's not in the van,' says Polly. 'I wondered where she'd gone when Reg woke me an hour ago but I thought she must be at the shower block.'

'If she was, I'd have seen her. I was in there for ages. There's oodles of hot water.'

Polly giggles. 'Yes, I'd forgotten about the unisex facilities when I went in there last night. I almost bumped into a man in the urinals. I don't know who was more surprised, him or me. He zipped up so fast he made his eyes water.'

'Must have been a Brit then,' says Isaac. 'The locals wouldn't bat an eyelid.'

'So Lucia isn't there.'

'No. Mum seemed a bit edgy last night when we got here though. Didn't you think so, Uncle Tommy?'

'I didn't notice,' Tommy says, concentrating hard on rebuilding the tower.

'Maybe she was just shattered from all the driving,' says Polly, frowning. 'I meant to wake up and take over but I was so comfy, and Reggie was out for the count. I didn't even realise we'd covered so much ground until we stopped.'

Tommy, Peter and Isaac pull up camping chairs and sit down to wait for Lucia. The morning sunshine warms their faces as they watch Reggie on his blanket rolling onto his tummy and attempting a kind of commando movement. He looks like a very round caterpillar that's forgotten how to move forwards, thinks Isaac, smiling down at the little boy who's red in the face now. His eyes meet Polly's when he glances up again and he can't help noticing she's not in a hurry to look away, for a change.

Tommy has his eyes closed against the morning sun now and Peter is reading an old Ian Fleming novel he picked up in the site office which doubles as the farmhouse kitchen. He doesn't react as Isaac reaches for Polly's hand. The tips of their fingers touch and the blood rushes to Isaac's face, and to several other places. He shifts slightly, hoping she hasn't noticed, but the movement draws her gaze. She grins, stroking the palm of his hand and making matters much worse.

Just as Isaac's wondering how on earth he's ever going

to be able to ever get out of this chair again, they hear a shout. Lucia is strolling across the grass, accompanied by a chicken, two ducks and a small white Jack Russell.

'This place is amazing,' she calls. 'And look who I met on my walk.'

Reggie hauls himself into a sitting position, entranced, as the bravest duck waddles almost up to the rug. He claps his hands and lurches forward, banging his nose hard on the ground as he lands. The ensuing howls frighten the poultry away but the little dog sits down hopefully, cocking its head to one side. One ear is folded backwards. It has a black patch over one eye, giving it a vaguely piratical air.

Polly, busy cuddling Reggie, doesn't see Isaac adjusting his shorts, and the moment passes safely. He bends to make a fuss of Lucia's new camp follower.

'What's it called?' he asks, deeply glad of the distraction.

'*She* is called Pickles,' Lu says proudly, as if she's created the dog herself. 'The sad thing is, she's got no home. The farmer's wife says she's taken her in. She belonged to an old man in the next village who died recently. He was an ex-pat, originally from Worthing, but Pickles was born here last year.'

Lucia looks at Isaac expectantly. Oh bugger, it's happening again. She's trying to tell him something without words. Surely his mother must know by now that's an uphill struggle. Light dawns.

'Mum, you can't be hinting you want us to take her home with us? Can you?'

Peter laughs. 'I rather think that's exactly what's on her mind. Hello, Pickles. How do you feel about being adopted?'

'But Mum, we can't. What about quarantine and stuff? Don't animals have to have passports these days? And what would Nigel and Petunia say?'

Lucia smiles at him, the picture of serenity. 'I'm sure we can get around all that,' she says. 'If nobody takes pity on her, Pickles is going to have to go to the local dog's home soon. The three Alsatians who live here don't like her, apparently. I don't know why. How could anyone not love Pickles?'

The little dog has settled herself on the rug now and is nuzzling Reggie's toes. He whoops with delight, squashed nose forgotten.

'You see that? Reg loves him already,' says Lucia. 'Leave the details to me. Pickles is going to live with us, even if we have to come back for her later in the year.'

She folds her arms and stares at Isaac, daring him to argue. He shrugs. Resistance is useless, and anyway, Pickles is already melting his own heart as she snuggles up to Reggie and goes suddenly to sleep.

When Peter and Polly have had showers, the whole party wander over to the café, equally hindered and entertained by Pickles who insists on circling their ankles, barking happily.

'Now, don't hold back. This is on me,' says Peter, peering at the chalk board. 'I can't read French as well as I can understand it, sadly, and I've left my glasses at the van. Does that item at the top of the list translate as *blood sausage?*'

Isaac and Polly both shudder. 'I'd like some of that wonderful crusty bread and lashing of butter and jam, preferably cherry,' Polly says, getting up to place her order. 'What about you, Isaac?'

In the end, they all opt for baguettes fresh from the farmhouse oven, with a dish of sunshine-yellow butter and a selection of preserves that are almost too pretty to eat.

'This is heaven,' mumbles Polly though a mouthful of bread. 'I want to stay here forever.'

'Déjà vu,' says Tommy. 'You said something very similar when we were in the pub in Pengelly, and you had your mouth full then too. I bet you say that to all the campsites.'

'Mmm,' agrees Lu, reaching for the mug of hot chocolate that's just been placed in front of her, 'I don't blame her. This is wonderful. Anyway, we're not going anywhere until well after lunch.'

'How come? I thought you'd want to get on and visit . . . you know . . .' Tommy tails off.

'Yes, I did, but I've just been talking to the farmer and he's very kindly offered to be our driver if we can wait until later when he's finished his work.'

'But we've got our own transport,' says Isaac, frowning. 'Why do we need a lift?'

Lucia waves a hand around their encampment. They've put the awning and tent up, the chairs are all out and the barbecue is set up ready for the evening. 'Do you really want to unhook the awning and pack things away?' she asks. 'You moaned enough last time when you and Polly wanted to go shopping. If we can get a lift, we can leave everything like this.'

'Perfect,' says Peter. 'I must admit to being rather jaded this morning. A lazy start to the day is what we all need. Especially you, Lucia, after your long drive last night. I can't believe we all slept for so long. So what are we aiming to do when we reach Dieppe? Do you know exactly where you want to be?'

Lucia reaches for a baguette and tears off a chunk, taking her time to butter it. She chooses apricot jam to spoon over the top and eats half of her bread before she answers. Polly's feeding Reggie a bowl of mushy cereal and Peter's working hard not to lose a tooth on a particularly resilient crust. Eventually she looks up.

'Yes, I'm pretty sure I can direct us to the right place. And before you all start clucking again, I want to go there. I need to.'

The farmer's wife emerges from the kitchen at this point, offering more hot chocolate, a pot of coffee, croissants and advice on how to get Pickles home to England. The moment passes in a flurry of extra drinks and Reggie upturning his cereal bowl on his head. The resulting spluttering as milk cascades down his face distracts Polly, but Isaac, deeply affronted at the insinuation he's clucking and filled with a growing sense of dread of what's to come, stares his mother straight in the eye.

'I can't help thinking this is a very bad idea,' he says.

Chapter Twenty-Nine

The rest of the morning passes peacefully. Tommy sets off rather suddenly to walk to the nearest village, Peter dozes in the shade for most of it and Isaac and Polly take Reggie for a stroll to a nearby lake and on to a local village for lunch in a bistro. Lucia does some necessary laundry and pegs it out on a washing line she's rigged up between two trees. Pickles has attached herself to Lu's side, as if she instinctively knows this is her best hope for the future. The comfort of the little animal resting her nose on Lu's foot when she finally sits down to rest is something she knows she must hang on to at all costs.

'Can you tell me what I need to do to adopt Pickles?' Lu asks the farmer's wife, Amelie, when she's mustered the energy to go over to the main building sometime later.

'Leave it with me,' the woman says. 'Jean-Luc and I are visiting with my friend in London next month. I will deal with the necessary paperwork, get the small Pickles vaccinated and chipped and bring her to England.'

'Oh my goodness, would you really do all that?' Lucia is almost overwhelmed by this kindness. 'I'll pay for everything, and you can either come and stay with us

234

in the Midlands or I'll meet you somewhere. Anywhere!' she adds recklessly.

Amelie smiles. 'We will work something out. Maybe Jean-Luc and I will extend our stay and visit Stratford-upon-Avon. We have always wanted to go there. Is that near to where you live?'

'It's not a million miles away.' Lucia sees the puzzled expression on Amelie's face. 'Sorry, that's just a silly saying. What I mean is, Stratford is within an hour and a half's drive from Chandlebury. I would love you to come and stay.'

'And we will meet your husband? The one who you say does not like to travel with all of you lovely people?'

'You might. Or on the other hand, you might not.'

The two women exchange looks. No more words are necessary. Lucia goes back to their pitch knowing she's made a friend.

By three o'clock, Jean-Luc is showered, dressed in his best with bushy hair and beard combed neatly. He brings his seven-seater pick-up around to where Lucia's party are waiting. Reggie is already strapped into his seat and Jean-Luc takes great care to make sure he's securely fastened in.

'Are you sure you don't mind picking us up again?' Lucia asks. 'We can easily get a taxi back from the town . . . or I guess that's possible . . .'

He laughs. 'Please don't take away my excuse. Our neighbour is having a party this afternoon and evening for his fiftieth birthday and everyone will be there.'

'But what about you, Jean-Luc?' Shouldn't you be at the celebration?'

'Perhaps I *should,* but there are a hundred things I would rather be doing. Amelie and I will go there early for a little while with the children and then be home in plenty of time to fetch you. It is a good excuse to leave before the dancing. Last year my neighbour's wife fell off the table and the party ended early. It can get, as I believe you English like to say, *messy.*'

Tommy climbs into the front of the truck and they're soon chattering away in a mixture of French, English and some strange in-between language that they both seem to find extremely amusing. Lucia is suddenly overwhelmed with gratitude for the others, all here to support her. There is no way she could ever have done this on her own.

Peter echoes Lu's thoughts when he says, under cover of the howls of laughter from the front, 'I'm so very glad we took this trip together. There's no group of people who could make it as perfect as this, from my point of view. Thank you all for making this new family.'

Polly looks as if she's about to cry and Lucia grabs her left hand as Isaac reaches for the right.

'I'm so sorry,' Peter says, his brow furrowed now. 'I've said too much, my dear. I didn't mean to upset you.'

'No, it's fine. It's just that I was thinking the same thing. You lot are amazing. I feel as if we're a team now. Me and Reggie . . . well, we were drifters until we met you. Now it's as if we belong somewhere at last. At least for a while,' she adds quickly.

'For as long as you need us,' Lucia says, giving her a hug.

'For always.'

Lu can see that Isaac's words are out before he can stop them, as usual. How's Polly going to react to this? She holds her breath, but Polly just smiles and squeezes Isaac's hand.

After a few miles, Jean-Luc announces that they have reached the nearest parking area to the place Lucia has described to him.

'You can walk to the cliffs from here,' he says. 'And later, there is a path to the beach, or you can follow the lane down to the village where you will find a very good café. My cousin Gerard runs it, and if you mention my name, he will make sure your bill is reasonable and your food and wine is excellent.'

'That sounds like a marvellous plan,' says Peter, when it's clear that Lucia is lost in her memories. 'The café sounds ideal.'

They fix on a time for the pick-up and Jean-Luc departs, while Isaac and Peter follow Polly to a handy toilet block. Lucia thinks for a minute that she's alone but Tommy is soon by her side, and without speaking, he joins her as she sits down on a nearby bench in the shade of a sycamore tree. For a few moments, neither of them break the silence. The dappled sunlight through the leaves is mesmerising, flickering as a light breeze moves the branches.

'Are you sure you're ready for this next step?' Tommy

asks. 'It's going to be so hard, visiting the place where Eddie had his accident. I'm not sure if it's wise, darling.'

Lucia still isn't clear how much Tommy knows about the events so long ago when Eddie, wilful at the best of times, was allowed to join his friends on what turned out to be his last ever trip. Des may have filled him in, she supposes. But even Des doesn't know everything.

'I've got to do it, now we've come this far. If I don't go, I'll always regret it. I . . . I asked the compass.'

'Yes, I thought you must have done. Tell me more.'

'Well, not only did the compass needle point in the direction of the site of Eddie's accident, but the barometer swung around madly until I settled down and held it in my hands and just let myself think about him. It finally stopped moving when it reached *stormy*. Then I got the strongest picture in my mind of Eddie waving goodbye from the back seat of my dad's car. That was the last time I saw him. I need to say a proper goodbye, Tommy.'

'Okay. Well, if you're determined to go through with it, I'll be here to prop you up,' he says. 'The only times I ever got the *stormy* reading were when my thoughts were pretty tormented too but it always ended well, to be fair. I can see you're sure.'

'Yes, I am. It's a terrifying thought but that doesn't mean I shouldn't go there. I've spent way too much of my life being scared to take risks. It's time to jump off the highest diving board.'

He laughs. 'You go from one extreme to the other, Lu. You've spent years paddling around in the shallow end and now this. I'm very proud of you, darling.' He seems about to stand up but Lucia puts a hand out to stop him.

'Tommy . . .could I just ask you something? Why did you make that CD for me all those years ago?'

'Oh . . . I had my reasons.'

Lucia hesitates. Tommy looks as if he'd very much like the subject to be closed now. Does she really want to go any further with this line of questioning? But it's always going to bug her if she doesn't press for proper answers here. 'Tell me the reasons, Tommy. I'm . . . interested,' she says.

Silence falls. Even the birds seem to be slumbering in the afternoon warmth. A butterfly lands briefly on Lucia's arm and she's momentarily distracted by its shimmering beauty. Tommy clears his throat.

'I thought you needed some romance in your life. Des wasn't providing it. And I've always loved collecting my favourite songs. I thought you would appreciate the gesture.'

So that was all. Lucia has built up this crazy image of Tommy sending not-so-hidden messages and it turns out he just felt sorry for her. Shame at her own big-headedness makes her cringe. Tommy hasn't finished though.

'Embarrassing really, now I look back. You were married. You still are. I should never have sent it. That was just me thinking I knew best, as usual. I realised afterwards that you were probably so contented with Des that you didn't need a soppy CD to make life more fun.'

'Contented? I suppose so. Some of the time at least. It wasn't the life I expected. But that's both our faults.'

The bleak words are out before Lucia has thought them through, and Tommy turns to look her straight in the eye. When she doesn't look away, he slides a tentative arm around Lu's shoulders and pulls her close. She leans against him, feeling his strength and warmth sending shivers all over her body. Suddenly, he lets her go, and the shock of the cooler air between them makes Lu gasp.

'The others are coming,' Tommy says. 'I guess giving you a hug isn't so wrong at a time like this, but I don't want them to get the wrong impression.'

Lucia stands up and tries to collect her thoughts as the rest of their party approach the bench. The wrong impression. Well, that's her told.

Chapter Thirty

Isaac still can't understand why his mum seems to be desperate to visit the actual spot where her brother died. For years she's been avoiding even the slightest mention of Eddie, but now, she's talking about him even as they walk towards the cliffs.

'We weren't particularly close by the time he went on that last school trip,' Lucia tells Peter and Polly. 'I was fifteen and getting interested in boys, and Eddie was just a kid.' She pulls a face. 'He was what the newspapers always call *a loveable rogue*, when a young lad who's never been out of bother dies too soon. Eddie gave trouble a whole new meaning.'

Isaac's heart goes out to his mum, rattling on about the worst moments of her life.

'I think you're doing a very brave deed, Lucia,' Peter says. 'Your brother would be proud of you, I'm sure.'

Lucia pulls a face. 'I hope so. He wasn't the kind of boy to be very aware of what other people were doing though. Are you okay, Polly? You've been looking a bit peaky today.'

Isaac is glad to see some colour returning to Polly's cheeks. Her freckles were standing out way too clearly earlier, a sure sign she's anxious. He realises with a start that he's beginning to read Polly's body language, something he's always had issues with. Her strong brown hands fascinate him. Her fingers are long and slim, so she's got what his gran would have called *pianist's hands*. Polly's nails are unvarnished and bitten.

As he watches, Polly lifts one hand and brushes back a strand of hair from her forehead, tucking behind her ear. She's wearing tiny gold sleeper earrings. Her face is devoid of make-up, smooth and unlined. Everything about her is straightforward, honest and beautiful. Isaac swallows hard. He has a sudden urge to touch the long, shining locks that are flowing loosely over her shoulders and down her back as usual.

'You look nice today, Polly,' he says, hearing the banal words leave his lips and immediately wishing he'd been more imaginative.

'Why, don't I usually?'

'Yes, I didn't mean . . .' Isaac sees that Polly's grinning. Oh, only joking then. He presses on, trying to think of something a bit different. 'You always do. You could be a model. . . if you wanted to . . .'

Polly's laughing now. 'Oh yeah? Maybe as the *before* picture. I could manage that. Never the *after* though. Now your mum, she's the pretty one. She's got that inner glow, you know what I mean?'

Isaac looks across at Lucia. She's walking along briskly, hair blowing in the breeze and eyes wide as she contemplates the task ahead. It's hard to look at your mum objectively when you're so used to seeing her but Isaac thinks she's changing. She's altered her style of dress so subtly he's hardly noticed, but on this warm afternoon her cut-off jeans and vest top show how tanned she's become over the few days. Isaac can see that his mum is more energetic and carefree, even weighed down by the echo of her brother's last hours on earth. He considers, with a pang, whether she needed to be away from his dad to find this new version of herself.

'What are you thinking about, Lucia?' Tommy asks, happily going where Isaac dare not intrude.

'Getting out of my comfort zone, I guess. The feeling of escaping. Leaving your troubles behind.'

'Is that possible?' Isaac wonders aloud.

Polly nods enthusiastically. 'I think you're doing that already, aren't you, Isaac? I've seen you on this trip, dreaming about the future. I didn't realise what you were doing at the time but now I can see that your computer game is taking up all of your thoughts.'

Isaac knows this isn't strictly true. His thoughts are largely bound up with Polly. But since they talked about the bluebird game, he certainly has given it a lot more consideration as a proper business proposition. He considers all this as they follow the well-trodden path that will take them right to the top of the cliffs. Is he really leaving his troubled past behind? And if he is, can he take Polly and Reggie with him? Would he be enough for her?

Reggie's wide awake and waving his arms about happily. The bluebird is still going everywhere with him, and as Polly takes the baby from Isaac, he accidentally bashes her over the head with it.

'Ouch! That hurt, Reg. Be careful, love,' she says. Reggie's eyes are huge as she rubs her head and one fat little hand reaches out to pat Polly's arm. As she looks at him in astonishment, he leans towards her and nuzzles his face against her shoulder, his lips meeting the bare skin below the short sleeve of her T-shirt. She gasps.

'Isaac, did you see that? Reggie gave me a kiss, He's never done that before. Wow, that's so lovely.'

Isaac looks down at her happy face and in that instant, he knows there will never be another woman for him. Polly is everything. Her clear green eyes that seem to be able to smile even when her mouth doesn't, the way she cares for her little nephew even though she knew nothing at all about babies when she took the job on, her quirky sense of humour, all of these things and many more make a person that he just cannot live without.

Polly puts Reggie in his buggy and stands up, still grinning, and Isaac impulsively reaches out and hugs her. She leans into him for a second, before Reggie's wail of dismay at having the attention snatched away from him makes her disentangle herself and bend down again to soothe the baby.

The scent of Polly lingers. Isaac can still feel the warmth of her soft skin. He gives himself a shake. This won't do. Lucia is looking back over her shoulder to see what's keeping them. Isaac smiles down at Polly and Reggie and together, they head for the cliff top.

Chapter Thirty-One

Lucia stands on the cliff path with the others clustered around her. The beach is far below, the wide expanse of shingle stretching right down to the shore. It's cooler up here but a few brave swimmers are in the water and a group of children are paddling, squealing as they make their way over the sharp pebbles.

They are nearly at the site of the fateful fall. It's not been easy to work out the exact spot, but she's put together as many half-remembered clues about the disastrous school trip as she can, mostly from photographs and articles in the newspapers after the event. The accident made front page news in all the nationals at the time and almost caused their school to close.

While Tommy strides ahead, clearly keen to get Lucia's ordeal over with, Peter has walked by her side whenever the cliff path is wide enough, making sure he's on the side nearest the sea. He hasn't said much but Lu's heart goes out to him in gratitude for his earnest sympathy.

'How are you feeling, brave lady? I'm so proud of you for facing this ordeal, ' he says quietly.

'Well, I haven't tackled the worst part yet, but I think

I can do it,' she answers. 'And whatever happens now, at least I've gained more family.'

'You mean Polly and the boy? You already had Tommy.'

'Yes, but I was really referring to you.'

Peter's thin face is radiant and his hands shake slightly as he reaches for Lu's. 'Oh, my dear, I think that's one of the nicest things anyone has ever said to me. I'm honoured to be part of your extended family. I hope we'll share many more journeys together. Probably closer to home next time though. I expect we'll all need some recovery time after this very big adventure.'

'Maybe. Anyway, I think we're nearly there. I need to do the last bit on my own.'

Peter smiles down at her. 'We all understand that. I remember seeing you wandering around my estate in your blue coat the very first time we met. A lot has happened since then, and all of it good. Come on, you can do this. And you're not on your own. You never have been on this trip.'

Lucia pauses to gather her thoughts. Now she's finally here, the pain is as raw as ever. Her eyes sting with unshed tears but she's determined to do this. She turns to face the others.

'There were fifteen in the party. Not everyone wanted to do the hike along the cliffs but Eddie was first on the list, of course. What actually happened is a bit hazy because there was such a panic when he fell, but it looked as if he'd ignored what the guide told him and dashed off to scramble up onto one of those rocky outcrops

247

over there before anyone could stop him. Seconds later, he'd disappeared over the edge. It's a sheer drop.'

The sentence ends with Lucia's voice cracking, but she still doesn't cry. 'I'm going to go just a little bit closer,' she says. 'I'll be quite safe.' This last part is for Isaac, who's grabbed her arm and is holding on tightly. 'Let me go, love, I'll not go near the edge. I need to do this.'

He moves a little way from the others with Lucia. 'Are you sure?'

Lucia nods, and reluctantly, Isaac releases her. She walks very slowly to a vantage point overlooking the beach and now her tears begin to flow. She lets them drip down her cheeks unchecked. They're for crazy, unpredictable Eddie and for herself, the sister who has spent so many years grieving for someone who was such a loose cannon that something like this could have happened at any point in his life.

'Eddie,' she says quietly, so the others can't hear. 'I couldn't stop this happening, I know that now. I loved you even when you made my life hard, and I always will. I'll never forget you. Anyway, here I am, and this is goodbye.'

Lucia unpins the little brooch that she's been wearing on the collar of her coat. It's a tiny bluebird, bought from a craft fair not long after Eddie's accident. She holds it in her palm. Kissing the bluebird, she holds her arm up, and hesitating only for a split second, flings the brooch out in a wide arc. It seems to hover in the air for a moment before dropping out of sight.

Lucia wipes her eyes and turns back to her huddle of supporters. They're wearing identical anxious expressions so she dredges up a smile as she heads back. They reach for her in an impromptu group hug and her heart is bursting with love for them, this mismatched band of travellers, all with their issues to resolve.

'I've done what I came for. Let's go home,' she says.

Chapter Thirty-Two

The journey back to England is much more straight-forward than the outgoing one. They take their time, sharing the driving, making regular calls home to check on Nigel and Petunia, camping in Calais for a night to give Isaac a chance to keep up with his work, and generally enjoying the feeling of freedom and lack of pressure. Taking the scenic route wherever possible, they wind their way through countryside populated only with long rows of vines, along tree-lined lanes mainly used by farm vehicles and through deep forests where no birds can be heard.

Lucia feels deep peace finding its way into her very bones, something she's never experienced before, or at least not since the accident. Tommy avoids being alone with her, or maybe it's the other way round, she can't be sure. In any event, they seem to have reached an unspoken agreement to put their personal lives on hold and just enjoy the road trip.

As they drive, the group talk and talk as if they'll never run out of words. Peter tells them about the ups and downs of life on the Meadowthorpe estate, Tommy spins tales of his many travels and even Isaac waxes lyrical about his new business. Polly is the only one who seems to be holding back. She's happy to mention her sister but never gives any real details of what happened before the tragedy or the circumstances of how Reggie came into being.

On the final day, as the van trundles towards Calais and their first experience of the tunnel, Peter makes an announcement. 'I've been thinking,' he says, glasses in their usual place on the end of his nose as he unfolds the last French map of the trip.

The others all cheer and guffaw loudly. Everything's making them laugh today. 'Shut up and let him speak,' Polly says eventually. 'I know we're pleased he's been thinking, but give the guy a break.'

Peter bows to her and continues. 'And what I've been thinking is this. I'm feeling so much younger since we started on this adventure. What I'd really like is a good long walk. Where exactly are we going next, Tommy?'

'I was going to suggest we go straight to the seaside, maybe Weston-super-Mare or Burnham-on-Sea, but my favourite hills in the whole country are nearby. How do you fancy exploring the Quantocks?'

'It sounds like a nasty disease,' says Isaac. 'As in, *I'm feeling okay apart from a slight touch of the Quantocks?*'

Polly splutters but Peter frowns at Isaac. 'I can see you have yet to experience the splendour of those particular hills, my boy. I agree with Tommy. An experience everyone should have,' he says. 'Let's go hiking!'

The windows of the van are open and the cheers that

greet this suggestion make a cyclist that Isaac's overtaking wobble so much he nearly ends up in a ditch. Lucia, checking in her mirror to see that he's recovered his balance, gives the man a wave. The resulting gesture could be understood in any language.

'I think it might be a good job we're leaving France,' she says, laughing. 'We're starting to outstay our welcome. Next stop, Somerset and Tommy's hills. We can share the driving, stop every hour to give Reggie a break from his car seat and be there by teatime. Can someone find us a campsite?'

'Mum, are we getting the hang of being impulsive at last?' Isaac whispers to Lucia as he follows the signs for the tunnel.

'Do you know, Isaac, I rather think we are,' she replies. 'And about time too.'

Chapter Thirty-Three

The long drive from Dover to the Quantocks takes six hours including all the stops for refreshment and Reggie's needs. By the time they reach the caravan site, Tommy is aching with exhaustion and he can see the others are feeling the same, apart from the baby who is chuckling and trying to grab handfuls of Tommy's hair as he lifts him from his seat.

'It's alright for you, my little mate,' Tommy says, wincing as Reggie manages to bop him on the nose with that pesky wooden bird he's still hugging, 'you've been napping on and off all the way from Dover. The rest of us are ready for a shower, a beer, some chips from that wonderful van parked over there, and an early night.'

'A chip van? I haven't seen one of those for years,' Polly says. 'We used to get one round our village when I was younger. I was allowed to take my sister with me to get some if she'd been good. She wasn't always.'

Tommy looks down at Polly, noting once again the deep sadness in her eyes. He thinks it must be progress that this sister of hers is being mentioned more and more often but each memory takes its toll on the girl.

253

'From what I can gather, brothers and sisters can be a real mixed blessing,' he says. 'I never had any, neither did Isaac, and Peter's younger brother's long gone. He was neither use nor ornament by all accounts, anyway, was he Pete?'

Peter turns from his task of getting the chairs out of the van. 'Archie? No, I'm afraid he was the black sheep of the family. What point are you making, Tommy?'

'I was just thinking aloud. It's an interesting subject. Let's get set up and we can talk about it some more.'

There's a pause while the team make camp. They've done this often enough now for it to be easy, even though they're all shattered. Lucia goes to check in at the reception room taking Reggie with her in his buggy and by the time she's back with a carrier bag full of steaming packets from the chip van, everything is in place.

'It's getting like home from home, isn't it, this camping lark?' says Tommy with satisfaction, as they sit around the picnic table in the gathering gloom. Dusk is falling at the bats are starting to wheel and swoop overhead. An owl calls and another replies. Isaac passes around the beer and conversation ceases while everyone tucks in. Even Reggie is quiet, sitting in his buggy with a tray clipped in front of him. He sucks each chip before he finally swallows it, looking around at the trees blowing in the light breeze as he eats. Occasionally he rejects one and throws it over his shoulder.

'Reg is going to wonder what's hit him when we go home,' says Polly. 'He's got used to this new sort of life, moving from place to place, settling down in his travel cot full of food and fresh air, and having this big family round him.'

'Ah, that's what I was talking about earlier, sort of,' Tommy says, batting away one of Reggie's cast-off chips before it can hit him in the face. 'I think we've got the basis for a very sound family support group here, us six, don't you?'

'I've been mulling over what you were saying too,' says Peter. 'I reckon you were suggesting we're all brother-and-sister-less so we need to up our game and look after each other as if we really were what we're starting to feel like, one big family?'

Polly looks across at Peter, raising her eyebrows. 'A baby covered in chips, a flaky twenty-something, a reclusive computer-game buff and his mother who thought she didn't want adventures, an extrovert re-born adventurer and an aristocrat? We're a mixed bunch.'

'But that's what real families are like. They rub along together even though they're all different kinds of people. Sometimes they argue. Sometimes they infuriate each other. But one thing they should always do is have each other's backs.'

'Is that us then?' Isaac asks.

'Do you want it to be?' Lucia can't imagine the Isaac she used to know being up for being absorbed into a brand new extended family, but he's surprising her every day at the moment in all sorts of ways.

Tommy waits, astonished at how much he wants

everyone to agree with his idea. If he can't have Lucia for himself, the next best thing will be to be properly part of the inner circle surrounding her. He's pretty sure Des isn't coming home, and he knows Lu will be absolutely fine without him. What sort of idiot leaves a woman like this one?

'I like it, Tommy. We're a gang of six. All searching for something new and better in our lives. And all on the way to finding it, if I'm not mistaken.'

'We've got a good big age range between us,' Peter says, nodding. 'Eldest eighty-six, youngest not even one year old yet. We should be able to tackle most things. Let's shake on it.'

A round of rather sticky handshakes follows, with Polly insisting on cleaning Reggie up before anyone touches him 'It's time this chap was in bed,' she says. 'And by the look of you lot, we should all turn in now. All that travelling and then Tommy's emotional stuff on top of it. No wonder we need to sleep.'

It's not long before everyone is tucked up in bed. As Tommy drifts off to sleep, his last waking thought is that tomorrow he'll be able to show his all-time favourite lady one of the most atmospheric places he's ever been to. If he plays his cards right, this road trip could be the first of many. And if it's a gang of six involved rather than a romantic adventure for two, so be it. Compromises aren't always a bad thing.

* * *

The said gang toil up a very steep hill from the tiny car park the next morning, already far too hot. Reggie is in his sling on Isaac's back because Tommy knows part of the walk is way too rutty for the buggy. Isaac doesn't seem to mind having his head patted continuously, which is lucky, but the sweat is already trickling down his back, Tommy notices, relieved he didn't offer his services for that job. He offers Lucia a hand on the steeper slopes but she shakes her head each time, drinking copious amounts of water but managing fine without his help.

Tommy is leading the way now, striding out ahead. Every step is taking him further back into his memories. Lucia is clutching a couple of his old photographs of the wood, some of the few that don't feature past girlfriends. This is somewhere he's preferred to visit alone prior to today. Like an ancient village church or an art gallery, time to think in peace is needed to appreciate an atmosphere so rarefied.

The deep silence hits them all as they stop for a drink of water. Once catered for, Reggie slurps juice from his feeder cup enthusiastically and Isaac shouts when some of it runs down his neck but when those sounds die away Tommy realises that it's not quiet because the birds are twittering even more loudly than the ones in Lu's garden. The shade from the twisty ancient oaks is dappled, and the narrow lane winds upwards underneath the strangely contorted branches.

'How old must these trees be?' Polly wonders aloud.

'They look almost timeless. Like guards protecting the land.'

They trudge on, listening to the birdsong and Reggie's happy gurgles. Suddenly, Tommy holds out a hand to stop Lu, who's the nearest person to him. 'This is it,' he breathes, 'this is the spot. Could you pass me the photographs? Yes, we're in the right place. Look.'

Lucia leans over to see where Tommy's pointing. He shows her a glimpse of bright blue sea and church steeple through a gap in the trees. The land drops away here and a path weaves through the oaks down towards the nearest village. The same one is in the pictures, from three different angles.

'Bingo,' he breathes.

Lucia hands Polly her phone. 'Quick, record the moment. We've completed another challenge. Well done, Tommy. You're very good at showing us your world.'

Polly grins and does as she's told, and the others pose under the trees, making sure the church steeple is in the background. 'One more for luck,' Lucia says, swapping places so Polly can be in the picture.

'Right, that's the photo quest ticked off, and we've still got the rest of today to play with before we head home in the morning. What do you all want to do next? Any ideas?' Lu asks as they meander back down the hill to the van.

'Picnic lunch on the nearest beach, a paddle, bit of a drive to see some more of this lovely place if you're all not too tired. We could pick up a takeaway on the way back and have a glass of wine when Reggie's asleep?' says Polly decisively. She looks round, suddenly anxious. 'Is that okay? I didn't mean to sound bossy.'

'Perfect,' says Tommy. 'I like a person who knows their own mind. Let's do it.'

Much later at the campsite, Polly takes Reggie into the washroom and bathes him thoroughly in the sink while the rest fall into their usual pattern of getting ready to eat. There is no take-away nearby but luckily Tommy remembered just before they reached the site that there used to be a very good local delicatessen and luckily it's still there, so he stocked up with what he calls party snacks. He sets out a range of cold meats, salads, a roasted vegetable quiche and (what Isaac comments is) enough olives and similar treats for the whole campsite.

'Wow, what a feast,' breathes Lucia, opening the wine. 'It's just as Polly said about Reggie, we're all going to find it hard to go back to living a normal life after this, aren't we, Peter?'

'You're so right. Far horizons, exploring new places. I've quite got the wanderlust back in my bones.'

After dinner, when Reggie's tucked into his cot and fast asleep, exhausted by all the fresh air, the others wrap blankets around their shoulders and sit just outside the van with their wine in plastic goblets.

'It doesn't have to end here, you know,' says Tommy.

'I know it doesn't. We haven't finished this trip yet, Polly and Isaac get their turns next,' Lu answers, topping up everyone's glasses. She glances down at the compass in the bag at her feet. The leather flaps have fallen open and she can see the needles clearly. Should she tell the others what they're pointing to? She hesitates and Tommy carries on.

'No, I mean even after we get home. This is only the beginning. We've got so many other places we could explore, and most of them are much nearer than France or Cornwall. I think we should plan ahead.'

'Definitely. But for now, which of you two is going to choose first?' says Lu.

Polly is busy unfolding one of Tommy's less tatty maps. 'This is South Wales,' she says to him. 'It doesn't look as if you went there as much?'

'I did more touring in North Wales, but that's the map with Cardiff, isn't it? I had a great time there.'

Isaac joins Polly to look at the map. 'Are you thinking of us going here next?' he asks, running a finger along the coastline.

'Yes, I think it's something I need to do. One of my sister's best friends, Sheena, lives somewhere near Barry Island and she's always asking me to visit. I think she wants to talk. I've been putting it off. They were very close. It'll be hard.'

The others wait. After a few seconds, Polly nods briefly. 'Well then, decision made if everyone's okay with South Wales. It's quite easy to get to from here, across the Severn Bridge. Sheena's got rooms over a pub in a little village by the sea. I'll check the postcode and text her when we get closer.'

'Great! I've never been anywhere near there. Let's do it!' Lu says. 'Yes?'

The others all raise their glasses to Polly. 'This trip is the best thing that's happened to me for years. Maybe ever,' Tommy says thoughtfully.

Nobody answers, but their faces tell him they agree. Polly and Peter deserve to have more good times and Tommy's not about to let Lucia and Isaac get away with digging themselves back into their old rut when they get home. No way is that going to happen.

Chapter Thirty-Four

When he looks back on the final leg of their trip, it seems like a wonderful blur to Isaac, especially the drive to South Wales, with everyone so sunburnt and happy.

'It's taken a long time for me to make this visit, but I'm so glad we came,' says Polly, as Isaac takes over the driving so she can give them a guided tour of the area. 'It's just that now we're here, I'm realising I don't want to see Sheena at all. It was the place I was nostalgic for.'

'But I thought you were keen to catch up with your sister's friend?' Isaac is still finding it hard to have plans adjusted at a moment's notice, but he tries his best not to sound grumpy about it.

'I honestly thought I was. We came to see Sheena together just the once and it was the most perfect couple of days. That didn't happen often in my family. I don't want to spoil the memory by having to go over . . . old stuff . . . with Sheena. Let's just have a good time.'

They walk along the nearby beach, wander through a picturesque town and finally reach Barry, where everyone except Peter rushes to have their picture taken by the amusement arcade. Polly and Lucia lag behind, and Isaac guesses Polly is having some kind of unburdening session with his mum. He wishes for a moment that she'd chosen him to confide in, but thinks this is probably a good thing. If only Polly could let herself see what a wonderful surrogate mum she's turning into and how happy Reggie is in her care.

When Polly and Lucia catch the others up, Isaac's already feeling at home in this little town.

'Who are Gavin and Stacey anyway?' he asks.

'I was just about to ask the same thing,' says Peter, as Tommy rolls his eyes.

'I'll introduce you to them when we get home,' promises Polly. 'I can't believe you've never watched the programme.'

'Have you actually got a TV, Pete?' Tommy asks, frowning. 'Because if you haven't, it might be an idea to get one for your new apartment. A nice bit of selective viewing might while away some of the lonely evenings. It worked for me. Never resorted to the soaps but I like a good comedy or drama.'

Peter looks dubious at the flood of suggestions that Lucia and Polly pour out to start his future viewing. Isaac grins. He thinks Peter wants to shudder at the idea but is far too polite to offend them all.

They pitch camp as near to the beach as they can get, and Tommy insists on barbecuing again as Peter rummages for his indigestion tablets. After they've eaten, peace descends. This is the part of the day Isaac likes best, if he had to choose. The general laziness brought on by too much food is soporific and deeply relaxing. It suits him down to the ground.

'I don't want to go home quite yet,' he says. 'Is there any chance we could go further north before we head back? I'd really like to see a bit more of Wales now we've come this far. I saw a TV programme about Snowdon once. You can either walk up or go on the train, I think, and then the coast to the north is supposed to be good. Let's just explore, shall we?'

Lucia looks at her son in amazement. 'You really have got the wanderlust, haven't you?' she says. 'But I'm afraid Rowan might be ready for us to come home. She's done such a lot for us.'

'We can ask?'

As it happens, Rowan is more than happy to stay on in Lu's house for as long as she's needed. The decorators have been dragging their feet so they've not finished her flat yet and even then, it'll need thoroughly airing to get rid of the smell of paint, she says, when Lucia rings her.

'That's cool then,' says Isaac happily. 'The ones of us who'd like to can hike up Snowdon and the others can take the train. We'll meet at the top for a picnic. How does that sound? I'll book a campsite nearby. Don't worry,' he says as Lu starts to remonstrate, 'I'll check that clothes are expected to be worn at this one.'

The next site has such spectacular views over the mountains that they all spend most of the evening gazing into the distance, snapping a series of very silly photographs of each other in various poses when they've finished recording the view.

'The weather forecast's great for tomorrow,' says Isaac, taking great energising gulps of the fresh evening air as he and Polly wash up the dinner pots. 'Mum says she'll take the train up the mountain with Peter and Reggie if you want to walk up with Tommy and me?'

'That doesn't seem fair. She might want to do the climb.'

Isaac laughs. 'Nah. My mum likes walking, up to a point, but clambering up mountains isn't her scene.'

'How do you know? She's never done it, has she?'

He frowns. 'No, I guess not. We used to go for picnics to our nearest high hills though and she always let Dad take me to the top while she stayed at the bottom and looked after the food.'

Lucia shows her approval of the plan for Polly to walk in no uncertain terms, and the next day they pack a picnic and pile into Flora.

'It's really beginning to feel like the key to freedom now, isn't it Lu, this old van?' Tommy says, patting the rainbow painting as he climbs out of the van at the car park near the train's starting point.

'Definitely. I'm so glad you made it possible for me to buy it. I can't wait to try out some places closer to home when we go back. This is only the start of the adventures.'

'I've decided to go up on the train with you. Let's give the young 'uns a bit of space, shall we? Is that okay, Isaac?'

This is music to Isaac's ears. He and Polly set off

without further ado to climb to the top. To begin with they walk in silence, and Isaac is content just to cast occasional glances at Polly, loving the way her hair lifts and ripples in the fresh breeze and the rosy glow of her cheeks. She seems preoccupied with the ever-changing views from all angles, stopping every now and again to take photos.

After a while Isaac clears his throat. 'I've got something to tell you,' he says, carrying on walking. It's much easier to talk to Polly when they're side by side and she can't fix him with that clear, penetrating gaze of hers.

'Oh yes?' Polly puts her phone in her pocket and prepares to listen, which touches him. It's good to be the centre of attention but it makes him more nervous. He takes a gulp of water from his bottle.

'I was thinking about the computer game and so on . . . the future, and my bloody awful job.'

'Yes?' She sounds as if she's genuinely interested and Isaac presses on.

'I emailed my friend Nick last night. The internet was rubbish at that last site but it came back on quite late so I just did it. I wrote a quick pitch covering the aims of the game and a plan for the next two.'

'Did you? Wow! That's fantastic. I guess you'll need to be patient now while he considers if it's viable and so on?'

'Well, that's the thing. I switched my phone on this morning and there was a message waiting from him already.'

Isaac pauses, overcome with wonder at what he's about to say. Polly waits, matching her stride to his as they scramble over a rougher part of the path. He holds out a hand to steady her and she keeps hold of him as they carry on. It's a good feeling.

'Go on then. Don't keep me in suspense.'

'Polly, he loves the idea. He wants me to send the whole thing over to him and he'll test it out while we're away and then meet up with me when we're home to talk about marketing it. And he said "Get your finger out, mate. The next one won't write itself. There's an opening for this if we get a move on." So . . . that's what I'm going to do.'

'That's amazing!' Polly comes to a standstill and lets go of Isaac's hand, grabbing him by the shoulders. She has to stand on tiptoe to do this. He stoops slightly and on impulse, kisses Polly's cheek. Her skin is soft and she smells of fresh air and Nivea cream. Isaac has the overwhelming urge to bury his face in her hair. They stand like this for a few moments, both uncertain what to do next, and then Isaac wraps his arms around her. How has he never realised how good it can feel to really let yourself go? To hold someone tight, letting your heart beat with theirs and the scent of them get right into your soul.

Polly is the first to break contact. 'We'd better get moving,' she says. 'We told the others we'd meet them in the café and they'll have eaten all the cakes if we don't hurry up.'

Isaac swallows his disappointment at the abrupt end to his first proper hug. While he was holding Polly close he should have been telling her how she made everything in the world seem brighter and more exciting.

Polly is gaining height now. 'Come on,' she shouts over her shoulder. 'Race you to the next bend.'

They complete the climb in record time, trading stories about their worst school experiences and making loose plans for places they might visit in the future. Isaac feels warmed by the knowledge that Polly is assuming they'll be seeing these together but he still can't believe he let her go without taking the chance to tell her how he can't imagine life without her now.

In the café, the others are waiting, already on their third cup of tea. Polly asks Isaac if it's okay to share his good news and her glowing account of Nick's email makes him feel ten feet tall.

'So you might be able to ditch the dead-end job?' Tommy says, beaming all over his face. 'You can use my cash to keep you going and I guess your mum won't throw you out any time soon if the board and lodgings is a bit slow appearing?'

Lucia hugs Isaac and kisses him on both cheeks. He submits to this unusually fulsome show of affection, not wanting Polly to think he doesn't like that kind of thing. One of these days he'll show her he can do this. It needs to be soon before he explodes with longing.

Chapter Thirty Five

Isaac's plan of exploring the north coast of Wales has taken root with Lucia and the other two men while they've been drinking endless tea and arguing the merits of toasted tea cakes over rock buns. Peter has plenty of suggestions of places to include in their whistle-stop tour and while he and Tommy visit the gents, Lucia takes the compass from her bag and opens the case, half-cross with herself for what she's about to do. She'd wanted to see how the next part of the journey would pan out without its help and sure enough, the choice to travel to Wales had been made by Polly and Isaac anyway. Now though, Lu has a sudden yearning for home and her own bed. Will the compass back her up?

She takes it out and places it on the table in between the teapot and the sugar bowl. It's as beautiful as ever and she cups her hands around it and stares into the centre of the two dials. Before she's had chance to make sense of what she's seeing she hears the men come back, and looking up furtively, she makes to put it away again but Tommy stops her.

'Hang on, darling, you've got the right idea. Let's see

what my old friend says about the next part of our jaunt,' he says.

Peter sits down and leans forward. 'This must be what you started to talk about, back at the Manor when we first met,' he says. 'My goodness, what a beautiful thing. Tell me more about it.'

'I think we should let Tommy explain,' says Lucia, feeling Tommy's bright blue eyes on her face. 'We've never really discussed it properly, have we?'

She waits, feeling as if she's on the verge of something that she might not understand, but desperate all the same to know what the significance of this strange instrument is. Tommy sighs.

'It's very hard to express what it's meant to me,' he says. 'But I'll try. The compass and barometer were given to me by Angelina a long time ago. To be honest, I had to convince her to let it go for her own good. She was completely reliant on it to make even the smallest decision, and that's not how it's meant to work, in my opinion.'

Peter reaches out and touches the smooth marble outer casing of the beautiful thing.

'It's got powers then, Tommy?' he asks.

'You don't seem surprised.'

'I've travelled a lot in my time and seen some odd occurrences, sometimes involving what seem like inanimate objects . . . but aren't. Go on, I'm all ears.'

'I tried to get Angelina to divulge how she came by it, but she's closed up every time the subject is raised in the past. All I know for sure is that the compass only has one owner at a time. It has to be freely given to the next person. After that, if it's used in the right way, it can provide simple advice about the right way to act or the way to go. Lucia is just at the start of her relationship with it.'

Lucia frowns. 'But are you trying to tell me it might get a grip on me? Have too much power if I'm not careful? *Really?*'

'It could do. I was ready to let it go, but even then, it wasn't easy to give it up. So what is it saying to you now? Full interpretation takes a long time and a concentrated effort but you've made a start.'

She takes the compass in both hands again and stares down at it. The needles begin to move immediately but to begin with, they spin crazily, not settling on any place in particular. At last they slow down and stop. The compass needle is pointing due north and the barometer is set to *stormy*.

'What does it mean?' Lucia asks, frustration at the immensity of her task getting the better of her. 'How am I supposed to get better at knowing what the message is? There's no instruction book.'

'It's saying we're right to be travelling to the north of this lovely country,' says Tommy. 'That's the easy part. But the other reading really depends what you were thinking about when you were asking it a question.'

Lucia ponders on this. It was Polly who was on her mind, and has been all day. There's been an underlying restlessness in the girl ever since they she decided not to meet up with her sister's friend in South Wales.

Lucia's thoughts about the compass reading are forgotten until later when, exhausted by their frantic tour of the North Wales coast, camp is finally made on the outskirts of Rhyl.

'Let's just sit here and play with Reggie while the others get the water and so on. Everything else is done,' Lucia says to Polly as they set up the camping chairs in the shade of a giant sycamore tree. 'I want to talk to you.'

Polly looks at her in some alarm. 'Have I done something bad?'

She sounds so much like the worried little girl she must have once been that Lucia's heart twists painfully for her. The anguish she's suffered is still only just under the surface, however bright and breezy she appears most of the time.

'Not at all, love.'

Lucia realises suddenly that she's reached the point where Polly might have to be told about the compass. Her mind shies away from more revelations and possible doubting. Peter's acceptance of it surprised her but he's clearly had a wealth of unusual experiences in his own travels. Now doesn't feel like the time to be asking Polly to suspend disbelief.

'It's probably just me being silly and fussing,' she begins, trying to find the right words. 'But I've been having the strongest feeling that someone I cared about had some sort of . . . storm brewing in their life. The others all seem fine. Could it be you?'

Polly doesn't answer for a moment. Her frown deepens. Then she takes a deep breath. 'My dad lives in Shropshire, not far from a little town called Church Stretton. I've never been there but I've looked on the map and it'll kind of be on the way home. I haven't seen him since he tried to come to Alice's funeral. I've been wondering if now's the time. But Lu, I'm scared.'

Lucia slips an arm around the younger girl, amazed at how slender she feels under the big woolly jumper. 'Tell me about it?'

'I've always assumed that he left because he couldn't stand living with us. I'm afraid if I go to find him and we talk, I'll find out things about my family that I don't want to know.'

'Does he want to see you?'

The question sounds brutal but Polly doesn't flinch. 'Yes. He's got my mobile number and he often texts news about what he's been doing and asks how I am but I hardly ever answer. Maybe it's time to face up to it. Could we?'

'Of course. I'll tell the others. We'll plan a stop there and then head for home. We can take Reggie for a walk while you go and find him.'

'No, I need to take Reg with me. He's never seen his grandson.'

They look at each other and Lucia is horrified at the pain in Polly's eyes. 'In that case, we must go,' she says firmly.

* * *

The coast of North Wales is very easy to fall in love with, and as they make their leisurely way along it the next day, Lu begins to think seriously about the future. Parking the van behind rolling dunes, she's overcome with a wild desire to run and run.

As the others get ready for a more gentle stroll, Lu kicks off her trainers, rolls up the legs of her jeans as far as they'll go and begins to jog down the wide expanse of firm sand. She can hear Isaac's surprised cry at the sight of his mum hurtling towards the waves. By the time Lu splashes into the shallows, she's out of breath and every muscle in her body is telling her to have a rest, but her mind feels freer than it's been for months.

Perhaps it's time for a complete change? The thought of going back to the house she's shared with Des for so long, whether he's in it eventually or not, doesn't fill her with joy. Lu paddles along the shoreline, thinking about all the places they've visited so far. Might it be fun to come and live by the sea? Would Isaac relocate? How about Polly? Lu has no idea how long the girl is planning to stay with them. Polly's said she chanced on Chandle-bury by accident but Lu still feels there's more to it than that. Her mind moves on at a pace and she feels a sharp pang of loss as she wonders what Des is doing now. They need to talk, and soon.

As the rest of the group draw nearer, Lu makes the decision to shelve all these thoughts for now and just enjoy the moment. The future can look after itself. Today is full of sunshine, sea air and friendship. That's quite enough for the time being.

Chapter Thirty-Six

Two days later, the well-oiled camping machine swings into action. It's not long before breakfast is over and they're ready to go. They've spent the night on a site near Barmouth, having worked their way down from Rhyl, and everyone is glowing with fresh air and exercise. Isaac insists on making a brief detour to say goodbye to the sea and then they're off, taking one last look at the promenade and the rows of genteel guest houses and flats before they head in the general direction of Shropshire.

Lucia sings as she drives, and when they do their now-slick changeover, she entertains Reggie happily and chats to Tommy about people they both know from their village. Flora eats up the miles, and before too long, the Sat Nav is telling them that they're almost at Polly's father's smallholding.

Checking the younger girl in the driver's mirror, Lu isn't surprised to see her face is white and there are dark circles under her eyes. She's been glancing at her phone repeatedly. Messages from her father have been coming through thick and fast. He's obviously delighted at the prospect of Polly's visit but it's not hard to see that she doesn't share his joy.

When they reach the outskirts of Church Stretton, they're directed out into open country and finally down a long, rutty lane, with the holes in the surface of the road getting deeper as they head into what looks to be an alpaca farm.

'They're branching out,' says Polly briefly, as the motorhome trundles into a wide courtyard surrounded by apples trees and fruit bushes. 'Here he is.'

A tall, well-built man in a blue boiler suit is coming towards them, arms open wide in welcome. He takes the group in with one piercing gaze but then sweeps his daughter into a bear hug that almost knocks her off her feet.

'My girl,' is all he says, but his voice is warm and husky and Polly doesn't try to resist.

Behind him, Lucia spots a tiny figure dressed in jeans, wellies and a work shirt. Her hair is tied on top of her head, reminding Lu of Nigel when he's been to the grooming parlour. Her eyes are as bright as those of Lu's little dog and if she'd had a tail, she'd probably be wagging it.

'I'm Vinnie,' the woman says, coming to shake them all by the hand. 'Come into the kitchen and have some tea. These two won't need us for a little while, I'm sure.'

Later, when Lucia thinks back to that hour spent around the battered oak table in the farmhouse kitchen, with chickens wandering in and out and an impromptu visit from a curious goat, it has a dream-like quality. Vinnie is so welcoming that nobody feels the slightest awkwardness, and although nettle tea is probably an acquired taste, the welsh cakes that come with it are fresh from the oven and utterly delicious.

'I can't believe you're actually here,' Vinnie says more than once. 'Jack has wanted this for so long. It'll be a new beginning for them both, I'm positive.'

When Polly, Reg and her father finally emerge, blinking as if they've come out into the light, it's not easy to refuse the offer of a vegetable curry and more chat, but Polly is adamant that Reggie needs to go home.

'We've been away ages. It's been amazing fun but it's time to get ourselves organised again. I like him to have at least some sort of routine, Dad,' she says, kissing Jack goodbye with more warmth that Lu would have thought possible when they arrived. 'I'm doing my best to give him the sort of upbringing that Alice would have wanted. She'd have been such a good mum if she was here.'

Jack appears to be on the point of commenting on this but meets Vinnie's stern gaze and says nothing. Tommy ushers the party into the van and they begin the final leg of their journey, winding their way through stunning countryside until they reach more built-up city areas.

It doesn't seem long before the motorhome, on its last quarter tank of fuel and looking dusty and fly-spattered, is pulling up at the side of Lu's home. Polly has driven the last lap, having dropped Peter back at what he lovingly calls his ancestral pile. Rowan is there to meet them. She tells them she's left Joe in charge of the post office for half an hour, and has provided a huge lunch of salad, crusty bread warming in the oven and an extensive cheese board so they won't need to cook. Tommy sets off immediately to walk to the corner shop, because although they've bought French wine home with them, he says he's craving a bottle or two of bitter.

When Rowan's safely out of earshot, Isaac groans. 'I know she means well, but I feel as if I never want to see cheese again after all we've eaten on this trip. We overdosed on it in France.'

'Button your lip, Isaac,' says Polly, giving him a playful slap. 'Just be glad you haven't got to do a supermarket shop before we eat. We're going to be busy all the rest of the day unpacking and getting the washing done. I'm sure after that your mum will be ready to relax.'

'Well, it's funny you should say that.' Lucia says slowly, relieved that Polly's colour and usual bounce has returned but preoccupied with the next steps. 'I've been thinking.'

'Not you too? All this thinking's getting to be a habit,' says Isaac. He sees his mother's expression and mimes zipping up his mouth.

'I've already said I need to see your dad and sort a few things out,' Lu continues, giving him her best mean stare. 'I can't settle here until I've done that.'

'You're not going off again, are you?' asks Polly, frowning. 'You really need to kick back for a little while, surely?'

'I'll do that when I know what he's playing at. Don't worry. I won't be away long. He's obviously not going to

279

come here to me, so if I want to get some answers, I'll have to go to Huddersfield.'

When Tommy returns from the off licence, he's less than impressed by the news of Lu's trip, but she won't be dissuaded so he consoles himself with a pint. Isaac pours wine for himself and Polly, but Lu refuses both.

'I need a clear head for the next few days,' she says. The others say nothing but their expressions leave no doubt as to how they feel about this.

'Could we just have a quick chat before you start packing again, Lu?' Tommy asks. 'Come into the garden. I won't keep you long. I can tell you're itching to be off.'

Tommy's expression is unreadable as Lu starts to prevaricate but he's clearly not taking no for an answer so she follows him outside, noticing absent-mindedly that the lawn badly needs mowing.

'Shall we sit on the bench under the apple tree?' Tommy asks.

Lu nods. 'What's all this about?' she says sitting down at the opposite end of the bench to Tommy. There's something very unsettling about the way he's looking at her today.

For a few moments, Tommy is silent. Then he turns to face Lu. 'So, what are we going to do about you, darling?' he says quietly.

'About me? Why would you need to do anything about me? I'm fine.' Lu sees his face and adds, 'Well, obviously not completely fine, but I'm getting my head round Des leaving and I'll be okay eventually. I just need to speak to him face to face. I'm sure we can sort something out.'

'And I need to speak to you. I've tried several times while we were away but there's always something or someone distracting you. Don't put me off this time, just when we're on our own at last.'

Lu stands up suddenly, looking towards the house hopefully, but Tommy's on his feet too now. He takes a step forward so that Lu is looking right up into the bright blue eyes that usually twinkle but are now serious, and clearly trying to tell her something important. He takes her by the shoulders very gently. She can feel the warmth of his strong hands, reassuring and yet disturbing.

'Lu, this is really important. Just listen, would you?'

Lucia takes a few deep breaths to steady her jangling nerves but makes no further move to leave. Tommy's eyes are mesmerising. He clears his throat.

'Darling, when we were in Pengelly, Angelina made me face up to a thing or two, most of all the fact that throughout my adult life I've constantly flitted from woman to woman. Oh, to start with I know it was mainly because I didn't feel the need to settle. I haven't left a string of broken hearts behind me, or anything like that though.'

'I wasn't going to say you had.'

Lucia is having trouble keeping eye contact with Tommy now he's so close. Her heart is pounding quite alarmingly but she's determined not to be the one to break this powerful connection between them. The more she looks into the familiar blue eyes, the more she feels herself drowning in a totally unexpected longing for Tommy just to hold her really tightly, to kiss her, to . . . but he hasn't finished talking.

'I've stayed single because . . . well, I think you know now that it was because of you, Lucia Lemon. We fudged around the issue of the CD I made for you . . . all those romantic songs . . . but you must have realised it was really just an extended love letter.'

So her first thoughts had been right after all. A burst of happiness takes Lucia by surprise but she squashes it quickly. 'What have I got to do with you playing the field? You can't blame me for you being a serial flirt, can you?'

'Okay, here goes. I love you, Lucia Lemon. Absolutely adore you. Always have. Des saw you first and I'm nearly twelve years older than you in any case, so naturally I backed off. But it's been there all the time underneath. No other woman has been right for me because I've always, always wanted to be with you. There's never been anyone but you for me, Lucia.'

Vaguely, Lu registers that Reggie is crying inside the house. The bedroom window is open and she can hear Polly singing to him. Isaac must be busy in the kitchen. They really are alone. Should she?

Lucia reaches up to touch Tommy's cheek. His face is tanned, and comfortably lined with echoes of all the smiling and laughing he's done through the years. She traces a finger down to his lips, and stops. He moves even closer, bending his head so their foreheads are touching.

'I know my timing isn't great,' he says. 'Dropping this on you when you're just about to go and fight for your marriage, but I couldn't let you go without just once telling you exactly how I feel. If you and Des decide to try and make a go of it, I'll back off, of course I will.'

Lucia leans back slightly so she can look at Tommy properly. 'We'll always be friends, whatever happens though, won't we?' she says, suddenly terrified at the thought of not having this man in her life.

His steady gaze is still holding Lu's but now Tommy's eyes are unbearably sad.

'I'll always love you, Lucia, that's for sure, but I think if you and Des are going to be together again the only thing I can do is to make myself scarce. It wouldn't be fair for me to hang around here like a lovesick teenager.'

'But . . . but I'd miss you. I mean . . . we'd all miss you. Don't go away. Where would you go anyway?'

Tommy smiles, but the deep sadness is still there, making Lu want to cry. 'I've always had a yen to buy a narrow boat and just sail off into the sunset,' he says. 'Explore the waterways of Britain, meander around and stop wherever looks interesting.'

'That sounds wonderful,' Lu breathes, her head full of a vision of Tommy on the back of a boat steering with one hand and with his other arm firmly around her waist. Wait, she shouldn't be putting herself in that picture, should she? As Lu tries to clear her mind of the disturbing image, Tommy leans down and kisses her, putting all other ideas firmly out of her head.

For a long, blissful moment, Lucia leans into him, warm, flickering excitement growing as their bodies move together. Tommy's lips on hers, his arms around her waist, the mingled feelings of intense safety tinged with danger . . . no, this can't happen. Summoning up every ounce of willpower, Lu pulls away from him.

'Tommy, I'm still married to Des and I've got no idea what's going on with us. This can't happen. It just can't. I'm so sorry. I really am.'

Arms by his side now, Tommy nods. 'I guess I knew that all along. It's okay, darling. You go and find the silly bugger. I'll be fine. Another adventure is maybe just what I need. Off you go and pack.'

Lu hesitates for a second or two but makes herself turn and walk back to the house. She should be proud to have resisted such powerful and unexpected temptation. She ought to be happy that even if Tommy loves her as much as he claims to, he'll still be able to have a perfectly good life without her and follow his dream. Somehow neither of these thoughts is even remotely comforting.

Chapter Thirty-Seven

Lucia sets off for northern parts two days later. She's done all the necessary sensible jobs first: checked the van's tyres and filled it up with diesel, packed an assortment of clothes because the weather is spring-like rather than summery today, restocked the fridge and freezer and left instructions that they should call her immediately if anything goes wrong.

Her final task, in the privacy of her bedroom, is to get out the compass. Checking it after Polly's visit with her dad, she saw that the *stormy* setting had returned to the more neutral barometer reading of *fair*, and the compass was pointing in the general direction of Chandlebury, but now, her mind full of the coming encounter with her husband, not to mention the recent burning memory of Tommy's kiss, the *stormy* warning is back. The direction is North, which is reassuring if she's heading for Yorkshire, but worrying when she thinks what might lie ahead.

'Mum, are you sure you're ready to do all this driving so soon after the big trip?' Isaac asks for what seems like the twentieth time as she comes downstairs.

'I've been driving since I was eighteen and I've never

had even the tiniest bump,' Lu says, through gritted teeth. 'I've got Nigel for company this time and my phone is fully charged. Just back off, will you?'

Lucia sees Isaac's face fall and is filled with remorse. 'Look, love, I know you're fussing because you care about me but honestly, I'll be fine. I need to do this. And I have to do it on my own, you see that, don't you?'

'I guess so.'

'But if you get too tired, you could always ring and one of us could come to meet you on the train and take over,' says Polly, hugging Lu and presenting her with a large container of sandwiches and other assorted snacks.

Tommy stands on the drive to wave Lu off. His offering is a large bar of chocolate and some barley sugar sweets.

'Will you call me? Or at the very least text?' he asks.

'Yes, don't worry. Are you staying here?'

'No. When I was out earlier getting your journey treats I saw an ad in the post office window. There's a bed-sit to rent over the village shop. Sandy's an old mate of mine. I'm going to move in there for a little while. It's crowded enough here at the best of times and I've got a feeling Isaac and Polly need their space.'

'Oh. Okay.' Lucia can't decide if she's relieved or disappointed that Tommy won't be in the house when she gets back. At least he's not dashing off to look at boats for sale. She pushes the thought away for now. This isn't getting her anywhere. At this rate she'll still be here at lunchtime.

Finally, Lu and Nigel make their escape, driving down the lane with the radio playing seventies hits and the windows open to let in the fresh morning breeze. It's chilly as yet, but the weather forecast promises a warm spell later. Nigel, in his travelling cage, lifts his head and sniffs the air rapturously. He may be elderly, but he hasn't lost his inbuilt pioneering spirit, Lucia thinks happily.

As she heads out towards the motorway, Lu makes a snap decision to make a detour. There are no deadlines to meet and she's a free agent, after all. She turns left down the lane that leads to Meadowthorpe Manor. Peter's been on her mind ever since they got back, and now she won't be able to ask him round for dinner for a few days. She hopes fervently that his decision was the right one and he's not regretting giving up the ownership of the Manor now he's home.

Pulling up as close to the house as possible, Lu jumps out of the van and hurries round the back to the entrance she used last time. She knocks and then tries and ringing the ancient bell, but nobody arrives to answer. Just as the feeling of panic threatens to overwhelm her, a voice calls, 'Is that you, Lucia?'

Lu swings round to see Peter striding towards her across the grass, clad in a very battered wax jacket, some new-looking cords and wellies. 'There you are,' she says, hugely relieved. 'I thought you'd done a flit.'

'I'm just about to, as it happens,' he says, coming forward to kiss Lu on both cheeks. 'I've booked a very last-minute rail trip around the cities of Europe. They had a cancellation so they were more than happy to take my money. Never done anything like this in my life but the Trust have swung into action much more quickly than I expected. They still need to be in the house to do their surveys and the groundwork for the takeover for a while, so I thought I'd give Mrs Jacques a break and have one myself.'

'Good for you! It's all going ahead then? I was worried I'd pushed you into the wrong choice.'

'Not on your life, my dear. I've never felt so footloose and fancy free. Can't wait to get away for a while and see a bit more of the world. I've even bought myself some natty new togs.' He gestures to the trousers and opens his jacket to reveal a very smart sweater.

'Is that cashmere?' Lu asks, impressed, reaching out to touch the soft wool.

'Yes, I decided it was so long since I purchased any clothes that I deserved the best for this trip.'

'That's wonderful. As soon as you're home, give us a call and we'll have a fabulous reunion dinner and a good catch up.'

'I most certainly will. It's been quite strange being without you all. I loved our time together.'

'You're one of our new-look family now. We've missed you too.'

'Thank you. That's a perfectly lovely thing to say. You're a strong, brave woman, Lucia Lemon. Anyway, enough of that, you must all come for tea as soon as I'm settled in again after my holiday. Can you stay for a while now? I can't offer scotch pancakes, but I make a mean pot of Earl Grey.'

'I'd better not, I'm on my way north to have it out with Des, but I'll definitely come as soon as you're organised in your new rooms. You've got my email address, haven't you? Will you send photos from your trip?'

'If technology allows it, you can be assured I shall. Bon voyage, my dear, and good luck with the showdown. It's very good at my age to have made such splendid new friends.'

'Ditto.' Lu says goodbye, somewhat alarmed at the frailty of Peter's thin body but reassured by the warmth of his hug. 'I'll see you soon, I promise. Safe journeying.'

A heady sense of recklessness hits Lu as she finally reaches the sign for the motorway and settles into the slow lane behind a stream of lorries. She sings along to an old Rod Stewart song, 'This Old Heart Of Mine'. Well, Rod, hers has definitely taken a battering lately but today's trip is going to mark the start of a whole new chapter. A different Lu needs to emerge. Someone who won't let anyone trample on her heart. Someone who can make new friends. And also, a woman who knows how to let one of the most precious ones go, but that thought can wait. She can't bear even thinking about losing Tommy forever.

There's no rush to overtake anything, which is lucky because the van isn't keen on that sort of manoeuvre, but as soon as it's practical Lu plans to leave this horrible noisy motorway and take the back roads. She's got every map she could possibly need for this excursion into the unknown and there is nothing to say where she should be on any given day. Not only that, but the compass is on the seat by her side. If ever she's going to need help with decision-making, Lucia reflects, this is the time.

As long as Lu can remember, she's never had this kind of open-ended adventure, and until now has never felt the lack of it. Before she met Des, she was a creature of habit, stuck in her self-imposed rut of guilt and regret. Now, as she swings onto the slip road that's going to take her away from most of the traffic on this bright morning, Lu's spirits soar. She's only briefly outlined the first part of her scheme to Isaac and Polly. It's not far to Huddersfield. It's high time she faced up to the fact that she and Des can only go forward if they're brave enough to talk about what's happened in their past. After that it's anybody's guess what'll happen.

When the road she's following turns into a winding lane, Lu stops to check her directions, opening Tommy's map more fully. She sees various intriguing village names, and soon finds the one she's looking for. Bob lives outside the city so she's only a few miles from Des now. She gets out her phone, takes a deep breath and calls her husband.

'Lu?' Des is quick to answer and sounds alarmed.

'Hello. No need to worry, there's no crisis. It's just that I wondered if you'd like to meet me for a picnic?'

'A picnic?' Des repeats the word with as much surprise as if she's asked him to go bungee jumping.

'Yes. I'm not far from you, and it's nearly lunchtime.' She waits as he takes this in. 'You're . . . in Huddersfield?'

'Well, almost. I could meet you near Holmfirth. There's

a place marked on the map just above the town that looks like a good place for a walk.'

'But Lu . . . why are you here? I'm not saying you shouldn't be,' he adds hastily. 'I'm just a bit taken aback, that's all.'

She sighs. 'I decided that there was no point in trying to sort out our problems on the phone so I'd drive up here to try it face to face. So, are you coming to meet me or not?'

'Give me directions and I'll be with you in half an hour,' he says.

Lu tells him the exact place she's aiming for and heads further up into the moorland. With every mile she feels more alive, and Nigel seems to pick up on her mood. He sits up in his carrying basket and shakes his head until his ears flap. The birds are singing, the sun is shining now and there's hardly a car on the road. The van chugs rather alarmingly as she reaches higher ground but she's soon pulling into a deserted car park with picnic benches and lots of shade. Nigel is delighted to be outdoors, sniffing around ecstatically as she steers him towards the nearest bushes.

When Lu hears the rumble of Des's Skoda, her stomach clenches and she almost wishes she hadn't come. What if he's still distant and unreachable? What if their marriage really is in injury time? What if . . .

'Hello, love,' Des says, as he parks next to the van and winds his window down.

The familiar endearment nearly finishes her off, but

Lu is determined to stay strong until she's said her piece. She smiles at him in as cool a way as she can manage.

'It's good to see you,' he says, getting out of the car. 'I've got to admit it was a surprise to hear from you, but the best sort. I've been doing a lot of thinking.'

'Really?' She raises her eyebrows, unsure how to take this return to civilised chatting.

'Yes, *really*. We should talk. Make plans for the future, that kind of thing.'

Lu's heart sinks. This sounds ominous. 'Shall we go for a walk?' she says, trying to keep the wobble out of her voice.

He nods, and Lu clips Nigel onto his lead and heads for the waymarked trail that winds upwards, puffing slightly as it gets steeper and steeper. Hill walking has never been her thing. Tommy's Somerset walk was much gentler. Her mind shies away from this thought. Today is about her marriage. They walk in silence for a while, and Lu turns over various outcomes in her head. Does her husband want a divorce? Does he plan to live in Yorkshire for good? Maybe he's met another woman and he wants them all to be friends together and be civilised about all this. By the time they reach a plateau of heather-covered moorland, she's covered most of the options. Or so she thinks.

Chapter Thirty-Eight

The little dog runs free at the top of the hill, yapping delightedly as he chases butterflies. There are no sheep around and certainly no other people. Lu flops down onto the ground out of breath and wraps her arms around her raised knees. She leans her chin on them and wonders where to begin, but Des beats her to it.

'How've you been?' he asks. 'I mean, tell me honestly. I know I did the wrong thing taking off like that.'

'Yes, you did,' she agrees. 'It was cruel. Brutal.'

'I'm so sorry, Lu.'

The sadness in his voice brings a lump to Lucia's throat. They watch Nigel following a brightly coloured moth and failing spectacularly to get anywhere near it. The sun is warm on Lu's neck and she can smell the familiar scent of oily wool that always rises from Des's ancient fisherman's sweater. There's a long, awkward silence. An aeroplane cuts across the sky above them and Lu wishes she was on it, far from this difficult situation that doesn't seem to have a hope of sorting itself out.

'Maybe we need to go back a bit,' she says, after a while.

'How do you mean?'

293

'Back to when we started to get on each other's nerves. When we retired?'

Des heaves a huge sigh. 'You regret it, don't you? Finishing at the school?'

'No, not at all. Is that what you think?'

'It's obvious. You still can't tear yourself away from the place.'

Lu turns to face him. 'I've taken a long holiday from the volunteering,' she says, 'but now I've made the break, I can't see why I carried on so long. I think it was all tied up with my feelings about letting Eddie down. What about you though? There doesn't seem to be anything you want to do with all the spare time you've got now.'

'Hang on a minute before we get on to my problems, although now you mention it, I have got plans. You've actually finished at the school?'

'Yes. I'll tell them when I get home that they need to find someone else.'

'Ah. In that case, you'll be stuck there forever while they try.' Des sounds defeated.

'No, I mean I'm not going back. They'll cope. But tell me how you're feeling.'

There's a long pause. 'The redundancy hit me hard, Lu. All those hours with no routine to fall back on. It was terrifying at the start,' she hears Des mumble, eventually. 'I was miserable.'

The words hang between them, a bitter accusation. Lu feels fury take over. 'You could have said something. You should have talked to me.'

'I tried, but you didn't want to hear. You were so intent on not breaking the ties with the children at school, and you just carried on with what you'd decided to do in your own sweet way.'

There's long, uncomfortable silence. Lu is the first to speak. She's come all this way. It can't end in a pointless row. Perhaps they're getting somewhere at last. 'So, you left because you thought I was too busy to want to be with you?' she asks, meeting his eyes steadily for the first time today.

'That's the simple version. The more complicated one is that I felt useless. At work, I was somebody. And then there was . . . the other issue.'

There's a pause, and Lu sees that Des is crying. The only other times she's seen tears in his eyes have been momentous occasions – his parents' funerals, the moment he first held Isaac and the school appointment where the words *mild autism* were first uttered in relation to his son. Now his face is wet, and he's fighting sobs. He buries his face in his hands as if he can't bear to look at her.

'Des, don't,' Lu says, anguished. 'Come here.' She kneels up in the heather and puts her arms around his heaving shoulders, holding him tightly as the tension of the last few weeks finally finds a way of expressing itself. They cling together, Des moving to hug her close as he cries out his pain. The dog whimpers as the storm abates, snuffling at Lucia's arm, and Des gradually begins to breath more calmly. He rubs his face angrily. Lu hands him a tissue.

'I'm sorry,' he says again.

'Don't keep saying that. And what do you mean by *the other issue?*'

Lu lets go of her husband and sits back down. She knows their next words are going to be game changers. Des's face is white now and he seems to be having trouble speaking. Lu decides it's high time she took the lead.

'Okay, this is the hardest part,' she says, putting a hand on Des's arm. 'We're going to have to be really honest with each other now. Our marriage has been going downhill for a long time, hasn't it, love?'

Des blinks and looks at the floor. 'What do you mean? We're just like any other couple. We have bad patches, and getting made redundant was just one of them, wasn't it?'

'You're closing your eyes again to what's really going on. You always do that.'

'I don't! That's just not true, Lucia.'

'Yes, you do. You try not to see things that'll upset you. I should have tackled it before now but I'm the same in a lot of ways.'

They look at each other properly now, both wide-eyed. This sort of conversation has never figured in their marriage. Des shrugs.

'You're right, of course. That's why I was afraid to challenge you about who was going to take over the ownership of the compass.'

'What do you mean?'

'Well it was obvious it was meant for you, but I had

a horrible feeling that if I had the chance to ask it where I should be, it would tell me to stay put. I like an easy life. A boring life. But I knew deep down it was time to go.'

Lu takes a moment to understand what her husband is saying. 'Charming. You're saying our marriage is boring?' she mutters, when his meaning sinks in.

There's a long silence which neither of them seems to be able to break. Eventually, Des turns to face Lucia. 'Yes, it is. How long is it since we even had a cuddle, let alone sex? We sleep in the same bed but we might as well be in separate rooms.'

'Oh, so that's it. You're annoyed because we don't have sex anymore?'

The fierce anger in Lu's voice surprises them both but there's no going back now.

'No, I'm not annoyed,' Des says wearily. 'That's the sort of word you use when someone keeps leaving the top off the toothpaste or forgetting take the bins out. Not for the end of a marriage.'

There, it's said. There's a distinct possibility that this is it for the two of them. Fear grips Lucia. She knew this was probably coming but it's another matter facing a life without Des, however stale things have been between them.

'The end? Why does it have to be so dramatic? Can't you just come home and we'll work at it?'

Des sighs, and the grief in his eyes makes Lu feel physically sick. It really is over, and she's not even going to have a say in her future. He's dumping her. How dare he? If their marriage really is done for, Lu very strongly feels that she should be the one to do the dumping.

'It's gone too far for talking things through. I've . . . well, I'm going to have to tell you sometime. I've fallen in love with someone else.'

Lu stares at him. So that's it. Another woman? A kind of late mid-life crisis then, maybe brought on by the redundancy. She's been trying not to think about this option. A younger woman, probably skinny? She hates her already. How dare he?

Des clears his throat and looks her straight in the eye. 'And . . . and it's Bob.'

The words lie between them, heavy as Lucia's heart. 'What did you say?'

'It's Bob. I'm in a relationship with him. We've always been close, but with not having seen him for a while, I'd forgotten how good it could be. To talk to him. To . . . love him.'

Lucia's head is spinning and she wonders if she might faint. She never has before but this is . . . this is crazy.

'But Des . . . you're not gay, are you? What about us? Isaac? We've been together for years and years and you've never . . . have you?'

'No. I've been faithful to you, Lu. I love you. But I've always been scared to admit I had awful yearnings for something different. That's partly why I didn't hanker to go away from home. There's only one place I'd have wanted to go. Here. Bob and me, we go back a long way. We had a bit of a thing many years ago but neither of us was brave enough to keep it going. And then you came along and it all got more complicated.'

Lucia tries to think of something to say but the mixture of fury and grief that's poleaxing her makes speech impossible. Des ploughs on, and her world crumbles a little bit more with each word.

'Bob got married before I did, but it didn't last very long. Since then he's had a few flings, but it wasn't until now that he was prepared to be truthful with himself. His mum and dad are elderly now. He thought the shock would be too much for them.'

'And wasn't it?' Lucia isn't even nearly elderly but she's still trying to get her breath back and cope with the wave of rage that's threatening to swamp her.

'No, they've admitted that they secretly suspected it and they're happy for him to tell the whole world if he wants to. You can never tell, can you? I'm going to live with Bob permanently, Lu. I'll come home and pack up my stuff, see Isaac, that kind of thing, but then I'm moving up here for good. I'm sorry.'

'Will you stop saying that?' Lucia is shouting now, and it feels good. 'You bastard. You waltz off leaving me high and dry and then drop this bombshell on me. Sorry? You don't know the meaning of the word.'

She leaps to her feet and begins to stride away down the hill, and Des follows her, with the little dog galloping along beside him.

When Lu reaches the car park, she pauses, out of breath. She can feel the tears starting, but why shouldn't she cry? It all seems such a waste. Years of marriage, putting up with Des's grumpy moods, his lack of understanding of Isaac's complex needs, his . . . yes, his dullness. She finally admits it to herself. She has been bored out of her mind. The reason she's spent so many hours volunteering at the school and all the other stuff is that she'd rather be there than stuck in the house with Des.

He's caught up with her now. 'What are you going to do?' he says.

'Do you mean at this moment, or for the rest of my life?' she says, calm enough not to yell now.

'I guess I was meaning at this moment. You can't drive home when you're so upset.'

'Upset? That's a bit of a feeble word for how I'm feeling. But I think you'll find that from now on I can do any bloody thing I like, Des. And trust me, I'm going to start right now.'

Chapter Thirty-Nine

Without Lucia, the house seems very quiet, until Reggie decides to have a full-scale screaming bout and won't be soothed by anything or anybody.

'I don't know what to do with him,' whispers Polly during a short lull, her eyes wild and her hair tangled and messy. 'He's been like this for ages now, and it's even upsetting the cat.'

'I know,' Isaac says, 'it's hard to work with all the noise.'

As soon as the words pop out of his mouth, he realises they were unwise. Why can't he learn to think before he speaks? It's true though, and he's on a mission to get the updated game version to Nick later today. But Polly doesn't want to know about deadlines. She takes Reggie out of the kitchen and bangs the door behind her. Isaac sighs. He had been trying to make some lunch for a while, but the wailing made it hard to concentrate. He thought if he had a break and cooked a big Spanish omelette, they could all have some and it'd distract Reg, but now it's burnt.

'Polly, come back down,' Isaac shouts up the stairs. 'I'll make something else instead.' But she can't hear for the howling. What can he do to put things right?

301

In desperation, Isaac throws the ruined omelette in the bin and slumps down at the table, leaning his head in his hands.

'Oh Mum, I wish you were here to help me. What shall I do?' he whispers. 'Should I go upstairs to try and help Polly or keep out of her way to let her calm down? Please, just give me a clue. I don't know how to read her. I really thought I was getting better at this.'

Isaac focuses all his energy on trying to imagine what Lucia would say if she were here. He works hard to make his breathing calm and even, and to think about nothing but Polly. He knows without a doubt that he loves her, but surely she's never going to want to be with him if he carries on being so emotionally stunted. The counsellor he'd been sent to in his latter school years had told him over and over again that none of this was his fault, but life has always seemed tough. After what happened at university, he's accepted he's not the sort of person to have a proper relationship with a girl.

Before he can stop the flow, Isaac's treacherous mind catapults him back to the worst two months of his life. Settling into a new place had been hard enough, but when he found himself getting obsessed with one of the girls on his campus, Isaac had known for sure that he was totally out of his depth. The pain of that abortive relationship, his headlong dash for home and his refusal to communicate with the few university contacts who tried to keep in touch afterwards have left him emotionally battered and bruised. He forces his thoughts away from those dark times and back to the matter in hand.

After a few moments, when no inspiration is forthcoming, Isaac has to accept this is entirely up to him. He has to take charge for once in his life. Trembling slightly, he stands up and heads for the stairs.

Polly's door is closed, so he knocks gently and waits. Maybe she can't hear him over the noise. He tries again, more forcefully.

'Oh, you'd better come in if you can stand the row,' she shouts, above Reg's cries.

Polly's sitting on the bed with the baby clutched to her chest, and she's crying too now.

Isaac's stomach flips. He's always been useless with tears.

'Sorry, Poll, I didn't mean to be rude,' he mumbles, staring at the floor.

'It's okay, I know you can't help it.' Polly sounds so exhausted that Isaac looks up in alarm.

'Why don't I take Reggie for a walk to the park?' he hears himself saying.

Her face brightens and then she shakes her head. 'What will you do if he won't stop crying though?'

Isaac thinks back to everything he's ever heard Mum say about babies, which isn't much, and only stems from them accidentally watching one of those super-nanny type documentaries while they were waiting for *Morse* to come on.

'The first thing to do is this,' he says, trying to sound

as if he knows what he's talking about. 'Eliminate the obvious causes for Reg to be making this godawful row . . . I mean, crying,' he adds, seeing her expression. She doesn't comment but she doesn't tell him to shut up, so Isaac perseveres doggedly, willing himself to get it right for once.

'Is he hungry?'

'No.'

'Is his nappy dirty?'

She sniffs the baby. *Yuck*, thinks Isaac. 'No.'

'Do you think he's got a tummy ache?'

'How do I know?'

Polly bites her lip. Strangely, the little boy chooses this moment to stop howling and fall suddenly asleep, still hiccoughing. Reggie's long eyelashes make delicate half-moons across his rosy cheeks. Polly waits for a moment to make sure he's really out for the count, then gets up and places him gently into his cot. She rubs her lower back and winces, motions for Isaac to follow her onto the landing and takes a deep breath.

'I am completely rubbish at this, aren't I?'

Polly's face is pale now, and she sways slightly. Emboldened by the way she's looking at him so pleadingly for reassurance, he puts his hands on her shoulders and brings her round to face him. She doesn't resist, so he nerves himself to try and get to the bottom of the mystery of Reggie.

'Definitely not rubbish, the opposite of that, but how do you feel about having to look after him because he has no mother?' That didn't come out how it was supposed to, and Isaac can feel Polly's whole body tense.

'I don't *have* to, I want to. My mum took charge to begin with but she's not very well at the moment. I can usually cope. He's not normally this noisy, is he? I think he must be teething, or something.'

Isaac struggles with burning questions, but he's got to ask. 'Um . . .but what I still don't know is . . . who is Reggie's dad?' he says, when the silence becomes unbearable even to him. 'And why isn't he getting involved with all this?'

The silence that follows this goes on for far too long and Isaac's almost ready to give up and go downstairs when the answer comes. It certainly wasn't one he was expecting and it shakes him to his core.

'Well, that's the thing, Isaac, and it's why I came to Chandlebury in the first place. I'm pretty sure Reggie's dad is . . . you.'

'What? Are you joking?'

'Would I joke about something a serious as this? What do you take me for? I think you're the most likely person to be Reggie's father.'

'But . . . no! That's not possible . . . '

'Oh come on, don't try and wriggle out of it. The evidence is all there. I've tried to make excuses for you, but I can't do it any more. You need to be honest with me now.'

'Honest? I don't understand . . .'

'Neither do I. You don't seem like the sort of person

to leave someone in the lurch like that, but all the people I've spoken to since say you were most likely to be the one.'

'Polly, this is stupid. I really don't know what you're talking about.' Isaac rubs his eyes. Is this some sort of mad nightmare? He'll wake up in a minute, surely? But Polly hasn't finished.

'When I first arrived here, I was absolutely sure you must have known my sister was pregnant at the time when you were together at uni.'

'Together? I wasn't with anyone when I was in Leeds. Well, not in a baby-making kind of way.'

Isaac gestures to the sleeping baby, his mind whirling. He can't think straight. Why on earth would Polly think that *he* was anyone's dad? Chance would be a fine thing, he though bitterly.

Polly's eyes are narrowed now as she glares up at him, hands on hips. 'I've been doing my hardest to think of a logical reason for what you did, Isaac, ever since I came here and started getting to know you. I told myself you weren't the kind of man to do the dirty on Alice and the others must have been wrong, but . . .'

'Hang on a minute. Did you say *Alice*?'

'Of course I did. Who did you imagine I was talking about? You know very well what my sister's name is . . . was . . .' she corrected herself.

'But . . . but I've never heard you say her name.'

'You must have done.'

'No, I definitely didn't. I know you think I'm slow on

the uptake sometimes, but it's not that common a name. It would have rung a bell. Does my mum know where your sister was at uni?'

'I've tried not to mention it, but I guess I could have accidentally let it slip.' Polly stops for a moment, as if unsure. 'No, I'm sure she doesn't, she'd have asked more questions, wouldn't she? Anyway, all Alice's gang say you were involved with her. I can't believe you didn't know she'd died if you were such close friends.'

Isaac's mind flinches away from the time after his escape from Leeds. He'd cut himself off from every possible link with the place, even changed his email address and mobile number. There was nobody there he'd wanted to keep in touch with. Especially not Alice.

'The more I get to know you, the less you seem like a man who'd do such a thing to my sister, but if you *did* know she was pregnant, how could you leave her high and dry like that?' Polly says, her voice breaking. 'Have you any idea . . . any idea at all what that did to her?'

'But Alice was . . .'

'Alice was *what*?'

This is the moment when most people would have had the sense to shut up. Polly's voice is icy, but Isaac has never been able to read the signs. He stumbles on, and the words that pour out of his mouth have the effect of seeming to turn Polly to stone. When he grinds to a halt, breathless, she gives herself a little shake and turns away.

'Well, thank you for that, Isaac,' she says.

Isaac watches helplessly as Polly goes back into her room. 'Can't we just discuss this?' he says, as she's closing the door.

'No, we can't. I've heard more than enough for one day. Just give me some space tonight. Maybe tomorrow we can talk. But really, what else is there to say?'

Isaac is about to say he's sorry for making her look so sad but it's too late. It feels as if there's an awful lot more than a door between them now.

Chapter Forty

Watching Lucia drive off to face Des was one of the hardest things Tommy has ever had to do, and even now he can still feel the ache in his heart and the longing to tell her again how much he loves her. He knows deep down he couldn't have gone with her because this is something Lu needs to do alone. Maybe he should have insisted he at least went along part-way for the ride though, and then amused himself in Huddersfield for a few hours. She was bound to be all screwed up afterwards. He has a gut feeling that this soul searching isn't going to end well.

Torn between sadness that Lu and Des's long marriage might be over and a burning hope that this might mean there's a chance for him, Tommy thinks back to the moment when he knew he had to leave the household, even if just for a little while. Space is needed for all of them. He remembers scribbling the note to Lucia, checking the cat was fed and packing his knapsack as fast as he can.

Ten minutes later Tommy was striding down the road towards the village shop, ready for this next stage in his varied life. Having already made the necessary phone call to secure a bed for a few nights, he greeted Sandy, took the bunch of keys that was waiting for him and headed round the back of the building and up the flight of steep steps that hug the back of the house.

Now he's safe in his temporary nest, Tommy looks around as he sips his wine. At the top of the stairs is a small area sheltered by a stone balustrade, with just room for a single wicker chair and a small side table. A gnarled clematis winds its way around the trellis that shelters this tranquil spot and there are pots of herbs either side of the chair. He might eat out here tonight, when he can be bothered to fathom the workings of the microwave. Inside the room is a double bed, a tiny en suite shower room leading off it and a kitchenette spread out along one wall. It's enough for one person, and the thought of some time to himself is rather refreshing, even though he's already missing Lucia badly.

Being with Lu and her extended family has only served to underline what a self-centred existence Tommy has had up to now. He's not really needed to think about anyone but himself for years. If the mini heart attack hadn't brought him up short, he'd probably be still travelling around the world, making new friends and discovering fresh fields and pastures new, as his dad used to say when they set off on a journey.

Tommy's already unpacked his bag and stowed his few clothes and possessions away in the cupboard, arranging his toothbrush and toiletries on a shelf above the shower room sink. He stirs himself, making the effort to find his wallet so that he can go down to the shop to buy a few provisions and pay for his accommodation. One bottle of wine isn't going to go far.

'Okay, mate?' asks Sandy, as Tommy enters the deserted shop. 'Is everything up there that you need? I was just about to close.'

'It's fine, I'll be as quick as I can. I just need to get a basket and stock up.'

Tommy bustles around the shop, already nostalgic for the meals shared around the campsite with his new almost-family. In the end he selects a sliced white loaf, butter, marmalade, milk and a lasagne ready meal. He adds a pack of salad from the chilled counter and another bottle of red wine. Might as well settle in for the night. There's no TV in his room but for all he said to Peter, he's always been happier with a book.

Much later that evening, sitting outside again on his lone chair listening to the owls calling and sipping a final glass of wine, Tommy finally gets a text message from Lucia.

I'm on my way home, Tommy. All sorted with Des, but I need a few days to get my head round everything. He's staying up there. I'll fill you in soon. Lu x

Tommy reads the text several times and still can't decide if this is good news. At least Lucia will soon be safely back and he's not impinging on her hospitality while she grapples with whatever rubbish Des has thrown at her. He seethes with rage when he thinks of

311

his proxy, or more accurately poxy godson and how the man seems to have trampled on Lu's life without a thought for her welfare.

Gathering up his glass and the almost empty bottle, Tommy heads for his bed. His book, an ancient P.G. Wodehouse omnibus that travels with him everywhere, lies open on the duvet and the babble of voices from downstairs is comforting. Jeeves always cheers him up. He'll leave Lucia to her thoughts and try to get some sleep. Tomorrow he'll go for a long walk to clear his head. Loving someone this much is hard work.

Chapter Forty-One

Obeying Polly's instructions, Isaac avoids going anywhere near her for the rest of the evening. He goes for a long walk and when he gets back it's dark and her door is still closed. The dishwasher is on and the kettle is still warm so he assumes she's had an early supper and gone to bed at the same time as Reggie. The house is very quiet.

The next morning, the reason for the lack of noise is clear. When Polly still hasn't appeared and it's a while after Reggie's usual breakfast time, Isaac plucks up his courage and calls up the stairs to see if she'd like a cup of tea. When no reply comes, he goes up, knocks twice and then tentatively opens her door. His stomach flips when he sees to his horror that her bed is neatly made, Reggie's cot is devoid of toys and her enormous suitcase is missing from the top of the wardrobe.

Panicking, he calls her mobile time after time but only gets voicemail. Her calm words asking him to leave a message makes him want to cry. Why didn't he insist they talked things through right away and more to the point, where has she gone?

If Isaac felt strange without Lucia, he revises his

feelings when Polly and Reggie go. Now it's much worse, in fact it's heartbreakingly lonely. When he hears the jangle of the doorbell, he leaps to his feet, convinced Polly's back even though she still has her own key, but the woman on the doorstep is taller and more elegant than the familiar elfin figure of their lodger.

'Rowan,' he says. 'What are you doing here?'

She laughs. 'Thanks for the warm welcome, Isaac, I've called round on my way to work to make sure you and Polly are managing without Lu.'

'Well, you can come in if you like,' he says rather ungraciously, 'but it's just me – Polly isn't here. I'm guessing she must have packed and called a taxi to the train station while I was out last night but I think she only took the basics, so she must be coming back . . . mustn't she?'

Isaac opens the door wider and Rowan follows him into the kitchen, sniffing appreciatively when she smells toast. He gestures to the bread on the board and she nods.

'You're changing, Isaac,' Rowan says, sitting at the table. 'At one time you'd never have noticed I wanted some toast unless I grabbed yours off your plate and started eating it. Where's my friend gone at this time in the evening? I hope nothing's wrong with Reg?'

Isaac cuts two slices of bread and puts them in the toaster while he tries to decide what to say. 'She's fine, just not at home at the moment. Rowan . . . erm . . . how much do you know about Polly's background before she came here?' he says in the end.

She looks at him with her head on one side. 'Pretty much everything, I think,' she says. 'We had quite a lot of wine the last time we went out and she needed a shoulder to cry on. I know about her sister and Reg and so on. Why?'

Isaac is starting to feel better. The comforting smell of toast cooking and the presence of kind, practical Rowan are going a long way to bring him back from the edge of despair, but the thought of Polly out in the world away from her new almost-family is still making his stomach hurt. He waits for the toast to pop up and hands it to Rowan, passing butter and marmalade out of the fridge before answering.

'Yes, but *how much* about all that did she tell you?' Isaac says, sitting down opposite his guest.

She shrugs. They look at each other as they eat, and Isaac can see that she's unsure about breaking confidences, just as he is. They've reached an impasse.

'Look, let's have a cup of tea and compare notes,' Rowan says, when they can't spin out their breakfast any longer. 'I know we've both got Polly's welfare at heart so it can't hurt to talk about her in private if we promise it won't go any further.'

Isaac nods thankfully, and they've soon got their hands around big mugs of tea, waiting to see who's going to begin. Rowan clears her throat.

'Here goes. As far as I know, Polly has no children of her own. Reg is her sister's boy. His mum was only twenty-one when she died last summer, and he was

315

around a month old then. Polly's mother has had a bit of a breakdown from all the grief and stress and has gone away for a while, so Polly's been left holding the baby, literally. It's all very sad.'

Isaac can see how affected by the story Rowan is, but he has to find out if she's been told the rest. 'Do you know anything else about Polly's sister?' he asks. He can feel the tension in his shoulders and a headache starting to pulse over one eye.

Rowan gives him a long, hard look and clearly decides there's no point in avoiding the next part. 'Polly told me that her sister Alice was at uni in Leeds when she got pregnant with Reggie. At first, she kept it secret but when Polly and her mum made a surprise visit up there to see why they hadn't heard from her, Alice blurted it all out. She hadn't told anyone else, so they persuaded her to come home with them, because she obviously wasn't going to any lectures. She was living in a total mess of unwashed clothes and wasn't eating properly. And after that Alice came back with them too and stayed at home, so she could have the baby there.'

Rowan gets up to pour more tea for them both from Lucia's substantial red teapot. She puts a hand briefly on Isaac's shoulder before she sits down again and he finds himself, unusually, longing for her to hug him. Perhaps he really is changing?

'Polly and her mum thought Alice was coping. She was very quiet most of the time, but she adored Reggie and she cared for him well. The day she . . . she . . .'

Rowan's eyes are brimming with tears now and Isaac passes her a piece of kitchen roll and waits.

'Anyway, that day, Alice seemed her normal self – well, normal for Alice – so the other two thought they were safe to leave her for a while. You know what happened next, don't you?'

They are both silent for a few moments, as if paying some sort of tribute to the sad, dead girl. Then Rowan stirs herself.

'And the burning question is, who was Reggie's father? Polly thinks it's you, Isaac. You were up at Leeds at the same time before you dropped out. You and Alice were friends, weren't you? You were seeing each other. Polly came here to find you when her other investigations came to nothing. You're her last hope and I think she's been pinning everything on you being the dad.'

Isaac can't speak for a while. He swallows hard and remembers the night before when Polly threw these same accusations at him. He's still reeling.

Rowan covers his hand with hers and the warmth is deeply comforting. 'Is it true?' she asks gently.

He shakes his head, still speechless.

'You're definitely not Reggie's dad? How can you be sure?'

Isaac's face is burning now, and the headache has grown to epic proportions. He wonders if he's going to throw up. Hopefully not, he hates sick. Rowan presses his hand and waits.

'I know he isn't mine because I never slept with Alice. I've never slept with anyone,' he croaks.

There, it's out. The shame, the embarrassment, the echoes of Alice's sobs of rejection after he tried and failed. He's twenty-one years old and he's never done more than kiss a girl. He can't look at Rowan. She must be laughing at him too.

'But you and Alice *were* friends?' Rowan persists. She seems to be skipping over his shameful confession for some reason.

Isaac nods. 'I thought we were more than friends. I wanted us to be a proper couple. She let me kiss her and then . . . anyway, nothing happened.' He risks a glance at Rowan. She carries on, frowning.

'What I can't understand is why you didn't put two and two together when you realised Polly was from up north and had a sister called Alice. Didn't it ring a bell? I know it could have been a coincidence but surely . . .'

'Polly doesn't like to mention her sister by name, so I didn't pick up on who she was. I assumed it was because the whole thing was so painful, but maybe she was keeping the details secret until she'd sussed me out?' Isaac says, relieved to have a different angle to explore.

'And you never heard rumours about a student having committed suicide after you left Leeds?'

Isaac shakes his head. 'I made sure nobody could get in touch with me after I got home. I was . . . pretty messed up.'

He gazes into the distance, lost in thought. After a

moment he says 'Alice always referred to her big sister as 'Lark'. The had pet names for each other. They wrote each other long letters and she'd show me them sometimes, but Polly only signed with a picture of a little bird. Her pet name for Alice was 'Owl'. I forget why.'

'It doesn't matter,' says Rowan, waving a hand dismissively. 'but the thing is, if you're not Reggie's father, who is? Polly says she's discounted everyone else in the gang of students Alice hung around with.'

Rowan waits for Isaac to answer her question for what seems like a long time, sipping her third mug of tea and leafing through a magazine she's found on the table.

'You might as well tell me the whole thing, Isaac,' she says eventually, when the silence is getting oppressive. 'You'll feel better if you do.'

'I doubt it. Okay then, if you must know, Polly probably went away because I hurt her feelings. I'm good at that,' Isaac adds, 'I don't have a stop button when I'm saying what I think.'

'I've noticed,' Rowan says drily, 'but that can sometimes be a good thing. It cuts out misunderstandings at least.'

Isaac considers this angle. 'Not this time. I told her too much about Alice.'

'Go on, don't leave me in suspense.'

'It's hard to explain. Alice was unpredictable. It wasn't just the mood swings; she got these weird obsessions about people. Her friendships never lasted long. She put people off by being so . . . so hard to get close to.'

'She was unfriendly?'

'No, it was the opposite. She was too intense. She'd fall for people in a big way, both men and women, and try really hard to make them love her. Then, if they did, she'd somehow manage to push them away.'

Isaac cringes as he remembers that last evening at the gig on campus, when he'd made one final attempt to get close to Alice, to put right the damage he'd done to her fragile ego. He'd waited until there was enough noise going on to mask what he wanted to say, and then told her he loved her, but as a friend. She'd not been able to hear him properly, so he'd bellowed out the words again, just at the moment when the band fell silent. In the split second before applause began, Isaac's voice rang out clearly across the packed room.

'It doesn't matter if we never get naked together,' he'd shouted, 'I bloody love you.'

Stunned by the roar of incredulous laughter from the crowd that followed this revelation, Isaac ran full pelt down the corridor and out into the open area near his halls. He packed his few belongings in minutes and was on his way to the train station before anyone had noticed the trail of odd socks and papers he left behind along the corridor.

'That sounds like a nightmare,' says Rowan grimly. 'What did you do next?'

'Came home. Dad wasn't impressed but Mum understood, I think. I only went to uni in the first place because Mum and Dad were so desperate to see me do well. I'm much happier now, especially with the new project taking off.'

Rowan gets up and takes the empty mugs to the sink. 'I've got to go in a minute,' she says, 'and we haven't even nearly finished. Who do *you* think the father is?'

This is a difficult one. Isaac still doesn't want to badmouth Alice but it's time for honesty at last. 'If it wasn't a student, I reckon it could be any one of three men. Alice was very good at covering her tracks, so her . . . well, her lovers, I guess, didn't find out about each other.'

'Really? I didn't get the impression she was that sort of girl from Polly.'

'She wasn't, but Alice *was* clever at being what other people wanted her to be, chameleon-like. I don't think she had any idea of the trouble she could cause. She just needed to be liked.'

'Right. Well, go on.'

He shudders. It still seems unbelievable that Alice has gone for good, but the bare facts need airing now. 'One of her men was a senior lecturer who was married with four children, another was the university bursar. He was a nasty piece of work and I think he might even have been blackmailing her in a half-hearted sort of way. She used to get weed for him. And the last possibility was the son of another tutor and he was only fifteen.'

'Wow. Alice certainly knew how to cast her net wide. No wonder Polly couldn't find the right one. Please tell me you didn't tell her all this?'

Isaac can feel himself blushing.

'You did, didn't you? Oh, man – why?'

'She asked me. And I didn't want her to carry on thinking I'd let her sister down by leaving her pregnant. I'd never do that. Actually . . . I'd love to be Reggie's dad. I think Polly might have gone back to her mum's house. I know it's in a village not far from Sheffield but I haven't got her address.'

'Have you phoned her?'

'Yes. No answer.'

Rowan looks as if she doesn't know whether to shake or hug him. Luckily, she goes for the hug, and Isaac relaxes into it, wondering why he's resisted this basic human comfort for so long.

'Right, I must go. Phone her again now. I'll call back later to see if you've heard anything and I'll ring her myself too. Look, I'll get out of your way. I need to get to work.'

Isaac nods. He wishes she didn't have to leave. The thought of another day without Polly is hideous. Isaac knows without the shadow of a doubt that he won't be able to even begin to relax until Polly's safely home with him for good.

Chapter Forty-Two

Lu has just stopped on her way home at the motorway services to search out some strong black coffee and a pastry when her phone starts to shrill. The caller display says *Isaac*. Instinct tells her this isn't going to be good news.

'What's the matter, love?' she asks, unclipping her seat belt and flexing tired shoulders.

'It's Polly. She's gone.'

'Gone where? Isaac, what's happened?'

'We had a row. She thinks I'm Reggie's dad.'

'*What?*'

There's a short silence. Lucia's head reels. Maybe she misheard him.

'I beg your pardon, Isaac? Did you say . . .'

'She thinks I'm Reggie's dad,' Isaac repeats more loudly. 'Mum, when are you coming home?'

'As soon as possible. But Isaac, is it true? Are you his father? Why didn't you tell me before?'

'She's got it wrong. Mum, please come back.'

'I'm already on the way. I should be there in about an hour, traffic permitting. Stay put and I'll be as quick as I can.'

'Drive carefully, Mum, please.'

Isaac's voice is shaky and he's disconnected before Lu has chance to say goodbye. She gets out of the van and heads for the main building. There's no time for coffee and her appetite's completely gone but she needs a loo stop and a leg stretch before she does the last lap.

Washing her hands five minutes later, Lu's tired brain begins to process what Isaac has just told her at last. Polly thinks her son is Reggie's dad? That can't be right. Or can it? Maybe he's just in denial. How can Isaac be expected to cope with this sort of crisis? He's only just beginning to get his life on track. But a grandson? She's always longed for her lovely boy to find someone to have a family with and it's seemed like an impossible dream.

This means that Isaac must have had a relationship with the elusive Alice when he was in Leeds. How did Lu never know about this? She recalls how withdrawn her son was when he returned home for good, so soon after his triumphant exit to join a course that ticked every box for him. And Reggie . . . as Lu thinks about the adorable little boy her heart swells with love. Could he actually be Isaac's son?

The tumble of thoughts rolls around Lu's brain as she sets off again, the radio playing classical music to settle her rising panic. Her mind is still reeling at the thought that Polly's sister must have been at uni in Leeds with Isaac. For some reason she's always imagined Alice to have fled the nest to somewhere further North. The relationship between Isaac and Alice has got to have been serious if that's the case because Isaac doesn't do trivial. And if so, why has he never mentioned her? She feels her heart begin to race alarmingly and does her best to push the worst of the worry to one side so she can concentrate on the busy motorway.

The traffic isn't too bad, and in less than an hour Lucia is driving past the post office at a crawl and turning into the lane leading to Jasmine Terrace. Home. It's such a comforting word, and Lu says it to herself several times. Now all she needs to do is sort out Isaac's issues and find Polly. She makes a rueful face at herself in the mirror as she pulls onto the drive. Simple? Not so much.

'Isaac? I'm home,' she yells, carrying Nigel's basket into the kitchen and decanting him next to a very surprised Petunia.

Her son comes thundering down the stairs two at a time. 'Can I borrow the van?' he gasps.

Nigel frolics around Isaac's ankles as he holds his hand out hopefully for the keys to the van. 'Hang on a minute,' Lu says, catching hold of her son's arm. 'Let's just calm down. Why do you want it so urgently and where are you planning to go?'

'I'm off to track Polly down,' Isaac says. 'I know the name of the village where she's staying but she never gave me the full address. I'm going to find her whether she wants me to or not.'

Lu's head's spinning now. 'But . . . but . . . if she doesn't want to see you . . . Is it because you've talked about you being Reggie's father?'

'I'm not his dad, and she knows that now. I bloody wish I was though.'

A wave of sadness washes over Lucia. So she isn't Reggie's grandmother after all. 'But . . . but if it's not you, who is it?'

'We still don't know. It doesn't matter really. I want to help look after him and watch him grow up. I don't care who his biological father is. I just want me, Polly and Reggie to have chance to be a proper family.'

Lucia takes a deep breath, swallowing her disappointment. 'That's wonderful, love. So I'll still get to be the grandma? I love Reggie anyway, it makes no difference to me if he's yours or not.'

He sighs. 'Look Mum, I haven't got time to talk about this now. I'm going to find Polly's village. It can't be that big and someone must know who she is, surely. I don't care if she wants to see me or not, we need to clear the air. I love her.'

Isaac says this with such an air of wonder and triumph that Lu hasn't the heart to discourage him, and maybe he's right. If she'd waited until Des was ready to discuss their marriage she'd still be sitting on the sofa feeling sorry for herself. At least now she knows what the next steps are.

'You'll need to fill up with diesel again and check the tyres and water and so on. Go and do that while I make you some food to take with you.'

'No need, I've just eaten, I don't want to waste any time. I can always stop on the M1.'

Lu is lost for words. Isaac has always scorned fast food restaurants on motorways. He must be desperate to get on his way. She fetches her luggage from the van as Isaac dashes around getting ready, and within fifteen minutes he's ready for off, a small bag packed and ready on the passenger seat. He comes back into the kitchen to say goodbye.

'You're absolutely sure this is the right thing to do?' Lu says, putting her hands on Isaac's shoulders to make sure he's listening.

'It's got to be right. I can't live without Polly. Stop trying to hold me up. It's time I stood on my own feet. More than time.'

Isaac pulls away but at the last moment, comes back and hugs Lu. 'Sorry, Mum,' he mumbles. 'I'm just scared Polly won't want to see me after all this. I didn't mean what I said. Well, I did actually,' he adds, his innate honesty battling with the desire to put things right.

'Not to worry,' says Lu rather stiffly, but she hugs him back and then gives him a gentle push towards the van. 'Bring Polly back as soon as you can. I miss her already, and Reggie too.'

Lu watches Isaac drive away, with very mixed feelings.

'Will he be safe?' she whispers. It's a question she and Des have asked each other many times over the years, every time Isaac has tried something new. It's odd to be saying it to herself. Her eyes are full of tears and there's a lump in her throat. Des isn't hers now. She hasn't had time to think how she feels about that, but one thing's for sure. Even a husband who doesn't want her anymore would be better than this echoing, empty house today.

Chapter Forty-Three

The next few hours are a challenge for Lucia. Torn between worry about Isaac and a strange, lost feeling when she thinks of Tommy, she tries desperately to find something to occupy both her mind and her restless body, but nothing holds her attention for long.

Finally, after tidying most of the house in a quick-fix kind of way, she decides to put some peaceful music on and tackle a job that's been waiting for her for years. The old blanket chest in the corner of the bedroom Lu has shared with Des for so long has always been a dumping ground for anything they can't bear to part with that's small enough to fit in there. The wicker chest belonged to Lucia's grandmother, who rather grandly called it her ottoman. It's been painted many times over the years, and now is a faded apple green with a padded lid, worn in places and covered with a chintzy fabric in green and gold.

Lucia kneels beside the ottoman and puts her hand on the lid. She can almost see her grandmother folding freshly laundered and aired sheets and pillowcases to stow away in it. The old lady had been proud that this was a genuine Lloyd Loom piece of furniture.

'You'll take good care of this when I'm gone, won't you m'dear?' she'd said several times, and Lu happily agreed. There's a chair to match and a small wicker bedside cabinet and they're probably the most precious items in the house to Lucia. She opens the lid and stares at the jumbled contents in dismay. Has she taken on too much when she's feeling so wobbly? But at least this will keep her occupied for hours, and then she'll be tired enough for a long bath and something comforting to eat, like poached eggs on toast or a bacon sandwich.

The thought of food encourages her and Lucia begins to carefully take out the contents of the blanket box, layer by layer. To the background music of Classic FM, she methodically spreads everything on the bedroom floor in heaps, trying to put them roughly in categories. There are lots of Isaac's early drawings, mostly of birds or cars, all signed with his signature flourish. Even as a small boy, he'd loved to write his own name, making eyes out of each lower case letter A, and giving them long eyelashes. The C at the end had become a half moon with a smiling face, the S was a snake and the initial letter always had a tiny bird perched on top.

Lucia smiles to herself as she remembers the chubby little boy who'd never been happier than when he had the kitchen table to himself to paint or draw. Des had hated to come home from work to a mess so she'd always tried to make everywhere look spick and span by tea time, but often this had resulted in an epic tantrum from Isaac, stopped mid flow in creating another of his masterpieces.

The next heap mainly consists of small items of clothing that she's not been able to part with. Isaac's first shoes, scuffed and shabby, a tiny knitted jumper which was one of Lucia's mother's few efforts to be a good grandma, and sundry other bits and bobs from Isaac's childhood.

Lucia moves on to toys and books next. She's always been fairly good and passing these on when they're not needed anymore but one or two treasures were too precious to lose. She places the battered copy of Maeterlinck's *Bluebird* on her bed so that it can be ready for when . . . if Reggie comes home. It's the board book version, much shortened, and it's held together with sticky tape now, but Reggie will like looking at the pictures. Lucia thinks about the baby, somewhere with Polly, maybe confused about what's going on. Is he old enough to know? He'll not mind his routine being changed after coping with all the travelling so well, but surely he'll miss the place that must feel like home in some part of his small psyche? Anger fills her mind when Lucia thinks back to how irritated Des had been to have Polly and Reggie around the house. Well, she thinks savagely, he won't need to worry about that now.

The last pile to be created is made up entirely of letters and postcards. When it comes to correspondence, Des is as much of a hoarder as Lucia, and some of these go back to the early days of her marriage. Sighing, Lucia decides to rationalise all this. She gets up rather creakily after having been crouched on the floor for so long, and goes into the tiny spare bedroom where she remembers storing several flat-packed boxes and some parcel tape, just in case Isaac should ever want to move out. Des had encouraged this plan, but his nagging seemed to have made Isaac dig his heels in even more.

When the boxes are constructed, Lucia piles all the toys and children's books into one for Reggie, taking it into what she hopes will still be Polly's room. She packs the little clothes into another, along with the dress she wore for her first date with Des. Then, biting her lip, she takes the tattered garment out again and throws it across the room into the bin. Why should she keep it? Des doesn't want her anymore, and he hadn't even liked the dress much. He said red wasn't her colour.

Last of all, Isaac's artwork goes into a third box. It can go in the loft when she's showed it him. It can't be thrown away. This leaves the tottering pile of letters, which Lucia bundles into a laundry basket and carries downstairs.

After a longed-for hot bath and some necessary comfort food, Lucia, snug in her dressing gown, lights a fire in the living room grate. The basket of letters is beside her as she settles down to watch the flickering flames. She gets up once more to makes sure it's burning properly and to fetch herself a large glass of chilled white wine from the fridge. The compass is in its case by her side and she gets it out. There's no advice needed but its presence is comforting. Then she gets started on what she knows will be an emotional journey. It's got to be done, though. This is the first step towards her future.

Chapter Forty-Four

To begin with, Isaac listens to his holiday playlist as he drives, but it brings back too many echoes of the road trip with the others and he can't bear the thought that they might never do it again.

What if Polly won't see him when he gets to Yorkshire? More to the point, what if Isaac can't actually find her? Since she's been away, he's realised how much she and Reg make the house come to life. He can't imagine being without her permanently. There has to be a way to persuade her to come home. Surely her mum's house will be easy to locate.

Three hours later, Isaac wonders what sort of deluded plan this was. He's eventually found the place where Polly said she used to live. The trouble is, when you get over the brow of the hill, the village spreads out all around. It's not the hamlet he expected. There are loads of houses here, and Polly isn't answering her phone so he can't ask her for help.

He tries the shops first. It's quite similar to Chandlebury in that way. There's a post office that's closed for the day, a butcher, also closed, and a general store where the owner has gone out and the girl behind the counter hasn't a clue what Isaac's talking about.

The charity shop is locked and has a note on the door saying it won't be open until tomorrow morning and the little craft store is no use either – they're just about to shut for the night and they haven't heard of Polly. She told Isaac her surname is Smith, and it occurs to him with a sickening jolt that of course this isn't her real name. Anybody else would have twigged this long ago. He must be even more gullible than he thought. Isaac never knew Alice's last name or home address. She liked to be mysterious.

A memory comes back suddenly, one of hearing Polly's sister telling someone who asked her that she didn't believe in giving out personal details to all and sundry. When the person persisted, she just laughed and said, 'Call me Alice Enigma if I've got to have a handle.' Now it's Polly who's the enigma. Isaac flops down on a bench outside the pub on the main street, exhausted. There's nobody around. They must be all cosying up inside their cottages cooking their dinners and chatting with their families. A wave of homesickness overwhelms him as his stomach rumbles. He almost wishes he hadn't come.

As he ponders his next move, he hears footsteps coming from the direction of the charity shop and a familiar voice says, 'Isaac?'

She's there in front of him, as beautiful as ever, carrying Reggie on her hip. Isaac jumps to his feet, unable to stop himself hugging them both. He can feel the tension in Polly's shoulders but Reggie gurgles with delight and reaches up high to pat Isaac's hair with both chubby little hands.

Polly steps back and looks at him more closely. 'Whatever are you doing here?' she asks.

'I've come to bring you home,' Isaac says simply, and she gazes up at him, looking like a lost little girl.

'This is the nearest thing I've got to a home,' she says, gesturing to the village street. 'Although to be honest it doesn't feel much like it these days. I don't live with you, Isaac. I was only the lodger.'

'You were *so* not only the lodger,' he says. '*Are* so not,' he adds, even more ungrammatically. 'Not just the lodger, I mean. Not only.'

'What?' Reggie's wriggling now, holding out his arms, and Isaac can see Polly's finding it hard to concentrate. It doesn't help that he's talking gibberish. He makes another attempt, desperate to keep her with him.

'I'm trying to say you belong with us now. Look, can't we go somewhere to talk?'

She sighs and turns away to walk down the street. 'Come on then, the house is only a few doors away from here. It's a bit of a mess. Reggie's been grizzling a lot since I came here. I can hardly get anything done at the moment.'

'Perhaps he misses us? We miss him. And you, of course.'

She doesn't answer this. They've reached a house in the middle of a row of five solid, stone cottages that look as if they were built to last forever. Polly gives Reg to Isaac and unlocks the door. He breathes in the little boy's adorable, familiar smell, a combination of baby shampoo and toast and Marmite, which he loves. Isaac's eyes are misty as Reggie snuggles into his shoulder.

Isaac follows Polly into the tiny front room but doesn't offer to give Reggie back to her. The baby sits on his knee on the sofa and claps his hands, saying *Uzzucuzzucuzzuc* over and over again, like a small engine trying to start. It's the nearest he ever got to Isaac's name and a feeling of pride almost chokes him.

'Why didn't you answer my calls?' Isaac bursts out, when Polly sits down opposite them. 'I was so worried about you.'

'I dropped my phone in Reg's bath and it's never recovered,' she says, pulling a face. 'I can't afford a new one at the moment. Anyway, I don't think we've got much to say to each other.'

'Because of what I said about Alice?'

She flinches at the name. 'You obviously didn't trust her. And you seemed to think she was completely immoral.'

'She . . . wasn't easy to trust,' Isaac says, knowing that this transparency is as unwelcome as it's ever been. He can't lie about this though, it's too important. 'And it was more that she was *amoral*.'

'Oh, words. What difference does it make? You made your point.'

'I can't explain it any more clearly than that. You must know yourself that your sister was complicated. She didn't live by the same rules as everyone else, somehow.'

Isaac falls silent as he considers Alice, trying to find a way of expressing his misgivings about her. She was a fey kind of person, as unlike Polly as you could possibly imagine. It's hard to believe they came from the same mother.

Polly's crying now, wiping away the tears as they fall with the back of her hand. Isaac doesn't know whether to put Reg down to try and comfort her but he's clinging on tightly and starting to whimper himself.

'I've never talked to anyone about how Alice was,' Polly says, between sobs. 'Sometimes I hated her for being so flaky, but I loved her too. Is that possible?'

Isaac nods. 'I felt the same for a little while,' he says slowly, feeling his way through a minefield of hurtful words, 'but the love didn't last. It was just a silly infatuation. Looking back, I think she treated her friends badly without really meaning to, but it was painful when it happened to me and I had very mixed feelings about her by the time I left. People have to deserve to be loved, don't they?'

She seems to be calming down a little bit as she listens. 'Do they?'

'Yes. *You* deserve it because you're generous and thoughtful and funny and beautiful inside and out.'

He runs out of steam, face burning. If only he didn't blush so easily. It's so uncool. Isaac's never said anything like this to anyone. Polly's wonderful green eyes are shining now, and her cheeks are pink.

'You forgot clever,' she says.

'Oh, I'm sorry . . .'

'I'm joking! Isaac . . . those are lovely things to say.

But I'm not the person you think I am. I've done some awful things . . .'

'I don't care what you have or haven't done in the past. You're amazing. I love you for what you are *now*.'

There, it's out at last, but Polly shakes her head. 'Isaac, when you say things like that that, it's the best feeling in the world but I can't let you go on thinking I'm amazing. You'll probably change your mind if you really get to know me.'

'That's where you're wrong. Anyway, you've never shown any signs of not accepting *me* for what I am.'

'What do you mean?'

'Polly, I know I don't say the word out loud much, or at least I haven't up to now, but you must have realised I'm Autistic. Do you even know what that really means?'

'Of course I do. I'm not daft. It means you're clever, funny, loving, quirky and very creative.'

'Yeah?'

'Absolutely. Look at the game you've made. Look at how well you got on with everyone on our trip. Peter thinks you're great. He told me he loved spending time with you because you have a unique view of everything. You're interesting. Tommy said the same.'

'Really?'

'Yes, really. And you've got the most fantastic memory. Not to mention the fact that you're never afraid to say what you think.'

It takes Isaac a moment for this to sink in. He's slightly unsettled to realise that the others were discussing him but the fact that they were saying good things easily balances any edgy feelings he might have had. He resolves to think about this more when he's not so preoccupied and turns his attention back to Polly.

'So come on, Pol, tell me what it is that's so bad about you. You'll feel better if you get it off your chest.' Isaac likes this phrase. He used to have a teacher who trotted it out when he was all wound up after the others had been mean at playtime and he'd lost his temper.

Polly doesn't answer immediately but Isaac tells himself to be patient. He feels Reggie relaxing in his arms and when he looks down, the little boy has fallen fast asleep, thumb in his mouth and clutching a handful of Isaac's t-shirt.

'Look, I can't move now or I'll wake him up so you might as well make the most of your chance to tell me your darkest secrets,' Isaac says. 'Who have you murdered?' Polly doesn't smile back. Right. Serious stuff then. Isaac waits again.

'Actually, I murdered Alice's tropical fish,' Polly says.

There's an awkward silence. He wasn't expecting this. 'Go on.'

She heaves a huge sigh. 'I'm going to have to tell you the whole thing, aren't I?' Isaac nods, afraid to say more in case he breaks the flow.

'It was after she left me to be cut off by the tide and I almost drowned,' Polly says, matter-of-factly. Seeing Isaac's expression, she adds 'Oh, but I haven't told you about that, have I?'

'Well, no, you haven't, but why would you? She left you on purpose, I'm guessing?'

'Who knows? I thought so at the time but she was very forgetful, so the generous view might be that she just wandered off and got distracted. We were on holiday. I fell asleep in the sunshine; I was thirteen and she was eight. We'd been exploring a cove somewhere in Cornwall and we'd walked a long way. I had hay fever at the time and my eyes were so heavy that I closed them for a minute and the next thing I knew, the tide had come right in and I was trapped. Alice had gone. I tried to climb the cliff, it wasn't too high, but it was crumbly, and I fell and sprained my ankle.'

The horror of that long-ago day is on Polly's face again now, and Isaac starts to speak, horrified at the image this conjures up, but Polly holds up a hand.

'No, let me finish. Eventually I managed to clamber over the steep rocks into the next cove but by that time the water was up to my knees. I was crying so hard I didn't see Alice and Mum running towards me. Mum had eventually managed to get Alice to tell her where I might be.'

'I blamed her totally for that. So, the worst part is, I did everything could to get my own back on Alice, in sneaky little ways. And her precious fish – I didn't mean to kill the poor little things. I turned up the thermostat on their tank just to scare her, and I wrote her a note to say what I'd done but she didn't find it, and I went out with my friends and forgot all about it. They . . . they boiled, Isaac.'

'Oh no. That's awful.'

'Yes. It was then I became a vegetarian. I never forgave myself.'

The silence between them when Polly stops talking stretches for far too long. Isaac can't think how to get past this barrier. Eventually, he says 'Well, that's in no way stopped me loving you, Pol. You'll have to try harder if you want to get rid of me. What have you done that's really bad?'

Polly laughs, and with that joyful sound some of the tension in the room evaporates. She stands up and reaches for Reggie. 'You're a glutton for punishment, Isaac. My nan used to say that.'

'I am where you're concerned, and I could say the same about you. We need each other. I know for sure we do.'

She smiles at him, and the relief on her face shows how much this memory has been bugging her. Maybe sharing it has gone some way to exorcising it, Isaac thinks hopefully. Her next words take him completely by surprise though.

'Are you staying tonight?'

Does she mean what Isaac think she means? He's half terrified, half confused. 'In the van, do you mean?'

'No. Here. With me. Because if you are, we need to bathe this grubby little scrap, give him his supper and get him into bed. Then we can make a curry. If you run up the road to the shop you can get a bottle of wine. How does that sound? And if you stay, we can talk more.'

Isaac is outside and jogging up the road before she can change her mind. The van's parked some way up the street so he drives it back down when he's picked a chilled bottle of Sauvignon Blanc from the shop and pulls up right outside Polly's door. Armed with his overnight bag and the wine, he waits to be let back in, heart banging against his rib cage as if he's run a marathon.

Back in the kitchen much later, with dinner out of the way and Reggie sleeping upstairs, Isaac blurts out the request he's been formulating since he left the house earlier.

'Polly, do you think we could stay up here together for a few days?' he says. 'I want to take you both back home with me really soon, but I reckon it'd be cool to have a bit of time up here, just us three? What do you think?'

'That sounds lovely. I can show you round all my old haunts. But now . . .' She yawns and stretches her arms out. 'I'm really tired, aren't you?'

Isaac's mouth is dry as Polly hangs the tea towel over the oven door and switches off the kitchen light.

'Are you ready for bed?' she says. Her voice shakes slightly.

Suddenly more aware of another person's feelings than he's ever been in his life, Isaac realizes that Polly is as scared as he is. Why could that be? She must have had lots of lovers, surely? She seems so confident most of the time.

His legs are shaking now but he reaches where she's

standing by the open door, one hand on the frame as if she needs its support. 'I'm as ready as I'll ever be,' he says. 'But I'm not sure if you are?'

Polly's smile is nervous. 'Isaac . . . I'm not very good at all this.'

'All this what?' Now he's really lost.

'You know what I mean. Oh, maybe you don't. I haven't been to bed with many people. Only two, actually. And neither of them seemed very keen on me afterwards. I don't think I'm cut out for rolling around naked. I don't really like my body much.'

'But Poll . . . you're so pretty . . . you've got a stunning body. Not that I've noticed . . . I mean . . .'

She laughs, and some of the tension leaves her face. 'Would you mind if we just went to bed and cuddled this time? I'm great at cuddling, if I say so myself.'

'Absolutely. That suits me fine. I'm sure we can manage that very nicely. And if later on we decide to see how the rest of it goes, we can always change the plan.'

They smile at each other and she moves into Isaac's arms as if she belongs there. He kisses her, and kisses her, and kisses her. In his head they're back on the beach at Pengelly, with the sound of the crashing waves in the background and not a care in the world.

When they come up for air, Polly takes Isaac's hand and leads him up the stairs. Before many minutes have gone by, they find that cuddling is just fine, but the rest of it turns out to be even better.

Chapter Forty-Five

Isaac, Polly and Reg arrive back in Chandlebury at lunchtime four days later and roll onto the drive with a familiar crunch of gravel just as Tommy approaches the house from the other direction carrying his faithful old knapsack.

'Welcome home,' Tommy says, helping Polly out of the van and reaching for the baby. 'I hope Lucia's in.'

'Where have you been?' Isaac asks.

'I told you, didn't I? Decided to stay in a room over the shop for a few days.'

'Did you? Why?' Isaac frowns at this idea but Tommy just shrugs and unlocks the front door. They go into the hall, but the only voices that can be heard are coming from the back of the house. They follow the noise and find Lucia and Peter in the garden trying to put together what looks like a new swinging seat. Nigel is running around barking, chasing his tail, and Petula is lying in a patch of sunshine washing her face with a paw.

'Isaac!' Lucia yells when she spots Isaac. 'Hooray, you've just come at the right time. And Polly and Reg too. Oh, Tommy . . . I wasn't expecting you until later, but I guess you can help us.'

'I can go back to Sandy's again if I'm in the way,' Tommy says, picking up his knapsack from the floor and turning to leave. He's never felt awkward with Lucia before, but now he finds he can hardly meet her gaze. The phone call to ask if he could come round just for today so they could have a good chat seemed to surprise her, but she'd agreed to his offer of cooking dinner for them both this evening and his bag is full of everything he needs to make the best cottage pie in the world. Now he's going to have to stretch the ingredients to feed not only his old mate Peter, who surely should have been railroading around Italy by now, but also a veggie version for the others.

Lucia stops what she's doing and smiles at him at last. 'Don't be silly, Tommy, it's fine. I'm sure one of you will be able to get this thing sorted. Peter's had it delivered for us from the garden centre this morning. The old one collapsed. I think there's something wrong with the instructions though.'

'Hello, Pete, great to see you again. I thought you were setting off on another adventure?' says Tommy, through gritted teeth.

'Yes, I'm still going away, but the dates were changed. I'm travelling next week instead. The holiday I picked was under-booked so they've combined it with the next one. A tour of Italy by train. I can't wait! Pompeii again after all these years, Sorrento, Naples and beyond.'

Peter shakes Tommy's hand warmly and kisses Polly on both cheeks, tweaking Reg's nose and making him chuckle. He turns to Isaac and envelops him in an unexpected bear hug, then Lucia takes over to do the rounds of hugs and kisses, avoiding getting too close to Tommy, to his disappointment.

'Lucia has very kindly offered me the spare bedroom and the camp bed until I go away,' says Peter. 'My apartment won't be ready until I get back.'

'Oh. That's nice,' says Tommy. He's beginning to get a headache, something that almost never happens unless he's really stressed.

Lucia and Peter abandon the random pieces of seat for now and go into the kitchen, where Polly produces a large tin full to the brim with cherry scones.

'Isaac made them,' she says proudly, 'from my mum's favourite recipe.'

'Polly's taught me lots of things.' As soon as the words are out of Isaac's mouth he blushes scarlet but luckily Lucia is busy finding jam, butter and so on.

Tommy watches as Polly puts a hand on Isaac's shoulder and gives it what looks like an encouraging squeeze.

'Mum, me and Polly . . . Polly and I . . . we . . .' Isaac falters.

Polly steps in, squaring her shoulders. 'Lu, we were wondering if Reg and I could live here on a permanent basis from now on? I could share Isaac's room and Reggie could move to the box room. He needs his own space now. I'm always accidentally waking him up. We'd pay more rent, of course. What do you think?'

'Of course you can, love, and Peter can have your old room for now. Are you two . . . I mean . . .'

Tommy sighs. All this shilly-shallying is getting on his nerves and his head is pounding now. 'It looks like they're an item, Lu,' he says. 'Which in my book is excellent news. Congratulations to both of you.'

Isaac's still quite pink in the face and is clearly uncomfortable that everyone is looking at him fondly. He raises his mug of tea as a distraction but Tommy hasn't finished speaking

'I was trying to decide whether to go down to Pengelly for a few weeks and visit my old friend Angelina,' Tommy says, looking Lucia straight in the eye. 'And now I've made up my mind.'

'You're not really going to stay with Angelina, are you?' asks Lucia. Tommy's heartened to see that she looks rattled. 'I'm not sure that's a good idea. She's still very attached to you, you know.'

'I'd go along with that advice, my friend.' Peter nods. 'She's a charming lady, but rather . . . well . . . alarming?'

Polly grins. 'You'd never keep up with the gin intake, Tommy. Don't go, we'd all miss you.' Isaac says nothing but leans forward and pats Tommy's arm.

Tommy laughs, suddenly feeling a weight lifting from his shoulders. Four people he cares about are making the effort to think about his future. It feels like a turning point.

'Okay, this is my news,' he says. 'I've put a deposit down on a narrow boat and I'm going to have a permanent mooring next to the Chandlery. It means I can go travelling whenever I like and still live in the village the rest of the time.'

'Really? That's great!' Polly is beaming now and Tommy carries on, encouraged.

'And I've been making some enquiries about joining the local driving volunteers. You know, the social car scheme? They take people to and from hospital appointments and shopping and suchlike? Sandy told me all about it. He's been part of the gang for years in his spare time.'

'But you haven't even got a car, Tommy,' Lucia says, frowning.

'Ah, there is that. I wondered if we could maybe buy some sort of vehicle between us, for us all to share? Maybe we'll go somewhere together again?'

'Sounds great. I'm not getting rid of the van but it isn't easy to park when you're at the supermarket. And I'm getting itchy feet again too. I'm planning another trip myself soon,' Lucia tells Isaac. 'So you and Polly and Reg will have the place to yourselves for a little while. Do you think you'll be okay without us?'

Isaac looks at Polly and they smile. 'Oh yes,' Isaac says. 'I'm pretty sure we can cope with that.'

Chapter Forty-Six

Early the following morning, Lucia takes her first coffee of the day out to the garden with the compass in its case and sits on the brand new swinging seat in the sunshine. It hadn't taken Polly and Isaac long to put it together while Tommy made two kinds of cottage pie and Peter entertained Reggie with a range of animal noises and a few books. Lucia had felt a bit useless for a while but then realised that this was her chance to re-read the letter that had preoccupied her since the great sorting out of the blanket chest.

Now, with the letter safely in the pocket of her jeans, she has time to give it even more thought. Most of the contents of the laundry basket ended up in the fire. The little notes through the years from Isaac had been saved and a few postcards from her grandparents dating from their travelling days, but the rest had been burned without a second glance. Apart from this one, that is.

Lucia checks that nobody else is about. Peter must still be fast asleep after the late night they'd all had, and no sounds have filtered down from Polly's room so far today. Reggie hasn't moved into the box room yet. Polly and Isaac are planning to decorate it first and then Polly

350

is going to paint a Bluebird of Happiness mural all along one wall. Lucia feels a ripple of joy at the thought of the old house being spruced up. She's sure when Polly gets the bit between her teeth she'll galvanise Isaac into carrying on right through all the bedrooms. And about time too. Meanwhile, Lu plans to begin downstairs. Decorating has never been her strong point but she's sure she can do it if she tries.

The compass is on her knee now and she tries to relax into her usual companionship with it. What lies in store? She thinks about Tommy, and the buzz of excitement is immediate, like the first gulp of an ice cold gin and tonic, the lemon giving it a sharp, enervating zing. The needles are moving. Lucia knows where the barometer one will end up. It's no surprise to see it settle on *change*.

The compass needle wavers for a while, spinning lazily, but never really rests on any direction. What can it mean? Suddenly, she realises that she doesn't care. It's time to make up her mind about the next steps, without constantly needing affirmation that she's right. The compass has been a crutch; a necessary comfort an support at a very tough time. Now she must begin to work out a way forward under her own steam.

Getting the letter out of her pocket, Lucia unfolds it and begins to read it again. She knows the sender so well that his voice comes through the words, making it feel as if Tommy is actually there in the garden with her.

Dear Des,

I use the term dear *for want of a better one because as I'm writing this, you don't feel particularly dear to me, and that's sad. We've always been friends, haven't we? But what you told me yesterday and your aggressive response to what I said in return, have made me think I don't really understand you at all.*

Hopefully you've thought more about this in the cold light of day now. Can you honestly say that marrying the lovely Lucia is the right thing to do? Des, that girl is more vulnerable than anyone I've ever known. She's still grieving for her little brother and you're not helping by taking her away from her parents when they all need to get through this together. I'm not daft, I'm aware Lucia's mum and dad aren't an easy couple to like but they're all she's got, and I'm worried that you're driving a wedge between the three of them.

The other thing is that in my opinion, if Lu is going to fly the nest, she needs to see something of the world before you tie her down to marriage and children. Des, you hate travelling, you always have. You're not the one for her. Let her go now. She's only 17 and getting married next year as you plan to do is just not right for Lucia.

Finally, let's not forget a reason that probably puts the rest into shadow. I am very much aware that you have already had a relationship that's rocked your world. Is it fair to let Lu commit to a lifetime of you looking over your shoulder?

I'll phone you later. Maybe we can go for a pint and discuss this?
Your almost Godfather,
Tommy

Lucia drinks her coffee and thinks hard. She's contemplated ringing Des to discuss what he said to Tommy all those years ago. The letter has touched her deeply. To care so much about a 17-year-old who he's only known for a few months is amazing. She remembers Des introducing Tommy to her parents at one of the few gatherings that they'd attended after Eddie died, to celebrate their neighbours' golden wedding. It was an open house, with half the street there, and her mum had the vapours after half an hour and had to be taken home and given smelling salts.

Des volunteered to go back with Lucia's dad to help. He was still in the phase of trying to ingratiate himself with them, no easy task. Tommy stayed at the party with Lucia to keep her company, and they'd found a quiet corner of the garden to share a bottle of disgusting Lambrusco and talk about travelling.

'Don't you want to see the world, Lu?' Tommy asked, passing her the bottle. 'There's so much fun to be had out there. You should have a gap year and go and get stuck in.'

'A gap year from what? I'm not planning to go to uni.'

'Why ever not? I had you down for a shining future.'

'I can't really leave Dad to cope with my mum. She'd

go to pieces if I wasn't here, or at least nearby. I'll get some sort of job in a school. There's one just up the road from the house Des is buying.'

'But you don't live with Des.'

She remembers the hot blush that must have been so unflattering. She'd already promised to marry Des at that point, and she was looking forward to moving into his house and helping to make it theirs.

'You're not going to actually move in with him, are you, Lucia?'

Tommy's voice was urgent in its panic. Why did he care so much anyway? They'd only met in the previous autumn.

She shrugged, something she could still get away with, as a teenager. It was almost expected of her. After that, she and Tommy had talked about neutral things. His next camping trip around Europe in the summer holidays kept them going for a while and after that, Lucia's dream of getting a puppy or a kitten.

Soon after that, Tommy had stopped coming round to see Des for quite a while. Lu had asked him several times why this was and Des had palmed her off with some story about Tommy being up for promotion and having to put in extra hours at his secondary school.

'He wants to be head of the Art department,' Des said scornfully. 'He's bound to get it. He always gets what he wants. Well, usually,' he corrected himself with a smile. 'I'm glad you don't want to do all that, Lu. We'll be happy together just being at home, won't we?'

As Lucia tucks the letter back into her pocket, she sees Tommy approaching from around the corner of the house. He looks better today. He'd refused paracetamol for his headache last night, saying the champagne would perk him up, and his dinner was devoured with many compliments to the chef.

'Morning, darling,' he says, and Lucia is relieved to hear he's back to using the term of address she's come to expect. 'How are you today? Looking as stunning as ever. Thanks for last night, and for all of you being so supportive about my next steps. We really are family now, aren't we?'

Lucia's not sure how to answer this. She's finding the closeness of Tommy disturbing as he settles down next to her on the seat. His mop of curly white hair still wet from the shower and the faint scent of shampoo and soap sets all her senses tingling.

'I'm glad you don't mind me saying I'm settling in the village for good,' Tommy continues. 'And Lu, I'm really sorry I made you so uncomfortable while we were away, with all that talk of . . . well, you know what I mean. We can be friends, can't we? Family friends? I can be around to help you with anything, if Des definitely isn't coming back. I'm happy with that. What do you think you'll do?'

Lu is suddenly unable to speak. What exactly is her life going to be like now? She's adamant she won't go back to the school. Those days are over. But there are so many other possibilities. Suddenly breathless at the thought of all that might be possible, she turns to Tommy.

'I want to go on a narrow boat trip, and I want it to be with you,' she says.

'Oh Lu, that's the very best news you could have given me. You'll love it. There's plenty of space. I'm going to sleep in the old boatman's cabin but there's a very decent spare bedroom too.'

'Right . . . well, thank you . . . and I also need to ask you something. Do you remember writing this letter to Des? I found it when I was having a sort-out.'

Tommy stares at the now rather tatty letter Lu has pulled out of her pocket again. He nods slowly.

'You mention that Des didn't react well when he told you we were engaged and you made some comment?'

There's a silence that goes on so long that Lucia has plenty of time to wish she'd just burnt this letter with the others. Then Tommy shakes himself, as if he's waking up.

'He accused me of having ulterior motives for trying to protect you. He said I was just jealous because I wanted you for myself. And it was true, darling, I was yearning for you more than you can ever imagine, but it was so much more than that. You were being caged before you'd even had chance to fly. I thought you deserved a taste of freedom.'

'I know. I was so scared, Tommy. The guilt about not having saved Eddie by going on the trip to keep an eye on him was eating me up. My mum blamed me until the day she died and my dad was almost as bad. The thought of leaving home to go right away from them was so exciting in comparison. Moving in with Des was an adventure.'

He pulls a face. 'Not much of one.'

'As it turned out, no. But I honestly thought I could change him, and later we'd set off on lots of exciting journeys. And there would be children, lots of them. It didn't happen though,' she says sadly, 'at least, there was Isaac but not for a very long time, and I didn't know you loved me like that. I assumed we were just friends.'

'And we were. We are.'

'Yes, but . . . anyway, since Des went away, I've spent a lot of time thinking about my life with him. It wasn't always much fun, to be fair, but we did have some good times and we had Isaac together. It wasn't wasted, after all. Did you know he's moved in with Bob and they're together?'

Tommy nods. 'He rang me.'

'You don't sound surprised?'

'That was another reason I told him not to marry you. I knew about his fling with Bob. He said it was just a phase, one of those things some blokes go through, and I tried to believe him after you were married. It wasn't though, was it?'

'No, and it must have been hellish pretending all those years. He adores Bob and the feeling's mutual. I'm getting over being so angry now. I'm hoping we can be friends again one day. Proper friends.'

The garden is full of birdsong now, and through an open upstairs window, Lucia can hear Reggie's whoop as he wakes up. Peter is singing some sort of operatic number in the kitchen as he makes tea. The peace is about to be shattered. She'd better move quickly.

357

Feeling as if she's right at the highest point of a giant roller coaster, poised to swoop, Lucia says, 'But after all this water under the bridge, Tommy, do you still feel the same about me?'

'Loved you then, love you now, will always feel the same. It doesn't matter though, I can live with that if you can. I won't embarrass you again.'

'I don't want you to stop saying it. Tommy, I want us to go somewhere in your new boat together.'

'You've already said that, darling. You know you'll always be welcome to come travelling with me. We've proved without a doubt we don't drive each other mad on a trip.'

Lu groans inwardly. He still doesn't understand what she's getting at. She tries again.

'That's great, but I mean together, as in . . . you know . . . *together*? I'm not intending to live my life by the compass but I get the feeling we've definitely got more places to go before we settle down, you and me.'

Tommy doesn't say anything at first. Then his arms go around her and the kiss that follows makes it very clear he's got the message. When they come up for air, he holds her so tightly that she has to push him away to breathe.

'My goodness,' she gasps. 'Before the other day in the garden I didn't know a kiss could be like this. Can we make sure we do it again, lots?'

He laughs, such a joyful sound that Lucia wants to cry with happiness herself. 'Oh yes, that's how a kiss should be, my love, and we're only just starting to get into training. You just wait.'

Tommy kisses Lu again and only stops when they hear the sound of the back door opening. They move apart. There will be plenty of time for explanations later.

Epilogue

Lucia stands beside Tommy on the back of the boat as he expertly swings his new home out of the mooring area and towards the lock. The sturdy craft is leaving its mooring as dusk approaches, slipping along between shadowy banks and sending ripples out into the darkening water.

When they reach the lock gates, Lu waits for Tommy to come in close enough to the bank and then leaps for the tow path, laughing as he gives her a round of applause. Lots of things make Lucia laugh when she's with Tommy, she reflects as she operates the windlass and watches the swirling water change levels.

Out the other side, when she's closed the gates safely, she navigates the leap onto the front of the boat without getting wet feet and makes her way through the galley to collect two bottles of beer from the fridge.

'You did that as if you'd been manning the locks all your life,' Tommy says admiringly, downing half his beer in one gulp. 'I thought I was going to have to train you up.'

'Ha. Train *me* up? You might find it's the other way round. I've spent so much time down here over the years watching the boats go by I could probably write a book about lock etiquette.'

'Really? You're full of surprises, but I knew *that* already.'

They sail on in silence for a while and then Lucia takes a deep breath and says 'Tommy, I don't want to ruin the moment but we need to talk about what happens when we get home.'

She sees the expression on Tommy's face and quickly carries on. 'Look, I definitely don't want to move in with you on the boat, lovely as it is, and I don't think I could uproot Isaac and Polly and sell my house at the moment even if you thought I should.'

She smiles at him, hoping he isn't going to be offended. It's been difficult to know how to word this important speech but Tommy doesn't look in the least bit upset. 'Go on, tell me more,' he says.

'My little adopted dog is going to be arriving in England in a few weeks. I wondered if Pickles could come and live with you on the boat. Nigel and Petunia would be pretty horrified by that little bundle of energy, I reckon, and you might even like the company.'

'You're not wrong there. I've really missed old Bruce. Walking an excitable Jack Russell will be a bit different from being dragged along by a German Shepherd but I'll soon get the hang of it.'

'Are you sure?'

'Absolutely. And if I have Pickles, I'll know you've got even more reason to come and stay with me on the mooring, or set off on lots of other adventures. It's an excellent idea.'

Lucia waits, feeling her heart swell with love for this man

who already seems to know her so well. He carries on.

'And we can divide our time between the two places. When Isaac and Polly need some privacy or you need a break, you can stay with me, when I get a yen for noisy family life, I'll come to you and sometimes we'll just sleep in our own beds. How does that sound? I don't want to tie you down. It's freedom, but with bonuses.'

'It sounds perfect, Tommy. I can't think of anything I'd like better.'

They fall silent as they sail on and night begins to fall over the almost-silent cut. This is the time when the birds are roosting and the bats are coming out to look for their first meal of the evening. The boat passes under the bridge that takes a narrow lane to Little Snoddling and then they're out into the open countryside, moving slowly between verdant banks and overhanging willow trees.

Lucia has never in her life felt such a sense of peace and well-being. She and Tommy seem like the only people left on Earth.

'Am I going to be enough for you?' Lu murmurs, almost to herself.

'What did you say?'

She repeats the question and sees a look of confusion on his kind face.

'Enough? What's that supposed to mean?'

'Well, you've travelled the world, met lots of people, loved lots of women . . .'

He holds up a hand to stop her. 'Correction. The

first two are right, but I've told you before, I've never loved any woman but you. Liked them, enjoyed their company, yes. But you, Lucia Lemon, are the love of my life.'

Lucia can't speak for a moment but it doesn't matter because Tommy hasn't finished.

'I wanted to give you your freedom, Lu,' Tommy says, 'but it turns out I also wanted to be with you when you found it. I remember thinking when I was marooned in Somerset that I was alive, but I definitely wasn't living the life I wanted. Well, now I am. This is my idea of heaven on earth. We're in this together now, aren't we? Partners?'

Lucia smiles at him and his answering grin tells her she doesn't need to say another word. She remembers part of a story she used to read to Isaac at bedtime to reassure him when he was small, and eventually had enlarged to hang above his bed, illustrated in azure and gold.

> *The bluebird flies above us,*
> *He's floating on the breeze.*
> *His wings are full of promises.*
> *His nest is in the trees.*
>
> *He holds the key to happiness*
> *Our dreams are safe and true.*
> *Tomorrow is another day,*
> *And I will be with you.*

The best is yet to come. There's no need for a compass to tell her that. The knowledge and the happiness are already right there in her heart.

Postscript

The compass is back in its box. Same house, but in a different room now. It hasn't been here before but the vibrations it's getting are positive. Underneath the leather case is a note. It's short and to the point.

Dear Isaac

I haven't the need for this beautiful object any more, but I think you may find it useful for a while. Treat it with care but never, ever let yourself rely on it completely. When the time is right, be sure to pass it on.

Good luck with your next steps, conquering the shiny world of high tech games, and always believe in yourself. Give my love to Polly and Reg, and to Peter when next you see him. We're a new sort of family now, and that makes me very happy.

With love,

Mum x

A glittering future is out there for the taking. The new owner might need a nudge to find and hang on to it, but that kind of challenge is exactly what the compass was created for. Lucia Lemon has found her own freedom, and Isaac's is just around the corner. The best is yet to come.

Acknowledgements

Each time I make a list like this, there are more and more lovely and essential people to thank. This time round, my brilliant agent Laura Macdougall (United Agents) has been very ably assisted by Olivia Davies to make sure that a little thing like giving birth to beautiful Thea doesn't get in the way of work matters. Their help, advice and cheerleading has been so very much appreciated.

Fabulous editor Sophie Burks was hugely instrumental in getting Lucia Lemon's story ready for the bookshelves, refining and polishing for all she was worth and never being afraid to say '. . . this bit must go . . . but why don't you . . .'. The copy-editing process was enhanced by the eagle-eyed Fran who was able to spot all sorts of glitches. Also involved in the latter stages has been my brand new and super-enthusiastic editor Lucy Stewart, and there are many others at HarperFiction to thank too, not least the design team. The covers of this and the previous two books are everything I hoped for, and more.

Matthew Broberg-Moffitt, a Sensitivity Reader for Salt & Sage Books was a valued and expert contributor to the editing process. He concentrated on authentic Autistic representation (through the POV of Isaac), as well as sensitivity issues that might derive from the exterior treatment of the Autistic character. His thoughtful advice was an eye-opener and Matthew also went the extra mile by giving his own review of the book, which got right to the heart and message of the story and made me cry happy tears.

I've borrowed dogs before in my books, and this time the focus is on Pickles, the real life canine companion of fellow Romaniac Vanessa Savage and her family (also a shout out here to all my Romaniac sisters who are always able and willing to give support and provide laughs). Christine Chandler and Vanessa Sutton came up with the names of minor characters Naomi and Janis after a competition in what seems like another lifetime when book launches happened in real life. (Incidentally, the village of Chandlebury was named after the gang of Chandlers, Christine, Terry, Simon and Mark, the team of four who do so much to hold our church's congregation together.)

My much-loved friends and family are the backbone of my life and never fail to encourage me when times are tough and celebrate when good things happen. Whether on Facebook, Instagram, Twitter, fellow members of the RNA or actually in the flesh – you are all amazing.

This book is dedicated to our two beautiful grandchildren, Levi and Ida, born in the midst of the pandemic and not cuddled nearly enough yet, but we're fast catching up. Huge thanks to Hannah, Mark, Laura and Hakan for making this joy possible and for all the love and fun you provide. And last but very definitely not least, to Ray; endless thanks for all the tea, ginger snaps, love, hugs, the excellent wine and gin choices and the regular votes of confidence. Writing a book is a team effort, and this team is the very, very best.